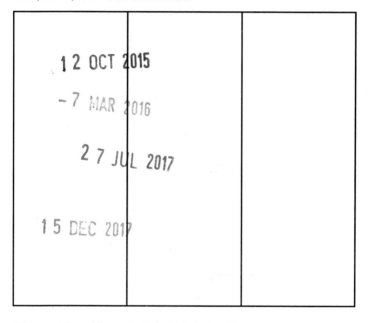

THE DAY BEFORE THE FIRE

The Day Before the Fire

MIRANDA FRANCE

Chatto & Windus

LONDON

2 4 6 8 10 9 7 5 3 1

Chatto & Windus
20 Vauxhall Bridge Road
London SW1V 2SA

Chatto & Windus is part of the Penguin Random House
group of companies whose addresses can be found at
global.penguinrandomhouse.com.

Penguin
Random House
UK

First published in Great Britain in 2015 by
Chatto & Windus

www.randomhouse.co.uk

A CIP catalogue record for this book
is available from the British Library

ISBN 9780701185817

Typeset in Stempel Garamond by Palimpsest Book Production Limited,
Falkirk, Stirlingshire

Printed and bound in Great Britain by Clays Ltd, St Ives PLC

Penguin Random House is committed to a sustainable future
for our business, our readers and our planet. This book is made
from Forest Stewardship Council® certified paper.

MIX
Paper from
responsible sources
FSC® C018179

To Susannah, with love and thanks

ONE

Somebody once told me that we never escape the patterns laid down in childhood. The urge to recreate those early bonds and rituals is so ingrained that even when we try to break away from them, we end up forcing new experiences into old moulds. I don't know if that's true but I'm often surprised by people's attachment to the past. In the studio I'll ask clients to consider whether a damaged heirloom is really worth the money it will cost them to repair it (our service is expensive, after all). They nearly always say 'yes'.

I'm a conservator. It's not as inhibiting a job title as 'traffic warden' or 'tax inspector', but it can still put a drag on party talk. People occasionally think it means you're into right-wing politics. Even among the ones who understand, 'conservation' bores some and scares others because it sounds like a word with no forward motion. It carries the weight of history, wagging a finger at anyone who doesn't know how to value or look after old things. Yet in a way all of us are conservators. It's a human instinct to collect and preserve. Who wouldn't want the precious elements and relationships in life protected, our lives themselves to be preserved – within reason – and everything good to stay as it is, immortal and unchanged? Of course there are also times that we'd like to run away from permanence, to let the past break down and turn to dust.

Usually I get a better reaction if I describe my work in terms of truth, or authenticity. Everyone can agree that truth is worth fighting for, and in a way that is the battle Frieda and I do every day in our studio in east London. We specialise in the conservation of paper and rare documents, lifting away stains caused by water or moulds, unpicking the damage done by bad restoration. We're about getting to the heart of what is true and then keeping it, stilling it for future generations. You have to have an eye for this work, you need to be able to distinguish what's real and what's fake. Several times we've been able to add to the national sum of knowledge, setting the record straight with a document or diary entry that couldn't be deciphered before our intervention. It was our work that restored the marginalia in Shelley's love poetry (the British Library marked the discovery with a lecture and a small display). Without us nobody would have known of Alfred Hitchcock's alternative ending to *The Birds*, recorded in pencil inside the back cover of a notebook. So much slips away, or is washed away by history. We're like divers sent into a wreckage. Sometimes we bring back jewels.

The world of paper conservation is small and a few, well-publicised successes have kept us busy, even in times of austerity. I don't worry too much about my prospects because this country's love affair with the past means there will always be a ready source of work. We even laugh about it sometimes, the way the English wallow in history: the Sunday-evening period dramas; that dash to a stately home on bank holidays. It's as though the future, with its undeveloped horizons, doesn't tempt them – or perhaps I should say 'us', because I admit that I like looking back, too. The past contains as many mysteries as the ocean floor – and it is everywhere beneath our feet, barely a square foot of land that wouldn't yield an ancient coin or a fragment of earthenware. Those objects, the relics of people whose lives were full of incident, dreams and disappointments, are like clues in a gigantic puzzle of human motivation. All you have to do is turn off a main road into an ancient alley and you can feel it on your neck – an ancient foreboding, a crowd of ghosts pushing towards an execution. The past is snapping at our heels, and yet as quickly as we move forward, so everything behind us dissolves into mystery. Even today, by the time you wake up tomorrow, will be breaking into fragments, while photographs from twenty years ago already show a world that's irretrievable. I love my work. For a long time I struggled to love anything else as much. It's been a problem, reconciling work and my life outside it. I never dreamed that they would collide in the way they did at Turney House, nor that in solving one mystery I would stumble into another that was going to change everything in my life.

It was a few weeks before Christmas, two years ago, and I was on Oxford Street, a coffee in one hand and my mobile in the other, weaving among harried shoppers and groups of boys in high-tops and skinnies, when the phone buzzed in my hand and made me jump. At that time I had good reason to avoid people – especially my husband, with whom relations had reached a low point and almost every exchange was reproachful.

This was a call from Frieda, so I pushed Accept and stopped walking, which isn't easy on Oxford Street with a Christmas crowd pushing you forward and a skinny latte burning into your ungloved hand.

'Hi,' I said. 'Can I ring you when I'm home? Only I'm in shopping hell.'

'It's just something quick,' Frieda said and her voice was layered with a ghostly acoustic I recognised from the studio. I didn't like to think of my colleague working on a weekend, although I knew that she often preferred that to being at home, now that her husband had died and her daughter moved abroad. The space around her voice rang full of that loss and she sounded like someone very small speaking from somewhere very big. 'I wouldn't call you now but I thought you would want to know about this straight away. There's been a fire at Turney House. It's still burning now, as we speak.'

Burning as we speak. I pictured the house wrapped up in flames, a dramatic still from an old movie. I even looked up, half expecting to see flames in the sky above us, and a pedestrian behind me tutted, it being a rule of London life that you don't stop moving. Stepping out of the traffic of shoppers, I moved to the corner of Selfridges which usually resembles a foreign embassy but had gone fully Nordic for the festive season. Store designers had filled the windows with pine trees and model deer frozen mid-leap.

'What happened exactly?' I asked, frowning at the pavement. Frieda explained how the fire had started in the roof space of London's best-loved eighteenth-century house and in less than two hours torn a way down to the ground floor. How the collapsing roof and chimneys had knocked out the second and first floors, how the alarm had not immediately sounded, but members of the public had been hurried out of the house after a volunteer spotted flames at an upstairs window. Furniture had been thrown from bedroom windows, curtains laid out, still steaming, on the lawn; the Van Dyck portrait was cut from its frame, the famous Turney Globe rushed to safety in the arms of another zealous volunteer. While dozens of firefighters had struggled to contain and direct the fire, others had gone through the house salvaging the most precious artefacts. Turney House staff had stood at the doors directing them, as though in a grisly television game show, towards the most important objects.

'They took out everything movable first, then the salvage team went back in to pull the fittings from the ceilings and walls – the mirrors and chandeliers, panelling. And with burning timbers falling all around them.'

'Christ. Is anyone hurt?'

'Nobody. All the people are fine. Only the things are damaged. But you know how people in this country get about *things*.' Frieda sighed and I could see her in the studio, leaning against the old iron radiator and tugging her left earlobe with her free hand. She finds the English weirdly sentimental about their heirlooms. 'I suppose we have to be philosophical about it. Damage is our business, after all. But you can't help feeling sad about such a beautiful house burning down.'

Dismay coloured her voice. I've always thought it a

lovely old-fashioned voice, detached from the pressure to sound a certain way, to strain for class authenticity, for glottal stops or metropolitan vowels. Frieda has lived in London for more than forty years, but she's still German in the details. Some of her sentences get turned on their heads or oddly truncated. Where are you going on *hol*? she'll say. I like that about her: it makes you see words differently.

'Is there anything we can do?' I said. 'I could get over there.' I glanced down the street towards the Underground station, over the heads of the massed shoppers. 'I could be there in half an hour.' Even as I made the offer I heard it sounding phoney. What would I really be able to contribute? But I wanted to say something. I couldn't make a connection between the shopping and the fire, two concurrent events under London skies.

'I don't think so. The fire crews are still there. I'm sure they will call us in to inspect the damage when things have settled down.'

I murmured something about the news being unbelievable and nonsensical but both of us knew it was neither of those things. Frieda and I often work in houses where there has been a fire. They can be started in seconds, by a television left on standby, or sparks from an open fireplace. Curtains hanging too close to an electric light caused the destruction of more than a hundred rooms at Windsor Castle. At Hampton Court one wing burned down in five hours and nobody will ever know the reason why. Considering how old the wiring is in many stately homes it's actually surprising that fires don't break out more often. In the battle between security and 'authenticity' the historians don't always lose to the health and safety officers.

'The good news – if there is any – is that some of the papers downstairs have been salvaged. I don't know how much yet but we'll talk about it at the studio on Monday, OK?'

'Yes, OK. And thanks for letting me know, Frieda. See you on Monday,' and just before cutting the line I called: 'Don't work too hard!'

I put away my phone and junked the coffee and stood for a moment, feeling purposeless without these habitual props. But soon I was fending off a gypsy selling lucky heather and a Hari Krishna toting spiritual guides. Waving them away I walked on towards Marble Arch. Evening was creeping into the sky and all of London seemed to be on the move, everyone racing home to watch TV, or caught up in the greater race, which was to be ready for Christmas, or the greatest of all, to make something of their lives. Courier cyclists and speed walkers, shoppers and students, people who had fallen in or out of love, lost or found their mojo, their agitation charted by satellite and closed-circuit cameras. The business of the day was devolving to the excitement of a Saturday night and the cold air was edged with perfume and an expectation of good times. Not for me, though. I was going home to eat a ready meal with my husband, off our knees, in front of the television, hoping to fill with synthetic noise the space that would otherwise be available for an argument. We'd been having rows for weeks now about the value of our childless marriage, painful exchanges in which he – on one particularly awful evening – had been reduced to biblical allusions about sowing his seed and I had defended my womb as though it were a territory under siege. We seemed to have stumbled on one of life's stepping stones and were now neither the people we had been, nor the ones we had expected to become, but stuck at some bleak impasse. Television and ready meals were both a means to some very limited contact and a way to avoid proper conversations. We still shared a bed, but distantly. At the entrance to the Tube station I stopped to look in my bag for my Oyster card and caught the eye of an African evangelist. 'Hasn't God done enough for us? What more do you want God to do?' he said, looking properly exasperated, hands spread wide. He seemed to be speaking directly to me and, as I prepared for my descent underground, I muttered, 'Where would you like me to start?'

I must have been fourteen years old the first time I visited Turney House. By then, I was living permanently with my grandmother, my mother having taken up with a property developer who lived in Brighton – and I spent a lot of time with my Uncle John and Aunt Mariel, and my cousin Natalie, who was in the same year and at the same school.

A tradition began – I don't remember how, perhaps it was simply my aunt wanting the house to herself – whereby Uncle John would take us out on Saturday afternoons, bundling us into his Morris Minor and off to museums or matinees for cultural enrichment. John believed that an artistic sensibility should be fostered, not left alone to shape itself, and he had no patience with the idea that culture was only for the upper classes. In fact impatience was his starting point for most beliefs, from faculty politics to the spreading of germs. It was forbidden to sneeze or cough inside his Morris Minor. 'Right, that's it!' John would say through gritted teeth. 'Open all the windows!'

Under Uncle John's tutelage, we visited most of London's public collections, Natalie and I providing a galumphing escort for our diminutive guide. We were immature fourteen-year-olds, given to giggles, easily disgusted by the Renaissance fondness for testicles and bottoms. 'Gross,' we murmured to each other, when Uncle John invited us to study the dynamic of Rodin's *Kiss*, dancing around it like a leprechaun while we cringed and pulled our fringes over our faces. My uncle pressed on with his project regardless and gradually we saw less that was embarrassing and disgusting and more that was intriguing. We came out from behind our fringes, I suppose. Visiting Turney House was a kind of revelation. Uncle John had marched us into the library to look at an eighteenth-century globe.

'See how the earth is in the middle,' said Uncle John, 'with all of the universe revolving around it. That isn't what really happens, is it?'

My cousin and I peeped through our hair and shook our heads doubtfully. Science wasn't our long suit. Uncle John suppressed a dyspeptic attack and went on. 'Think about it. The earth orbits the sun, doesn't it?'

'I was actually about to say that,' murmured Natalie, sucking on a few strands of hair.

'But the people who lived in this house at the end of

the 1700s thought that the world was at the centre of the universe. They thought that London was the centre of the world and that this house was at the centre of everything wonderful and magnificent in the universe.' He threw up his arms, drawing down far-flung points of the cosmos to this imagined centre, where we stood, a pair of torpid teenagers, caked in Boots No. 7. 'Think about it! No wonder they spent so much money. It was flowing into their coffers from the West Indies and the Americas. They thought there would never be an end to it. They thought the world revolved around them!'

I was far too absorbed in my own dramas to care much about other people's – but something of Uncle John's ardour must have penetrated my kohl-and-powder carapace that day. This family's arrogance intrigued me and the antiquity of the globe itself was moving. I started looking for books about history at the library and watching documentaries, which my mother, at a safe distance in Brighton, thought might be a sign of depression. I saw that there was a distinction between real people who were hard to love, and dead ones who were both more interesting and less complicated. Some sort of battle was enjoined, that Sunday afternoon in front of the Turney Globe, and although it wasn't quickly won, Uncle John must have felt his work had had its reward when I told him that I was going to stay on at school in the sixth form. My mother had wanted me to do a secretarial course; John raised my sights to a degree and a specialism in paper conservation. It's only now, looking back, that I see how successfully he intervened to stop me repeating my mother's pattern of dead-end jobs and attachment to feckless men.

It all started at Turney House – and now Turney lay in ashes.

The worst of the fire was extinguished within fifteen hours, but it took another week to tamp down every smouldering pile. Heaps of incinerated wood, black and soggy, were still steaming when the first specialists were taken in to inspect the damage. Frieda was among them, invited to supervise the storage of papers that had been torn off the walls by firemen working in temperatures of forty degrees. The upstairs papers, including an eighteenth-century Chinese silk, had been lost altogether, but in the drawing room about two-thirds of an early-Victorian flock designed by Pugin were saved. Frieda said they had been left in a warehouse – 'pretty much dumped' – covered in masonry and soot. We mourned that Chinese silk in a pub near our studio, tutting over another loss to the national stock of eighteenth-century, hand-painted papers. We questioned whether the Marchants, owners of Turney House, had done everything they could, what with their grants and their tax relief, to look after the precious objects in their care. Public sympathy, at least to start with, lay squarely with the Marchants. In the days following the fire a rash of newspaper articles and television items paid tribute to the courage of firefighters and volunteers who between them had managed to rescue almost all of the furniture downstairs and some of the more valuable items on higher storeys. Brave passers-by (those stalwarts of the popular press) had risked their own safety to help. Even as the fire raged above, a human chain had been organised downstairs to rescue thousands of books from the library, including an early edition of *Gulliver's Travels* and a Gutenberg Bible. Footage posted online showed how some rowers en route to the river had put down their boat and joined the human chain. Out of the wreckage emerged a very English story of pluck and determination winning out, of good humour in grim circumstances. 'We had worked through the night,' one member of staff told the *Richmond Times*, 'shoulder to shoulder with friends, with strangers, with people who had no motive to help other than their own good hearts. Finally there was nothing else we could do. By the time dawn broke we were sitting in the garden drinking whisky. The sun rose behind the burned-out carcass of the house we all loved. In one night we had lost everything. We had won everything too.' It was a perfect soundbite.

Brave sentiment only goes so far, though. The first critical response I remember seeing was a newspaper article that asked why more hadn't been done to protect the contents of the house and why the fire alarm was so antiquated. Priceless works of British art hadn't been properly safe-guarded, and neither had the lives of the visiting public. What if there had been a disabled visitor stuck on an upper storey? There were allegations, hotly refuted by the Marchants, that the evacuation procedure had been left to chance and to the goodwill of visitors who had joined in the rescue effort (not all of them with the best intentions: in the confusion a first-edition copy of *Hard Times* seemed to have been stolen). But it was the blithe assurance of a full-scale restoration that really got the public's goat. A few years earlier, that would have been less controversial. At a time of recession, with heart units and children's hospitals under threat, it infuriated the liberal middle classes as much as the retired colonels and socialist workers on either side of them. And while it was true that most of the reconstruction was going to be covered by insurance – at a cost of twenty million pounds – there were some significant extras the Marchants hoped to fund from the public coffers. A few streets away, locals had just lost the fight to save their library after a month-long vigil and a petition of five thousand signatures (library users staged a mass borrowing in an attempt to protect the books, but even that gesture hadn't moved the councillors to a change of heart). Meanwhile Turney's owners wanted taxpayers to save their chandelier, which had shattered into more than three thousand pieces, on the grounds that it was an 'object of national heritage'. 'Not repairing the Turney Chandelier would be like not restoring the Albert Hall,' said Alexandra Marchant. That was a bad soundbite that kept getting worse. Images of Lady Marchant floated over articles fingering her as a gold-digger. She was thirty years younger than her husband and very attractive, noted *The Times* Diary suspiciously, with shoulder-length blonde hair that was styled at one of London's most expensive salons. The *Daily Telegraph* praised her 'Diana factor' – saying that she had restocked the Marchants' depleted gene pool at the same time as 'refreshing the brand'. Lord Marchant had the same short legs and bulbous nose as his Georgian ancestors but his sons were fine-boned and leggy, like his wife. There were her expensive wardrobe and smooth forehead to consider, too, and the fact that she had once posed naked for an article about old houses in the *Tatler*.

'Everyone gets off their kit nowadays. It's almost an obligation if you want any publicity,' said Frieda.

'Gets off their kit? Gets their kit *off*. All the same, it's not strictly necessary to take your clothes off for a piece about stately homes.'

'Of course it is! Taking off your clothes is necessary for everything these days.'

'Better hope they never interview us for a piece on conservation.'

At the time of the fire we were working on Alan Turing's notebooks, preserving the calculations and annotations he had made in pencil seventy years earlier. So we followed the battle for Turney's future from our studio in the East End. There was an inevitability about much of it: that hum of indignation from traditionalists who wanted everything to be as it had always been, however nonsensical that equation; the modern architects railing against 'Disneyfication'. In conservation journals purists, opposed to any form of reproduction, argued for the preservation of the building as a shell, a blank space in which eighteenth-century paintings, trinkets and furniture could be displayed still charred as the forensic detritus of a long-gone age. The modernists wanted the building updated – why not combine what remained of its Georgian architecture with the very best contemporary design? The ruinists were all for leaving nature to take its course, in a gradual reclaiming of the once-grand house. Far kinder, they said, to let the building fall down than subject it to major surgery. Wild flowers would be allowed to displace the parquet. The walls that had witnessed parties and royal visits would be overgrown with ivy. The ravaged house could stand as a symbol of the greed and hubris of a bygone age brought down by the corrective tug of nature. Perhaps it wasn't so much the eighteenth-century greed that rankled, but something closer to home. A new puritanism was growing in Britain thanks to the excesses of an overpaid elite, the reviled '1 per cent', and some people detected the same sense of entitlement in the Marchant family that had come to define the world of high finance. They had been very rich for more than three hundred years. Why should British taxpayers help them to stay rich?

The arguments were fierce, but in a country like England restoration would always win the day. When tenders were put out for the work at Turney, we were awarded the contract to repair the mid-nineteenth-century silk flock that gave its name to the drawing room: the Rose Room. It was what we had expected. Frieda had few rivals in the conservation of historic wallpapers, and a reputation for sticking to budgets and completing work on time. She had also worked at Turney House before and, in our world, contacts are everything.

'The guiding principle is to use as much of the original as possible,' said Frieda. 'That goes for everything – papers, glass, wood, ceramics. Everything that isn't burned to a crisp has to be put back in.' It was fifteen months after the fire and we were on our way to Roehampton, negotiating traffic-throttled streets doused red and yellow by an alliance of cheap pizza and chicken joints. Wherever we drove we caused aggravation. Our white van infuriated other road users: cyclists thumped the roof; taxi drivers swore at us. People's expressions sometimes changed when they saw a woman at the wheel, though the sight of Frieda with her batty hairdo may have confirmed their worst suspicions, and she wasn't averse to giving them the finger.

'Things come full circle,' said Frieda, as we entered the more pampered streets of Richmond, passing a super-market that had been designed to look like a country manor house. Further along the same road at a private tennis club long-legged girls in minuscule shorts were lobbing a ball about, collapsing every now and then into photogenic laughing fits. 'Houses are like members of your family. You think you are finished with them, but you never are. A few years later you are back again, sorting out a problem, patching them up again. There is always going to be some new crisis.'

I was looking absently out of the window, thinking of the crises in my own family, the bouts of patching up, the pain, the tears. By now I was living apart from Chris. We were calling the arrangement a trial separation, though sometimes it just felt more like a trial, with me accused of not trying harder to become a mother. Moving out had been horrible, waiting downstairs with two packed suit-cases for the taxi to come while Chris hid in the bedroom, staring at his laptop. In what I feared might be a regressive step, I had moved back into my grandmother's house, into the room I had slept in as a child, while we decided what to do next.

'What a prick,' I murmured, as a lycra-clad cyclist streaked past us on the inside. Louder I said to Frieda, 'When was it that every woman in London decided they needed a manicure? These days there's a nail bar on every street.'

'First they persuade us we need to drink coffee all the time. Then it's nails. What next?'

'Botox on the high street. Conservation for the human face.'

'My God! They will have their work cut out with me.'

These days Roehampton is a lost corner of south-west London, cauterised by road systems, but in the eighteenth century it had been famous for the grand villas that sprang up on prized plots along the River Thames. I'd been reading about them in preparation for today's visit, how wealthy merchants, politicians and lawyers used to keep a town house in London's West End as well as a grand country residence that might be closed up for weeks while the family was away for the social season. Those estates could be several days' journey away from the capital, but when a bridge was built in 1729 over the Thames at Putney, it became possible to keep a smart house only two hours by horse and carriage from central London in a riverside plot big enough for formal gardens, orchards and kitchen plots. Architects and landscape gardeners rushed to line the river with villas. It became, perhaps for the only time in its history, wildly fashionable to be south of the river. This was the place to spend the season showing off to socialites who couldn't be lured out to the provinces. Some of the ones who didn't get an invitation came anyway to gawp from the road at the grand houses, the mazes and menageries. By one contemporary account it was a female version of the Grand Tour: women who couldn't go abroad toured Roehampton's architectural treasures instead. By printing tickets for the sightseers drawn to his own house, Strawberry Hill, Horace Walpole started a trend that grew into today's heritage industry.

After the First World War even England's grandest families couldn't afford to maintain two stately homes, and anyway, transport improvements had made the family seat easier to reach. So Roehampton's villas were sold for cheap housing, subdivided into flats or demolished to make way for tower blocks. In the 1930s they built one of Europe's largest council estates here, a brutalist development inspired by Le Corbusier. A different kind of estate. Those villas that remained intact were made over as golf clubs and psychiatric hospitals or swallowed up by Roehampton University. Post-war Britain needed public services more than aristocrats and this part of London quickly forgot its own glamour. The Marchants were the last aristocratic family left with a link to Roehampton's Georgian age and their house was often described as the only 'proper' stately home in London.

How had Turney House survived, despite the changing social scene and the fluctuating fortunes of its owners? Scale was a part of the attraction. Upstairs only two bedrooms were open to the public along with a nursery full of antique toys including a doll's house that may or may not have amused the young Princess Victoria. Downstairs the Palladian hall led on one side to a drawing room and on the other to a library that housed, along with books, a strange collection of stuffed animals. On

Saturday mornings children were encouraged to visit in animal costumes of their own while an entertainer read them stories. Beyond the library, in the dining room, was a table at which George III, on an excursion from his madhouse at Kew, was supposed to have thumped his fist and praised his dinner with the words 'By Jove it's good!' You could still see the prong marks made by the fork he had been holding. On the lower floor there was a kitchen and scullery rooms that had hardly changed since the nineteenth century. If toys, taxidermy and royals weren't enough of a draw, the clincher was brevity: it took less than an hour to get round the whole house, leaving plenty of time for the cafe and shop. There was much less walking than at Hampton Court and none of the queuing required at the Tower of London. To get this sort of return on your money without leaving London was unique. The fact that the house was still occupied by the original family made it especially attractive to visitors. 'This is not a museum but our home and we want you to feel at home here too,' wrote Lady Alexandra Marchant on Turney's website, her words presented in an italicised font that made a dainty allusion to her eighteenth-century predecessor Lady Isabella Marchant.

We pulled off the road and into the drive at the back of Turney House. This, the public facade of the house, was also the back of the building which had been designed to face the river and positioned at the top of a slight rise. A number of vans outside attested to the restoration project under way. Frieda left ours alongside the others and we got out. I had visited Turney House once or twice since my teenage years, but it still surprised me to see how much plainer the house looked than it had been in my memory. Essentially it was a red-brick rectangle, surmounted by a neat balustrade following the roof's perimeter, which had been broken in several places by the firefighters' ladders. Also missing was one of a pair of towering chimney stacks, which had plummeted through two floors on the day of the fire. In their efforts to draw the fire away from the rest of the house, the firefighters had made vents in the roof to funnel the flames through its central core. The new roof was completed now but the windows were not yet finished and scaffolding still surrounded the building.

'Some scene-setting,' said Frieda, catching my arm as we walked towards one side of the house, following the garden wall. 'Samuel Marchant comes back to London in the 1780s after making his fortune in the Indies. He's joined the aristocracy. He's landed one of the country's famous beauties even though he has a big nose and short legs. He's arrived in London society and he wants to make a splash, so he builds this great house and stuffs it full of things and in the garden there's even a zoo. And look at the materials . . .'

She paused, to let me take in the side view of the house. Overhead a jet plane tore up the sky. We were below the flight path and every minute brought a new air-quake.

'Red bricks,' I said, not getting it. I scanned the part of the house nearest to us, looking for more clues and screwing my eyes up against the noise. 'It's just London stock, isn't it?'

'Exactly. But bricks at a time when bricks are being taxed to pay for the war in America. Bricks at a time when nobody else is using bricks. None of that wedding-cake stucco John Nash used to cover up the poor-quality materials in Regent's Street. It looks simple, but this house was made of the best materials available.'

'How did Samuel Marchant get so rich?' I asked. We were walking now along the side of the brick garden wall.

'Sugar. Slaves.' Frieda shrugged. 'The usual.'

'And the title?'

'Anything can be had for a price in this country, can't it? Come on, Dr Watson. It's time to investigate the crime scene.'

There was a door, ordinary-looking, in the wall, and a security man on the other side of it who telephoned the house, pointing the way across a lawn to the main entrance. This was where eighteenth-century guests would have arrived from London after crossing the river at Putney. The Palladian hall that received them was a blank now. The niches which had displayed busts of Isabella Marchant's four children as classical gods with laurels in their hair stood empty. Two men were smoothing plaster on the walls and a radio carried some chortling exchange between a DJ and a caller. The smell was of putty, new wood and plaster, though the air retained a wisp of smoke. I remembered standing here with Natalie while my Uncle John negotiated with an elderly volunteer who was taking a long time to establish which colour ticket we ought to have. The grand elliptical staircase sweeping away to the left had been destroyed during the fire, when the hall and stairwell were used by firefighters to channel the flames away from other rooms and out through the roof. This was where the greatest heat had been recorded – temperatures so high that the paint on a seventeenth-century battle scene hanging over the stairs was seen to bubble even as salvagers tried to wrench it from its frame. The reconstruction of the staircase currently under way was one of the most controversial elements in the restoration programme. Purists had wanted it replaced with a modern design but the Marchants had argued – successfully in the end – that a replica was the only fitting solution. To the right of the stairs a small door was concealed in the wainscoting of the hall, intended for the use of servants who were either even shorter than their eighteenth-century masters or expected to appear that way. That door opened now, and through it came Lady Alexandra Marchant.

Advancing crisply over the plastic groundsheet, her head held high on the end of a long neck, Alexandra Marchant gave the impression of someone who was literally making an effort to keep her chin above the waves. She seemed uncomfortable, as though this haughtiness came at a cost. Her long hair, between white and blonde, had the appearance of being often brushed and she looked like the kind of woman who would carry a hairbrush in her handbag and produce it in the washrooms of upmarket restaurants. She was wearing a red cashmere polo neck and grey slacks that were close-fitting on her hips and loose around her ankles. On her feet were silver pumps, a stylish concession to the difficulty of walking on plastic floor coverings.

'Frieda,' she said, advancing with both hands outstretched. 'It's good to have you here.'

'Hello, Alexandra,' said Frieda. 'This is my colleague, Ros. I think you haven't met before.'

Alexandra nodded, drawing me within her compass and extending a cool hand to each of us – as though proposing a round of 'Ring-a-Ring o' Roses' – then snatching them away again. She turned to indicate a man who had followed her into the hall.

'Roger,' she called. 'Didn't I tell you there was only one person I could trust to work on the Rose Room wallpaper? Didn't I say it was a job for Frieda?'

'You did, you did,' said Roger, beaming at the idea of having lost an imaginary battle.

She turned back to us with a smile of triumph. 'Roger is our Visitor Services Manager. He is also joint chairman of the restoration committee.'

Roger, who appeared to be in his mid-forties, was smiling and solid, almost a perfect oblong in a suit that contained somewhere within its weave a metallic thread that made him shimmer under the temporary bright lights workers had installed. He had dark hair and eyes and the ready smile of a man who was used to encountering difficult people and winning them over. His eyebrows, unusually dark, were markers of a cheerful resolve. There was a mechanical regularity to the way they were raised and lowered every few seconds as he spoke – he could have been the novelty mascot of an oompah band – but the movement made his face lively; hands clasped behind his back, he rocked back and forth slightly where he stood, tracing a moderate sway that made his shoes creak on the floor's plastic covering.

'So tell me,' said Frieda, 'what is happening in the house at the moment?'

Alexandra Marchant cast around her in playful

astonishment. 'Where to begin! For a long time it felt as though *nothing* was happening, but now we are slowly getting somewhere. You should have seen it a year ago, Ros. The place was sodden. We had huge drying machines in every room. We still have them in the basement. The roof is just about finished.'

'The first phase of work is completed,' offered Roger. 'The roof, floors, stabilising the walls.'

'I had to fight like a wildcat for the roof! They wanted to use steel beams. I said to them this building is a living thing! It has to move and creak like an old person.'

Everyone laughed – encounters like this needed to be moved along with laughter – and it was easy to imagine Alexandra as a wildcat, her hair in disarray, fingernails sprung.

'But why are you having to fight, Alexandra?' asked Frieda. 'The insurance is not clear on every point?'

'The terms of the insurance are to use authentic materials where it can be *proved* that they are essential,' said Roger. 'It means we have to make the case for every job, no matter how small. It's a nightmare, actually.'

'I keep trying to make the point that it isn't just the look or feel of something,' said Alexandra. 'It's the sound, the smell. It's all about authenticity. So far one is winning the battles. But the war most certainly isn't over.'

It grated, that 'one', an unusual mannerism in somebody of Alexandra Marchant's age which I knew to be thirty-six – the same as me – because I had googled her before we came out. She seemed older than me, but that could have been down to poise, grooming and clothes. Her bearing was of an indeterminate age, the consequence of her marriage to an elderly husband perhaps, or of her two years at a Swiss finishing school.

'Why don't you come and have a look around?' said Alexandra.

I had seen the photographs that were taken of Turney a few days after the fire, its once opulent interiors bedraggled, its contents atomised. Some of the pictures had been taken from the second floor through two broken storeys into the rubble-filled basement. Now all the walls and ceilings had been rebuilt, and the debris cleared away. In each of the downstairs rooms tables were spread with plans, papers and photogrammetric photographs, with the detritus of stress and overwork: teacups and chocolate-bar wrappers, cigarette stubs ground into improvised ashtrays with a kind of sadism.

'So,' said Alexandra Marchant, tossing her mane like a rich child's pony. 'The plasterers are nearly ready to begin on the library ceiling. The staircase is close to finished, so is the Axminster carpet. Twelve ladies have been working on that for most of the year. What else? The wood carvers are working on finials and door panels in a studio in the garden. With any luck the panelling will soon be going back in the library.'

'Was all the panelling burned?' I asked.

'Actually it's surprisingly unscathed,' said Roger. 'But we couldn't leave it in place because the walls were so damp. Perfect conditions for fungi.'

Alexandra Marchant's folded arms lay neatly together above her waist and her long fingers were tipped with nail polish in the same colour as her lipstick and jumper. Her slim wrists sported several bangles dripping charms, love tokens from Lord Marchant, I guessed, or from her children.

'I suppose there is a silver lining to this tragedy, in that we get the chance to study Turney House from the inside,' said Roger. 'Behind the scenes as it were. It's not the kind of opportunity many people get to see the inner workings of a great house like this.'

'I hope you didn't start this fire deliberately, Roger,' said Frieda, characteristically deadpan. She was wearing one of her collection of girlish hair clips, the diamanté sparkling in her grey wiry hair.

Roger gave a yelp of laughter that rang out in the empty room.

The burst of jocularity made Alexandra, unsmiling beside him, appear rigid with displeasure. 'If there is one thing this terrible experience has shown me, it is that Turney House is so, *so* loved, a jewel in England's crown. Having it empty, it's like a wound that isn't healing, you know?'

I nodded quickly, knowing that Frieda wouldn't have much patience with the notion of metaphorical wounds.

'Shall we have a look at the Rose Room now?' she said. 'Of course.'

As we walked back to the hall and towards the door leading into the west portion of the house, I took my coat off, subconsciously engaging with the job. Stepping through the doorway into the Rose Room, I felt a stab of exhilaration at the sight of this once-grand room reduced to its skeletal state. Long ago I had learned to put emotions aside when visiting the scene of disasters. Work clothes went with a working attitude: this was a job, not a tragedy.

All the same, to enter a room where so much had been invested in creating character, where now no character remained, was a sobering reminder that the aura of a home is only ever an inch deep. The Rose Room was forty feet long with four floor-to-ceiling formal windows looking onto the front gardens and a curved wall with another window at its furthest end. Before the fire three of the family's best paintings had hung on its long interior wall including Gainsborough's portrait of Lady Isabella Marchant and her sister, made in 1765. Beside that had been a hunting scene by Van Dyck and another portrait, by Joshua Reynolds, of a seafaring relation of the Marchants. Now that wall was a mottled patchwork of charred wooden slats and clumps of plaster on which a few fragments of paper were loosely attached like scraps of burned skin. Here and there a glint of gold survived as a testament to Pugin's extravagant design.

'The windows were blown out, so this glass is new,' said Alexandra. 'We found the only factory in France that still makes glass in the same way as it would have been made here in the eighteenth century. Thank God for the French!' She tapped the glass with the back of her nails. 'See how the glass is bluish, with an uneven tone? The insurers wanted us to replace it with bog-standard modern glass. Luckily that was one battle we did win.'

It was moving in a way to look out of the window at the same view that would have greeted the Marchants' guests as they arrived from disease-ridden, smog-infested central London in the 1790s. They must have been enviously impressed. Georgian aristocrats thrilled to a good 'prospect', an unbroken, sweeping vista for which they even invented a new word: panorama. Beneath these windows was the Rose Garden, useful for ladies who needed to empty their bladders during the evening, under cover of hooped skirts. Beyond that, the view extended across gardens designed by Capability Brown down to a seamless boundary with the Old Deer Park, on the other side of which was the Thames. From this vantage point the formal gardens seemed to dissolve into an aspect of long grass and mature trees, as though the land and house had been miraculously hewn from nature and were still surrounded by wilderness. It was a lovely illusion, one the guests could dispel by climbing to the top of a folly in the garden, from which they would have been able to glimpse – and perhaps even to spy on with binoculars – other grand houses in the area, including one or two across the Thames in Chiswick. Looking out of these windows and keeping the eye straight, the view was now much as it would have been then. It was still possible to imagine a hunting party galloping over the tussocky ground in the distance. But the eye couldn't help drifting to the left, where five massive tower blocks stood on land the Marchants had been compelled to sell to the council in the 1950s.

'Better mask up, Ros, or shall I do the honour?' Frieda asked.

'It's fine – I'll do it.'

I took a pair of latex gloves out of my bag, pulled on a dust mask and walked over to the scalped wall. This was one of my favourite parts of the job: the clinical study, the moment of diagnosis. Moving my fingers over the denuded wall, palpating areas of bald wood, fragments of paper and horsehair, I tried to imagine what it must have been like to be in this room, which was now as cool as a mortuary, during the fire's tumult, with the light fittings shaking overhead as the ceilings began to crack under the weight of crumbling timbers. In the minutes before the ceiling collapsed, firemen working under a protective cover of water had managed to tear down twelve complete runs of wallpaper from this wall. A further eight runs were left behind and so damaged that they would need to be replicated.

'Apologies for the less than salubrious conditions,' said Alexandra Marchant. She was watching me, awkwardly craning forwards over her folded arms, like a mother watching her child being checked over at the doctor's.

'This is luxury for us,' Frieda said. 'Often we can't even count on a floor. We were working in the dark at our last job, wearing head torches and pulling the spiders out of our hair!'

Stepping back a couple of feet, I glanced to the left and noticed that on another section of wall beside the chimney much of the paper remained, blackened and bearing a ghostly imprint of the original pattern.

'They couldn't get to this part of the room?' I asked, lifting off the mask.

Alexandra shook her head. 'No, not into that corner. There was too great a danger of this chimney collapsing, like the other one.'

'It's quite safe now,' Roger interjected with a smile.

I walked over to that section of the wall and moved my hand over the carbonised paper, feeling it flake under my fingers. 'Do you know what's underneath this?'

Alexandra Marchant produced a kind of scoffing laugh. 'Rafters?'

'It feels different here, as if this paper was stuck straight onto the wall. It doesn't feel as if there's hessian behind it. I'm just wondering if it's possible that there is anything earlier than this paper underneath.'

'Ros is right to ask the question,' said Frieda. 'There could be an older paper. We have discovered some extraordinary treasures. And now is the perfect time to investigate. As Roger said, this is a chance to look at Turney from the inside –'

'We can't let ourselves get distracted by treasure-seeking,' said Alexandra. 'This room has to be restored and open to the public as soon as possible. Every day that we delay costs thousands of pounds.'

'It doesn't have to be a distraction,' said Frieda. 'The public love seeing restoration work going on. They're seduced by the idea of digging under the surface and finding secrets. We used to have to wait until the houses were closed to come in and work. Now quite often we get asked to do our work during opening hours – don't we, Ros? – so that the people can watch.'

'The public fascination with houses is quite extraordinary,' agreed Roger. 'They want to know every detail. I suppose it's because there's so much on TV about restoring old houses nowadays and visitors are better educated.'

Alexandra followed this exchange with an expression of baffled horror. 'Sorry, folks, but, *it's a Pugin.*' She pronounced the name with an upward inflection, as though it were a question, and I remembered that her mother was American and that she had spent some of her childhood living in California. She spread her hands in front of her and pushed out her chin to indicate that this was a no-brainer.

'Well, it won't be a Pugin by the time we've finished with it – it will be our reproduction of Pugin,' said Frieda. 'The public's sophisticated, you know – if they come here knowing that there was a fire, and there is no evidence of a disaster, they feel that what they are looking at is inauthentic, a fake. We shouldn't try to ignore the fact that damage has taken place. This wall is quite tucked away – it would be the ideal place to leave a panel showing the condition of the papers and the wall underneath.'

Alexandra Marchant said nothing for a moment, tapping her nails on her arms. 'Frieda, it sounds as though you're talking yourself out of a job!'

'No, no, that's not it,' said Frieda soothingly. 'I just want to look at different ways of *doing* the job. It would give the visitors a fuller picture. They will see what the effect of the fire was, and how we work.'

'Leave one wall as a testament to something we would all rather forget? Leave it as a mishmash of different styles?' Alexandra turned to Roger. 'I am not about to ride roughshod over two hundred years of history.'

'You wouldn't be riding over history,' insisted Frieda, 'you would be exposing it to view, for the first time in centuries. Actually I think people would thank you for it.'

'It's an interesting suggestion,' Roger said. 'You've always been very good at taking on new ideas, Alexandra. The children's story sessions. The evening tours by candle-light and so on.'

His words petered out because Alexandra had turned

her head towards him in such a way that a sheet of hair now shielded her expression from us. Roger's face appeared to be receiving a very particular message. He frowned slightly. Then his eyebrows moved quickly up and down several times, before coming together to create a reddened cleavage above his nose.

'The question may in any case be academic,' he said. 'We don't know that there is anything interesting beneath the rose paper. Besides, the insurance money that we have is for the restoration of this paper. We don't have dispensation to use it for anything else. We have to be conscious of budgetary constraints.'

'It's not as if we're part of the National Trust or anything. There aren't limitless resources at our disposal. Anyway, it's irrelevant,' said Alexandra, as if this word alone were enough to shut down a debate. 'The point is that I want the Rose Room back how it was. The terms of the insurance are very precise. The house is to be restored exactly as it was "the day before the fire". The money we receive is only for that. There is no budget available for any other investigation.'

Frieda nodded. 'I understand.'

'So, before we can go any further, we need to get security passes for you and Ros. Have you brought the photographs? Good. Would you come up with me, Frieda, and I'll introduce you to my brother? He does all the tech. I'm afraid it means using the servants' staircase.'

I waited for them in the library, where the oak panels were leaning against the wall ready for their reinstallation. This was the room from which two thousand books had been removed via a human chain that had stretched through French windows in the bay, across a side garden and into the old stables behind the house. In the spot where the Turney Globe had stood there was now a table with mugs and tools and, lying beside them, a visitors' book, which must have been retrieved from storage for reference. I picked it up and glanced at some of the pages, finding the same effusive comments common to all registers of this kind, praise intermingled with light sarcasm and plain rebuke. The coda to an afternoon spent looking at beautiful interiors and eating cake was to leave a remark in the book, some words of approval, criticism or one-upmanship. It eats at us, our love of the preserved country house. Alongside our admiration there is envy of these people whose homes and gardens are so much more beautiful and spacious than ours.

On the last completed page in the book, 'my favrit place in the wold' was written in a child's hand, dramatically sloping. Underneath it there was a comment from the child's mother: 'A WONDERFUL treat! LOVED the gardens!'

'Just a niggle' the next entrant had written, with a scratchy, niggled pen. 'Our guide told us that Alexander Pope was a near neighbour but of course Pope died in the 1740s, several decades before Turney House was built.'

There was more happy commentary, extolling 'this corner of Englishness', 'a taxidermist's delight!' along with the odd mocking admonishment. 'Might one suggest that the builders carry out their work less obtrusively? Loud rock music is hardly a suitable soundtrack for a Georgian house!!'

The effusive, the irritated, the lovers of heritage,

cake-eaters – every kind of enthusiast had found an outlet in this book. Entries stopped abruptly, though, on 6 December, the day of the fire.

I heard footsteps approaching through the drawing room and turned to see Lady Marchant moving quickly towards me, rounding on me almost, with a manila envelope in her hand.

'Frieda said I should give you these – some photographs of the Rose Room for research purposes. I'm afraid it's all we've been able to find, but hopefully it will be useful.' She handed the envelope over with a peremptory sniff. 'You're looking at our comments book. These last ones were made on the afternoon of the fire, at the very moment the fire was breaking out. In fact this guy helped to carry out the globe.' She pointed at the name of the man who had been niggled about Alexander Pope. I smiled at the thought of heroism being thrust on this man in the midst of his irritation.

'Did you see it on TV?' she asked.

I nodded. 'On the news.' I felt ashamed to have been a voyeur rather than a rescuer.

'We've got it recorded, but I can't bring myself to watch it. My husband and I had gone to see our son playing rugby. It was a Saturday and the men fixing a section of the roof had knocked off early. They left without checking that the soldering irons were all switched off. Our housekeeper was here but . . . She tried to call us, but the match was just ending, the boys were getting their medals and doing all their hip-hooraying and whatnot.'

I nodded again although these were foreign customs to me.

'I'd switched off my phone and . . .' she shook her head, 'I forgot to put it back on. I don't know why. I never usually do that. And of course Rafe doesn't have one – he lives in a different century! As we were driving back home I actually said to my son, "Look at that glorious sunset," and it was only when we got closer that I realised it wasn't that at all. It was fire reflected in the clouds. You could see, from miles away, the smoke hanging above the house, the flames pouring out of the windows, the *violence* of it.'

Suddenly her voice jumped up in pitch and she sounded like a little girl, trying not to cry. 'And, there was a popping noise like gunfire. Do you know what it was?'

Having been nodding for what felt like a long time, I shook my head. I felt unequal to Alexandra Marchant's lionising, the big hair, the red nails, the intense fixity of her eyes which now filmed suddenly with tears. 'It was the tiles popping off the roof in the heat! But I thought for a moment that someone had gone mad, shooting at our visitors. Or that there was a bomb! I mean, those things seem to happen quite a lot these days. I know it sounds silly. Why would terrorists want to target us? But the whole country is on high alert, isn't it? Besides, we stand for English history and English values and we have had threatening letters before.'

'Really? – threatening a bomb?'

'Not a bomb, but' – She glanced out of the window at the tower blocks. 'We have had do-gooders saying we're not trying hard enough to draw people in. That we should be targeting ethnic minorities and doing more work in the community – what do they call it? – fucking Outreach.'

Unlikely, I thought, that they called it that, though they would certainly reach a new demographic if they did.

'But look, I'm sorry –' she touched my arm – 'I'm being negative and there were so many amazing positives, too. The staff and the volunteers were just –' She shook her head; she couldn't think of words to describe the heroism of the staff and volunteers. 'I think all of us felt a determination to fight the forces of destruction – not to be beaten.' She cocked her head to one side as though this observation, which had probably been made many times before, had only now occurred to her.

'Look at this.' From her trouser pocket Alexandra produced a phone and gave the screen a few impatient taps, calling up a series of photos that replayed the rescue operation in vivid colours: men and women caught in the unnatural attitudes forced on them by speed; a flat-footed gardener struggling under the weight of a marble urn; white-haired ladies who had gone to work that morning expecting to talk about dolls' houses hurrying out of doors holding vases and ornaments – one of them had kicked off her shoes and was running in stockinged feet.

'These pictures were taken by one of the visitors. He sent them to me afterwards. Look, there's the Van Dyck coming out. The firemen had to cut it out of its frame. And Gainsborough's portrait of my husband's great-great-great . . . grandmother. Five greats or six, I can't remember. And look: here's how the house looked a few days later – disgusting. Sludge in every room. It's not just the fire that does the damage, it's the water. Of course, you know all about that. This house, it's not just our business, it's my husband's childhood home, the place where he grew up. I made a vow to get things back to how they were, for his sake and because – you know, he used to drive his little racing car through these rooms.'

Without warning, the little racing car made Alexandra's voice spring up an octave again and it was impossible not to picture Lord Marchant, as the elderly man I had seen in photographs, wedged into a racing car, pedalling through the derelict house.

'Where do you live?' asked Alexandra, with a suspicious knotting of her brow.

'Battersea,' I said. 'My grandmother's house, actually.' And then, because that didn't seem to explain the situation adequately I added, 'My grandmother's gone into a care home and I need somewhere to stay so I'm looking after the house for a bit. She thinks she's going to come back home but realistically . . .'

Lady Marchant feigned a two-second interest; she couldn't quite be bothered with my grandmother's predicament. Instead she concentrated on wiping her tears away, delicately touching her lashes and bearing off the tears on her fingertips as though they were too valuable to let fall. At some point in her life she must have learned how to cry without letting her mascara run. Perhaps it was something they taught in finishing schools, I thought, and I wondered what it was like – this great ache to have things how they were. Lord Marchant and I had one thing in common: we were both still living in the houses in which we had been children. I imagined a Turney-style rescue operation on my grandmother's house at the time when she still lived there: the heavy glass-fronted cabinet full of knick-knacks, the art deco teapot that was too special almost ever to be used, the Wedgwood dish on which my grandmother's jam roly-poly, an oozing beast, rested heavily on Sundays. The firemen may not have bothered to cut free from its frame the reproduction print of Pierrot smelling a flower, a three-dimensional tear glued onto his cheek like a perfect crystal globule. My Polish grandfather had given it to his wife and she cherished it. She had it with her now, in her bedroom at the care home.

'You see how important it is to have everything absolutely how it was?' said Alexandra Marchant, drawing me back from memories of my grandmother's roly-poly to the vases and Van Dycks.

'Of course,' I said. 'London isn't London without Turney House. It's a little piece of England.'

Alexandra Marchant smiled and her eyes narrowed thoughtfully. 'We might put that on a mug.'

TWO

There's a fashion now for saying that a marriage isn't a failure just because it ends. In this and so many other ways, we take our cue from the celebrities and their smiling assurances on TV that they will always love Tom or Nick or Jeff, that he's an amazing dad or friend or inspiration – just not someone you'd actually want to live with any more. The marriage vows are easily sloughed off; the tattoos are harder to lose. I have some sympathy with the celebrities, though. Like them, I didn't feel my marriage had been a mistake or a failure. For nearly fifteen years Chris and I had lived together, sharing more interests than many couples, and been busy in the way of Londoners: eating out, going to galleries and concerts or to friends' houses where we were, increasingly, the only ones not making rueful jokes about early nights and babysitters. We were happy, I think, even if our net gains didn't look good on paper. We never bought a house together. We didn't have a joint bank account. And although we always expected to have children, I made no particular effort to get pregnant. The steps I took were more like lapses: I stopped using contraception or worrying about dates. As time passed and no children arrived, and Chris began talking about the things *we* could do to improve *our* chances of conception, I found myself oddly resistant to doing anything at all. I dug my heels in you could say, and the more he proposed positive action, the more I matched him with negatives: I didn't want to eat extra zinc or check my temperature to confirm the monthly peak of fertility. I didn't want to choose sexual positions that favoured deep penetration, or lie with my legs up in the air for twenty minutes afterwards, urging the sperm towards its goal. And as time went on, and still no child came, so I tightened my grip on all the things I wasn't going to do. I wasn't going to try IVF or speak to specialists. I wasn't going to sit opposite a concerned professional, or lie on a hospital bed with my feet in stirrups or haunt fertility forums late at night. I definitely wasn't going to ask my mother for advice. What was wrong with accepting our lot? Well, everything, it turned out – at least as far Chris was concerned. It was a difference of opinion that had divided us first psychically and then physically, leaving Chris alone in our flat near Tower Hill and me on the other side of the river, back at my grandmother's house, in the bedroom I used to sleep in as a child.

It was comforting, in a way, to be here. Something about retreating to the family home at this stage in my life made sense, like a return to first principles. If childhood is where you learn about people and the world then maybe that is the state that requires scrutiny when things go wrong. Not wanting to be up alone, late at night in an empty house, I took to going to bed early and lay under the duvet as the room bulged with memories around me. I had spent hours playing in this room as a child, inventing stories for a ragtag collection of dolls and figurines. I used to have an incomplete Noah's Ark and a box of animals that were happy to parade into it any old how, never mind in pairs. The rug underneath, a deep blue, could be made to ripple like the sea. And on winter nights when wind battered both roofs, I had sometimes lain in bed and thought of the room itself as a boat, breaking free from the body of the house beneath it and casting forth into the night – a romantic expression of my feelings of separateness, perhaps, because I never felt as legitimate a member of the family as my cousin Natalie, neither as rooted nor as circled with love.

It was also in this room that I first heard about my father's death, though afterwards I could never remember the words that were used to convey the news. They must have blazed right through me, because all my memories of that day are sensorial ones to do with the mattress's capitulation under Granny Pea's weight and my efforts to stay upright next to her while she made her announcement, a feat complicated by her hand keeping a firm grip on my waist. Of course I had registered my mother's swollen face a few hours earlier when she came to pick me up at school; and I must have known that something was very wrong when she walked me past the newsagent's without letting me go in to buy crisps (Friday was crisps day), but it was left to Granny Pea to explain that there had been a motor-bike accident. The absence of any further details – nothing about injuries, hospitals, doctors, visits – left blanks for me to fill. I was nearly seven years old. I don't know if I would have been able at that age to add up the blanks, join them to the uncomfortable pressure at my waist and arrive at the idea of my father's death. The injustice of not

getting my crisps was probably a more immediate grievance. But the possibility of his death must have grown on
me over the following days, through his absence and other
peculiar things that happened, such as the school friend's
mother who arrived unexpectedly to take me swimming;
I can still see her standing in the doorway, smiling with a
desperate good cheer. Meanwhile my own mother went
to Ireland for a few days, presumably to take my father's
body home, and there – what? As I grew older, and knew
more about these things, I pictured a proper Irish wake,
with my father displayed in his coffin and relatives
murmuring 'bejesus', dabbing at their foreheads and falling
into swoons. I had to imagine these events, because nobody
ever told me about them. And now, back in my childhood
room for the first time in nearly twenty years, I found
myself going over the old territory almost obsessively,
looking for fault lines, testing the memories for weak-
nesses. I wondered if a relationship broken so early in life
sets a pattern of breakage. Having lived with the absence
of one man throughout my childhood, perhaps it was
inevitable that as an adult I would struggle to accept the
presence of another. The child had taught the adult self-
sufficiency. Could I only love a man who wasn't there?

I stretched and felt both feet protrude at the other end
of the bed, a giantess in a storybook room, gabled at either
side. It was already ten o'clock on a Saturday morning;
Chris would be out on a run. Friends my age would have
been assembling Lego with their toddlers for hours but
being childless freed me to behave like an adolescent at
weekends, moping in pyjamas, my hair in a sulky scrunch.
I got out of bed and walked, in a crouch forced on me by

the dimensions of the room, over to the chair where my dressing gown was, feeling an intimation of old age in the movement. Then standing up straight in its centre, I looked out of the bedroom window across the valley and up towards Clapham Common. The view, a patchwork of roofs in different shades of brown with red or brown coping, hadn't changed much in thirty years, except that every year more roofs were cranked up on one side as attics were converted into loft rooms. One by one the houses were easing open, like tombs in a horror movie. In the years I had lived away this neighbourhood had been acquiring a richer occupancy, though not so rich that the residents could afford to move house without settling for a less salubrious area, so three-bedroom houses must be made to grow another room. More recently people had started digging out their basements too, burrowing underground in search of a brave new world of cinemas and mini-gyms. A few streets away from here a house had collapsed during such a project, killing one of the men who was working underneath it. 'They knock out all the bleedin' walls then they wonder why the bloody house falls down,' observed the butcher – whose own hands were bloody as he had handed over my change without apology, as if blood, real and rhetorical, was what you should expect at a butcher's. When he said 'they' it was obvious that he meant the rich newcomers, who had to fiddle with everything, who couldn't be satisfied with an average house or car, an average child or life.

For all the changes underneath them, the roofs I could see stretched out before me preserved a higgledy charm that kept faith with the undulating streets below. The old tiles were spangled with lichen that caught the light and made them twinkle. From this high vantage point there was something fabulistic about the layout of the neighbourhood. These looked like the sort of streets Wee Willie Winkie might have run through in his nightgown, or from which the Pied Piper spirited away the children of complacent parents. There was in fact a fear of that kind of drama, evident in the Neighbourhood Watch stickers on many windows and letters to the local paper calling for more community policing. Every so often some rumour would take flight about an attempted abduction or paedophiles living in a local hostel. Here and there you might see a lone shoe, left at the side of the road, or a single balloon floating up into the sky. It was an age of fear, of cameras and criminal record checks. An age in which everyone was presumed to be dangerous, when a taint of suspicion attached to all Scoutmasters and children's entertainers.

Pulling my dressing gown tight around me, I picked up from my desk the envelope Alexandra Marchant had given me and took it with my laptop downstairs, where I had commandeered the dining table for research on Turney House. There was nobody to object – no family meals in the planning, no one urging me to clear away my 'project' (for my grandmother any kind of homework was a 'project'). In the kitchen I stood frowning at the espresso maker, willing it to a spluttering climax. It was a ritual repeated daily with no variation and I was gloomily aware of it as an axis on which the days piled up, undifferentiated. Making perfect repetitions was the focus of my work; it shouldn't govern my life. The kitchen was still almost exactly as it had been when I was living here. A tall, free-standing unit with cupboards at the top and bottom and a leaf that folded out to make a sideboard was home to her Wedgwood dinner service and royal-themed biscuit tins. She had always taken a close interest in the travails of the royal family, grieving over its broken marriages as if they were the misadventures of her own children. On a pinboard beside the fridge there were old Christmas cards, a bus timetable and Palm Sunday cross. I didn't want to remove these things – I didn't feel it was my place – but perhaps I should make some changes if I ended up spending any length of time here. I might buy myself a juicer; Chris had always said they were too much hassle. I brightened to think I could make decisions now without needing his approval.

When the coffee was made, I took my cup into the dining room. Then I emptied the envelope onto the table, laid the photographs out around me and sat down to look at them. The earliest was taken in 1860 when a number of improvements were made to the house. Summoning a photographer to take portraits of his family at home must have been a coup for Lord Neville Marchant – he of the stuffed-animal collection – who stood at the centre of this photograph wearing a black tailcoat and sporting the kind of mutton chops you would expect to see on a sinister hobbyist in a period drama. Beside him, his wife was trussed into a tight-fitting silk jacket and skirt, stiffly presenting her profile to the camera. A figure in the foreground was a blur of movement, but you could tell that it was a little girl from the glossy bounce of curls, the scrimmage of petticoats. They must have felt annoyed with the child for not managing to keep still, but another photograph showed this girl in finer detail, sitting motionless on a chaise longue in the same room, a confection in knickerbockers. She was posing with a violin I took to be a birthday present, since the violin's box lay open on the chaise, a ribbon beside it. This photograph had been taken closer to the wall and the rose wallpaper was clearly defined behind her with its angular curls, the boxy red flowers standing proud of a gold background. Even though it was a monochrome photograph, you could feel the density of colour, the newness of these forms. They were oddly masculine flowers; such stout leaves looked too proud to wilt or smell pretty. Next came a set of photographs from the 1920s that had been taken for a spread in *Country Life*. That era's Lady Marchant was a dark-haired, intense beauty and seemed to know it as she cast a wistful glance over one shoulder to show off her jawline. The same woman appeared in another photograph with a gathering of ladies in cloche hats and loose cream-coloured ensembles, all carrying tennis racquets. The arrangement of the paintings on the wall behind was much the same as it had been sixty years earlier. Gainsborough's portrait of Lady Isabella still on the left, catching the sunlight, and the Van Dyck canvas further towards the right, with two smaller paintings of dogs between them. It must have changed later on, accounting for the different areas of fading which were visible by the time of the fire.

Among some more recent photographs were several of Alexandra Marchant, taken for society magazines at the time of her wedding. In the *Tatler* profile she looked about twenty-five, her lithe arms wrapped around a man who appeared puzzled but grateful for the proximity of such a beautiful woman. Lord Marchant couldn't help but look like a hobbit beside her. Why had Alexandra, a beautiful young woman, attached herself to a short-arsed dullard thirty years older than her? Why did women still *do* that kind of thing? The black-and-white portrait showed the fine grain of her skin; her long straight nose leading to a full lower lip that could have appeared greedy in a smaller face: hers was a near-perfect oval. My own face was wider and shorter – practically square, I thought, resting my chin on my thumbs with my fingers at my temples. Chris had called me 'elfin', soon after we first met, a bashful compliment he immediately regretted because it had made me burst out laughing, though really I had only laughed to cover my own embarrassment. I did sometimes wonder if I could make my face look longer by growing out my bob. Alexandra evidently had no worries about her own appearance; she faced the camera with the level gaze of a woman who knows she is beautiful and has been prepared from an early age to occupy society's highest echelon with confidence.

I guessed that boarding schools and ponies were staples in such an upbringing but perhaps these were clichés – I didn't have much contact with the upper classes, in spite of working in their houses. Usually a project manager and other intermediaries acted as a buffer. Frieda and I might be invited to lunch once a job was completed, but somehow these gatherings still retained a social hierarchy and the sense of largesse being extended from patron to worker. I wasn't even sure what it meant to be an aristocrat nowadays. Did they still bother with deportment and elocution, with coming-out parties? It would be interesting to know how much the graceful appearance of someone like Alexandra Marchant was a matter of genetic luck and how much it was the result of diets, exercise and early orthodontic intervention. And here were more photographs of Alexandra, holding babies aloft for christening shots, receiving members of the Women's Institute and, in a recent portrait, surrounded by her family on Christmas Day. The golden-haired children sitting beside a ten-foot tree among stacks of presents looked unforgivably lucky to me, when I thought of my own childhood Christmases which had sometimes been spent in the noxious company of my mother's boyfriends in cramped rented flats.

This foreground story of privilege and beauty was distracting: I was supposed to be keeping my eyes on the background.

On the laptop I called up another picture of the Rose Room, sent by an archivist at the Office of National Monuments. This one had been taken in 1865 as part of a national survey of paintings. By now the room was more fully furnished than it had been five years earlier, though it looked as though the severely corseted Victorian Lady Marchant still wasn't getting much say in the redecoration. It was definitely a man's room – there was not only the jutting botanica on the walls but Lord Marchant's desk in the foreground with all its imperial paraphernalia, his cigar box and calendarium. His outsize blotter. I didn't like Neville. He looked like the kind to force himself on the parlourmaid and take a whip to the horses, or perhaps the other way round. In any case this photograph couldn't have been much use to the art survey: light flooding in from the left hand streaked across the mirror hanging above the fireplace, and the Gainsborough, directly opposite the window, was almost completely obscured by the glare.

I rubbed my eyes, and checked my phone, hoping for an interruption. Nothing: no messages and it was too soon to justify getting another coffee. I propped up the 1860 photograph against a vase and studied it together with the image on my computer. The earlier photograph was darker and foggier and mottled by age, but in both cases the light source was the same. Making an effort to focus only on the wallpapers – their condition and detail – I scanned the two images for any information that could be valuable when we came to reconstruct the wall coverings. Fiddling with the available light sometimes helped a mystery to reveal itself. I switched off the overhead light and focused an anglepoise lamp on the table down low over the picture, scrutinising a bare inch of the 1860 photograph through my hand-held magnifier. The stiff fronds of the crimson paper's curling botanical print were clearly visible, but in an area of shade the fronds look fuzzier. 'Obviously because the chimney breast is blocking the light,' I said aloud, conjuring Frieda's presence, or someone to talk to, in this too-empty house. But there was more to it than that. The pattern looked distorted uniformly. That couldn't simply be down to a play of light.

I squinted through the magnifier until my eyes began to sting, then swung back against the chair, noting the strain in my lower spine and with it the weight of my sole presence at this table which used to be so busy with people. If I tried to imagine my father here, I couldn't see him. But I could picture my mother and aunt, in their early thirties, laden with mascara and chattering about their secretarial jobs. And Natalie, who had seemed very much my inferior during those childhood years when eight months is an appreciable age gap, worth abusing. There was Granny Pea forever hovering at one end of the table, or going to the kitchen for more food. I couldn't remember her ever sitting down at the table – she preferred to wait on everyone and we always let her. 'Is that it? Have we had enough?' And however much we answered yes, we had had enough, and more than enough, Granny Pea seemed determined to feed us more roly-poly, more suet, more semolina – until everyone pleaded with her to stop and the women started fussing about their waistbands and threatening diets. My grandmother didn't think she was doing her job unless we all left the table with indigestion.

The phone rang. Chris's face loomed on the screen, anachronistically happy in Prague, in a photograph taken before we started having problems. I hesitated before accepting the call. I did want to speak to him – I missed him after all – but I was nervous.

'Hello.' I tried to sound reasonable and accommodating right away and felt the strain of that imposition in my throat. 'How are things? Are you OK?'

'Yeah, fine. I'm sorry to bother you –' He sounded strained too.

'Don't be silly,' I said reflexively. 'I'm doing nothing. I mean, trying to work but, you know, dreaming instead.'

'Dreaming?' He seemed to give the word too much weight.

'You know. Not concentrating,' I clarified. For years

now there had been a truncated quality to our exchanges that we seemed powerless to ease. Words bumped up against what we wanted to say, grazing the truth instead of expressing it. I don't know when that happened, or began to happen. Trying to pinpoint the moment when a relationship slips off balance is bound to be invidious. It's the culmination of a thousand words and silences, of mis-interpretations and missed opportunities. It was hard to believe now that we used to talk so much – about ideas, books, films, journeys, other people – that he had seemed like the friend I always wanted, as well as a lover, a partner.

'What work are you doing?' Chris asked.

'Looking at some photos for research,' I said. 'Bit sad to be stuck indoors on a Saturday, but never mind. What about you? Have you been for a run?'

'Yes.' He sniffed. 'Look, I'm ringing because there's stuff I don't know what to do with.'

The ache in my throat spread, encircling my voicebox. 'You mean actual stuff or – I'm sorry, what stuff do you mean?'

'Well, like the Otto Dix prints we bought in Berlin. Do you want them? Because I don't really mind.'

'I suppose I don't really mind either.' If there was to be a battle of not minding, I wasn't going to be easily beaten. 'Look, Chris, we don't have to decide this now, do we? I thought we were seeing how things go. Let's take it slowly. Don't start dismantling our home.'

'I thought that was what you wanted. I could say –' I heard him draw that sharp breath he sometimes took when he was making presentations, a quick top-up of oxygen before explaining somniferous data to drowsy businessmen – 'that you had already begun to dismantle it by leaving.'

'Not "leaving" – that's too definitive,' I said. My eyes passed over Lord Neville Marchant, the complacent dome of his abdomen encased in black serge. I felt a twinge of sympathy for Lady Marchant. Imagine sleeping with such a behemoth. Her expression was pained; I bet he was a brute in bed. 'Nothing is definitive. I just thought that we could do with some time away from each other. It's not the same as "leaving".'

'"Nothing is definitive"? You've been away three months now. At some point things have to be definitive. Otherwise –'

'Of course, at some point,' I snapped, immediately regretting my tone. I couldn't stand conversations that reverted to semantics, a particularly male form of argument. 'But I don't think – I *believe* we're not at that point. Look, why don't we meet up? Talking on the phone is never the same.'

'I could do this afternoon. Have you got time today?' There was a poignant echo of the lover, a reverberation from the past that made me wish we could be students again, looking for reasons to meet, with lectures that could be sacrificed to an afternoon in bed. It would be so good to say yes, fix a time and then spend the intervening hours sick with the anticipation of seeing him, the ecstasy of his skin on mine. Once it had been terrible to think of a time when we wouldn't be together. I remember an outburst of tears at the thought of death bringing separation. Chris had said: 'But we have our whole lives to live before then.' And we had managed so little: only fifteen years.

'I can't do anything this afternoon, love,' I said regretfully. 'I've already got an appointment with the redoubtable Granny Pea.'

He laughed, in spite of himself, and, encouraged, I let myself swim into the wake of his laughter. 'Next week I could do something,' I said expansively. 'What about Thursday evening? We could go to Amici.'

'No, neutral ground. Let's go to that cafe in the crypt. I could meet you there at six.'

'OK. It means I have to stop work early but –' 'neutral ground' stung – what an irritating thing to say, the petty utterance of a bureaucrat – and I could hear that 'work' stung him too; I wanted these not to be the opening salvoes in a row about my fixation on work and general inflexibility – 'but that's fine. I can do that. Let's do that.'

'So – see you then?'

'Yes, see you then. Take care,' I said – and I did mean it.

The family gatherings that had once taken place around Granny Pea's dining-room table were these days reprised at the Ravenslea Care Home, a nursing home near Balham High Road. The table was missing, but we still honoured its shape and jurisdiction, sitting either side of Granny Pea's armchair which governed the space. Without her housecoat, though, my grandmother seemed stripped of a purpose. Her hands idled on the arms of her chair, the reddened fingers itching to scrub something, or she plucked at the material of her skirt like an unhappy bird pulling out its feathers. Her legs, swathed in support stockings, were like a man's padded up for a pantomime dame and seemed to emerge at a comic angle from her skirt. I found it sad that these days my grandmother was always in slippers, as though shoes and a life in the outside world were now forever in her past. Her head, lying against an antimacassar, and her face, framed with lacy rondels and her own sparse curls, could have belonged to the dowager in a Victorian comedy. I greeted her with a kiss on the smooth dome of her forehead. Her cheeks were soft and papery now and I couldn't bear to feel the unresisting skin under my lips. And I handed her some home-made biscuits in a Tupperware box, hoping to jog a memory of her own industry.

'I hope they'll be allowed,' I said. 'They haven't got nuts or anything.'

'Nuts?' said Granny Pea quizzically.

'You know, some people have allergies to nuts.'

'Some people have memories of nuts?'

'Never mind, Granny, it's not important.'

Our family visits began in a spirit of purpose. We would all keep up a chirrupy exchange of news as GP listened, moving her head like a wintering bird from one bosom to the other. She made the odd contribution, often some-thing surprising, about Cliff Richard or the Prince of Wales, twin gods in her pantheon. A favourite theme was the boiler at Alma Street. Today, after about twenty minutes of this, her head sank into the soft layers buttoned over her chest and a throaty cooing ensued. For a minute or two we watched her in churchified silence, then my Aunt Mariel edged forward on her seat, watching the Tupperware box rise and fall until a low rumbling indicated Granny Pea's departure to a sleepier realm. In the second that her grip relaxed, Mariel pounced. The rest of us offered congratulatory smiles as the Tupperware was caught, secured and gently moved away.

Mariel made some anodyne remark about the previous evening's television, opaque to John and me, but instantly understood by my mother. They were less than a year apart in age and seemed sometimes to share the intuition of twins.

Uncle John twitched with irritation, tapping his toes and drumming his fingers on the armrests. 'Women. They speak a kind of code,' he said, not to me, but up through his wiry eyebrows. He was a physicist and an unbeliever, so this remark stopped at the ceiling. 'There should be a system. Why visit in the afternoon when all the inmates are going to be asleep anyway?' He looked disapprovingly at my grandmother, whose mouth had fallen open, her moistened lower lip quivering on every out-breath. John was neat and in command of himself. GP posed a challenge to his sense of decorum.

Mariel followed his gaze. 'I think you might find the same was true in the mornings,' she said unhappily. 'People of this age just do sleep a lot.'

'Have we decided when the house at Alma Street should go on the market?' I said, meaning to defuse tensions and inadvertently creating a new source of them.

'What do you mean "on the market"?' my mother said. She turned sharply towards me, moving only her head. The chairs in this room had noisy springs and Granny Pea's sleeps were movement-sensitive. Sometimes the four of us sat almost in silence for twenty minutes, doing crosswords or reading but, if anyone stood up even if only to reach for another biscuit, Granny Pea opened her eyes with a look of hurt bewilderment. So we kept as still as possible, speaking in stage whispers, moving our mouths in a near-soundless communication.

'We're not at that stage yet, Ros. At the moment there's a lot of back and forth with the council. Social services. It's all taking a bit of time,' said Mariel with a patient smile.

'Why, what do they say?' I said.

'It's not entirely clear that the house needs to be sold in order for Mum's care to be paid.'

'It makes sense to sell, though, doesn't it? The market's sky-high.'

'Yes – but not necessarily now. If we sell it then we would almost certainly have to contribute to the cost of the care.'

'Is she allowed to keep it? I thought the law was that you had to sell.'

'We're still not sure about that. If it's occupied by the family we may be able to keep it. Social services are dragging their feet a bit,' Mariel said apologetically, as though this were in some way her fault.

'Oh, so it's a game of wits,' I said. 'We have to seem to be occupying it.'

'Hardly a game.' My mother's eyes batted impatiently and she looked like an exotic bird sending out warning signals. Her eyelids were covered in iridescent greens and blues, with striations of silver and smoky grey under the eyebrow. The eyebrows themselves were plucked very thin, as they always had been, then reinstated with kohl. I knew that it took a long time to apply this make-up because I had often observed the process as a child, lolling on my mother's bed as she dabbed colour from the little pots around her eyes. At the time I accepted without question that this was the way an adult woman looked – parents being a child's pre-eminent models for life – and I expected one day to spend a portion of every morning creating the same effect, just as I had once expected to wear power suits and pencil skirts and to have my hair in a lacquered cloud around my head.

Aunt Mariel leaned forward, hingeing her upper body in a smooth movement calibrated to make no noise. 'Granny still thinks she's moving back home one day.' Her lips were painted a shade of taupe whereas my mother's mouth was bright red. Both sets of lips framed a snaggle-toothed denture that gave their faces a peculiar girlishness. Iris, who was more self-conscious about her teeth than Mariel, only ever laughed with her mouth closed. Mariel's teeth pinched her lower lip when she smiled, clipping a bloodless fold of skin between the front incisors.

'But we did agree that a time would come to sell the house,' I said. 'We talked about it with Natalie that time, remember?'

'Yes, but after she – you *know*.' My mother flung out her hand, open-palmed in an emphatic gesture as if Death were sitting there between Granny Pea and her, a solid entity you could point at but wouldn't want to name.

'I don't think she shows any signs of that,' said John grimly. 'She could go on for years.'

'She'll probably outlive us all,' said Mariel with a nervous smile.

We were keeping our movements small. Even Uncle John, who fizzed with energy all the time, was finding ways to expend it at his extremities, his feet tapping fast but noiselessly on the carpet, his hands simulating drumming on the chair arms, without touching them.

'It's actually very convenient that you're there, for the moment,' said Mariel. 'Because that way the property is occupied by our family which means –'

'Yes, but how long are you actually planning to be there for?' Iris asked crossly.

'Well, you know, I don't *know*, Mum. I'm there for the moment. I can certainly stay for a while and make myself useful, maybe start getting the place packed up.'

'It sounds very uncertain,' said my mother disapprovingly.

'Because it *is* uncertain at the moment. Sorry about that!' Forgetting to be circumspect I sat back sharply, forcing a squeaky gasp from the chair.

'Yes, the sweet peas are all just beginning to come out and are looking lovely,' said Mariel, flashing her eyes at me then rolling them like a mime artist back over towards Granny Pea, who was stirring in her chair. GP's eyes fluttered open.

'What's that, dear?' she said. 'A lovely time of year for the garden, did you say? Are you watering everything, chick?'

'Yes, Granny, don't you worry,' I said. 'I water the pots every evening.'

'That will be something nice to come home to, pet.'

As far as care homes go, the Ravenslea was not an unpleasant place to end your days. It was probably just the fact of knowing that this was it, that the onward journey was not an earthly one, that gave the air its sombre colour. For that reason, this sitting-room area, which was part genteel hotel, part children's activity centre, also had a darker aura of last-chance saloon. The aim of the staff was that no one must be upset – although there could be few things more upsetting than the thought of an imminent death – so there was an atmosphere of good cheer, even of a strained ebullience. The residents, my grandmother among them, had spent a lifetime brooking upheaval – bereavements, divorces, miscarriages, redundancies – and now all efforts were focused on keeping distress at bay. Paintings in the style of Impressionist artists were meant to induce feelings of a hazy well-being, maybe even stir up memories of times spent on the beach or in summer gardens. The carers moved around the space brightly, making whatever physical adjustments were necessary to navigate the many chairs and Zimmer frames. Here and there they bent down and made cheerful remarks at spooked-out faces. Jackie, the deputy care manager, had a small neat head, with chins cascading down to a large bust, several spare tyres and a vast bottom. Like a stackable toy, she would be hard to knock over. 'God moves in mysterious ways,' she said, as people often do, the difference being that Jackie completed the sentiment, 'His wonders to perform.'

'You perform wonders more like, Jackie,' quipped an old man, who had entered the turtle phase of life, with slow sideways movements of the eyes and head and a soft padding of his papery lips. His trousers were the same colour as his armchair and his torso appeared to be growing straight out of its seat, as if he had taken root there after so many years. His lap held a tray on which there was a very basic puzzle. Many of the residents were Jewish and sometimes a visiting rabbi tried to get people to dance with him. 'So many lovely ladies to choose from!' he said, whirling among the Zimmer frames. 'I am indeed a lucky man, a blessed man.' Those who didn't want to dance could make collages, memory books or attend creative writing sessions. Before entering Ravenslea, Granny Pea had never in her life made something simply for fun nor was she used to so much spontaneous cheer. Scheduled cheer was fine, for weddings and baptisms – something that you could put on with a brooch and a hat. She endured it well, but that might be because she was under the impression that her residence here was temporary, that one day she would return to the house in Alma Street and her beloved garden.

'The hollyhocks are taller this year than I've ever seen them,' I said. 'The buddleia is covered with butterflies. I've never seen so many cabbage whites.'

Without lifting her chin off her bust, Granny Pea fixed me with a sharp look, as though these details constituted vital information, of exactly the kind she had been needing to solve a puzzling case. I dared not look away. My grandmother had only recently acquired this piercing expression, the 'beady eye' that people spoke of in relation to the elderly and which I didn't understand until the day I felt my grandmother's pale blue eyes, like circles of glass, boring into my own face. She had never looked so alert in her housecoat days. Back then her face was placid and dozy, a reflection of the comforting puddings she produced on Sundays. Her responses to my chatter about school were rarely more expansive than a rising 'hmm' to denote 'what did you say?' and a falling 'hmm' for something like 'well I never!'

Compelled now to make the most of my grandmother's attention, I said, 'I thought I might not cut back the buddleia this year. If we leave it unpruned, we can attract more birds and butterflies. The foxgloves are going up like rockets.'

Granny Pea drank deeply of this information, then seemed immediately to feel its surfeit. She blinked heavily and when she opened her eyes again the perspicacity had gone and the cold blue irises were glazed with a sleepy warmth. Aunt Mariel lifted her hand from the chair arm, signalling no more talk of foxgloves. 'It's a pity,' said Granny Pea, but said nothing more. Two or three times she moved her lower lip sideways, looking unexpectedly girlish, then she let out a world-weary sigh. We watched the old head teeter on its axis before dropping by degrees towards her chest. Mariel's hand was still raised and all kept quiet. Finally a low rumble emanated from underneath the woollen jumper, a sound that I associated with night trains on the Underground. We waited for a moment, until Granny Pea's breathing had fallen into an even rhythm. Then Mariel eased herself back in the chair.

'What if you don't manage to sort things out with Chris?' hissed my mother. 'What if you divorce?' Her tone suggested I was bound to divorce, that this would be a tremendous inconvenience to her, though the truth was that my mother had never liked Chris. He was too reticent for her tastes and not given to flirting.

'If that happens I'll have to look for my own place, won't I?'

'In this market? Have you seen the cost of rents?'

'I'm not a child, Mum. If there's a hurry for me to be out of Granny's house, I can leave. I can rent a place, stay with friends – whatever.'

'No, no, darling, it's the opposite of that,' said Mariel quickly. 'We'd *like* you to stay. Otherwise the situation may become quite complicated.'

'You worry. You're a worrier,' announced John to his wife, not with sympathy but as a statement of fact, as though he were in his laboratory writing out labels for samples.

'Yes, I know,' Mariel admitted, adding with an anxious smile, 'sometimes I even worry when there's nothing to worry about. I think "I know there was something" but I can't –'

'Ros's got a right to choose where she lives,' interrupted John. 'There's no question of her having to sacrifice her own interests for ours. She's a young woman at the start of her life.'

'Hardly young,' my mother murmured, raising her eyebrows.

The years passed, I thought, but they are the same as they always were. My mother and aunt, who had never learned to swim or to drive. My uncle, so alive with nervous energy that he seemed to burn up calories as soon as he ingested them. In his younger days there had been no fat on him anywhere. Now he had a modest pot belly that was commensurate with his modest savings account, his modest insurance policy. His hands were always moving, whether drumming a tattoo on the arms of his chair, fluttering in the air to illustrate ideas of theoretical physics or jotting down invisible words. Sometimes, surprisingly, one would pop up behind his head, tapping at the hairline or clawing the skin of his own forehead as if he were about to whip off the mask of his face and reveal some horrifying visage beneath it: Professor Psycho. Aunt Mariel, in contrast, moved little, hingeing from the waist, now and then cocking her head to one side or another, apparently reluctant to investigate the full range of movements available to her.

'The thing is that there are implications, John,' she said. Her tone, though gentle, allowed that there was in fact a reservoir of good sense and useful knowledge hidden under the surface. She knew she wasn't as stupid as her husband made her out to be. 'If no one from the family is occupying the house we can't claim that it is a family home.'

'None of that is Ros's concern. We can move in there ourselves if necessary.'

'Really? Would you?' said Iris, incredulous.

Uncle John shrugged his shoulders very fast, like a child in a hurry to get away from a scolding. 'Why not? It's of absolutely no concern to me where I live!'

Mariel shot him a look of wounded exasperation, her house pride flung in her face.

'You've got a lovely house already!' said Iris, but it was a quiet remonstration, qualified with a few nervy movements of hand and foot, because my mother was frightened of John – at least that was my theory. I didn't know if that was because there was some history between them

– an altercation or embarrassment nobody mentioned any more – or if it was simply that John was the only man in the family and made her feel unhusbanded. In my mother's eyes, a woman without a consort risked looking like a spinster or a whore. She always seemed more confident in the company of a boyfriend, however awful, than she was on her own.

'A house is a house, Iris. If someone needs to live in it, I volunteer.' John sat low in the chair, his tapping feet drawing him lower, with Mariel primly upright beside him. For a moment they looked more like a mother and rebellious son than husband and wife. That 'I' with its implications that he would be happier alone was unnecessarily cruel. It embarrassed me, at times, that John was so quick to defend my interests, even when I didn't need or deserve support. He was kinder to me than he was to his own wife.

'I would like to go up in a rocket,' piped up a girlish voice and for a moment all of us froze, not sure who had spoken, then Aunt Mariel said in the tone of a dutiful daughter, 'Would you really, Mum? You mean up to the moon like an astronaut?'

'Not like a bloody astronaut!' snapped Granny Pea. 'My ashes, I mean. That's what Godfrey is going to do. She pointed at the old man who had complimented Jackie and who had been smiling foolishly at them since they arrived. 'He wants his ashes sent up in a firework so that bits of him end up all over London. He says he's had women all over London and he wants to leave a piece of himself in every borough.'

All eyes turned on Godfrey, the sexual conqueror, who

broke a toothless grin, and performed a little half-bow over his jigsaw puzzle.

In the car afterwards, I folded myself into a corner of the back seat, imitating the child I used to be, hidden behind Mariel, as John negotiated junctions with explosive bouts of road rage. You felt very close to the ground in John's car, especially now that so many road users travelled in Jeeps and Land Rovers, looking for an advantage in height, just as they looked for it in so many other places. That was the trouble with advantage – it was a crowded platform and the disadvantaged seemed to be slipping further and further below it. John's car was so low I had the sensation of skidding along just a few inches above the road. There was quite a draught in the footwell and I imagined that if I peeled back the floor mat I might see the road racing by beneath us.

'How's work, love?' said Mariel, turning to look over her shoulder. Ever since I could remember my aunt's kindly face had been filling this gap between the front seats with polite but worrisome enquiries. *How's school? How's college? How's your mum?* Years of unfocused worry had left a permanent crease between her eyebrows.

'Good, thanks. Frieda and I got this job at Turney House. I don't know if you heard about the fire –'

'Of course! What a terrible thing.' The crease deepened into an indentation, and even when she turned away to face forward again, I could see her in the wing mirror worrying about this event that had no claim on her thoughts at all but that was nevertheless going to occupy them until a new worry came to take its place.

I sat forward between them. 'John?'

'Yes, love?' said my uncle, looming up in the rear-view mirror. This indirect way of talking to a driver always felt awkward to me. John's eyes looked ferrety and suspicious when they were framed and separated from the rest of his face, as though they belonged on a swatch waiting to be fitted into a criminal photofit. I could imagine my uncle turning criminal one day, breaking bad after some particularly violent fit of anti-government rage tipped him into action. He also seemed to be getting hairier with age. Wiry curls, escapees from his beard, were sprouting in the wrinkles around his eyes. That isn't right, I thought. That's an odd place to have hair.

'Do you remember taking me to Turney House with Natalie? We must have been about fourteen.'

'To where, love?'

'Turney House. We looked at the globe.'

'Yes, I do remember it. Curious place. Was that where Natalie's contact lens fell out in the garden?'

'I'd forgotten that.' I smiled at the memory of my cousin's lumbering form in a black minidress and platform shoes, wodges of opalescent thigh shining through her tights as she bent over to inspect the path. 'She'd only just started wearing them and she hadn't brought her glasses as backup. She had to keep one eye closed the rest of the day to see anything.'

'Really, how silly. She should have known to take her specs,' said Mariel, shaking her head. 'Somebody should have reminded her.' I felt my aunt's worry working retroactively on this new scenario, gnawing at the edges of the anecdote with attributions of blame.

As we stopped at a red light a Land Rover pulled up beside us, spick and span as utility vehicles are in London, and the child inside it stared down at me from behind tinted glass. This boy, who looked about five, was wearing some kind of kit for judo or karate. The race for advantage began at an ever earlier age. In front his mother was frowning and tapping the wheel with manicured nails. I tried to imagine myself into her role, ferrying around children instead of rolls of antique wallpaper.

'I do remember that extraordinary collection of stuffed animals,' said John. 'There was even a dodo, wasn't there?'

'Yeah. They stuffed their pets too.'

'Peculiar people. I always felt there was something strange about the place. Something more than met the eye.'

'What sort of thing?' Now I felt compelled to meet my uncle's eye in the mirror, or risk looking shifty myself.

'Well, I always thought, I mean it's rather ironic that – wasn't the family fortune built on shit?'

'John!'

'Well, I'm afraid it's true, Mariel.' John's hands locked on the wheel, his body stiffening into a well-worn annoyance. 'In the mid-1800s the Marchants made *a lot* of money out of Peruvian guano.'

'That's not exactly the same thing.'

'It is precisely the same thing, *Mariel*,' said John, so much steel in the way he spoke her name you could hear the menace glinting off it. 'Guano *is* pigeon shit.'

'Really?' said Mariel quietly. 'I didn't know that. It's got such a pretty ring to it.'

Up he popped again in the rear-view mirror. 'I just think anyone who makes their money out of flogging shit –'

'John – please stop saying that.'

'– anyone who makes their money out of flogging shit to people probably puts money before principles. Once a shit merchant always a shit merchant.'

The merciless repetition had knocked Mariel back into her seat where she sat silently, simmering.

'And before guano it was sugar,' I said, hoping to sweeten the conversation for my aunt. 'In the eighteenth century they owned sugar plantations.'

'Slave drivers too. Well, it doesn't surprise me. As long as they're treating you all right, that's all that matters,' said John, beaming at me from the top of the windscreen, a tree air-freshener dangling beneath him.

They dropped me at Alma Street and I waved them away from the front doorstep feeling like an abandoned child. Sunday evenings with Chris had been companionably aimless. We used to ransack the fridge and eat strange combinations of things on toast, standing beside the counter with the toaster to hand, or we sat at the kitchen table with the Sunday papers spread around us. It was civilised, I always thought, perhaps too civilised compared to the cheerful mayhem of a family meal. These days my grandmother's house was even quieter – no Sunday papers and nothing much in the fridge. There was toast, at least. I switched the kettle on and walked into the front room to put on the TV, but catching sight of the Rose Room photographs I was drawn back to the dining-room table. I turned on the overhead lights, and the anglepoise lamp. Natalie and I had given this lamp to Granny Pea as a birthday present one year when she started to complain that she couldn't see her embroidery, but she always refused to use it, saying the light was too harsh. That last year before she had gone into the nursing home had been blighted by a growing impatience both with her circumstances and with all attempts to improve them, which had been frustrating for everyone. Now I realised that Granny Pea hadn't wanted an improvement in her lighting arrangement, she had wanted an improvement in her eyesight. It was the business of ageing that was too harsh, not the light itself.

Angling the lamp down low over the photographs, I set to studying the images again, 150 years in the life of a country house, laid out on my grandmother's dining-room table. I came back to the two photographs from 1860 and 1865, scrutinising one, then the other, then back to the first. This time, either the new arrangement of lights or my afternoon away from the job released the information that had eluded me that morning, and when I picked up my magnifier to look at the 1860 picture I saw straight away that there was a pattern underneath the rose paper showing through it. The uniform fuzziness I had spotted earlier was the weave of an underlying paper – a phenomenon conservators call 'ghosting' or the 'halo effect'. That underlying pattern would not have been visible to people using the room at the time, but the photographer's flash had brought it forward. 'A ghost', I thought, and smiling, I said aloud: 'There's a ghost in the Rose Room.'

THREE

People working at Turney House entered the site by a small door in the garden wall on the north side. On the other side of that door was Bob, or sometimes Cole, security guards and unofficial court jesters. Cole was young, probably not much over twenty, and full of smiles. He liked to refer everything back to his childhood in Barbados. The banana that I brought in for lunch was not as good as a Barbadian banana. A hot day in London was not as hot as a day in Barbados, a blue sky not as blue. Bob was thirty years older and favoured a more oblique approach, centred on subtle physical humour – head-scratching, chin-rubbing, eye-rolling. 'Call that a sandwich?' was more his style, with a sardonic glance up to the less-than-Barbadian sky. His eyes seemed more often to be directed upwards than down into the bags he was meant to be inspecting. He gave the impression of finding the Turney crew and their work too silly to warrant close attention.

Cole and Bob were the gatekeepers to a world of industry irresistible to anyone raised on that English lode of secret gardens, wonderlands, Tardises and magic wardrobes. The door they guarded was a portal to another dimension, an invitation to leave a grubby corner of the twenty-first century and step into a magical reworking of the past. Standing on the road outside, among kebab shops and nail bars, there was no guessing the scale of the enterprise behind Turney's high brick walls, where a hundred people were killing themselves to recreate an eighteenth-century home, on time and to budget. We were going to bring back sconces and casements, cornicing and pilasters. We were going to resurrect friezes and bas-relief. Bodily we would transpose one century onto another. All we needed were power sources and an infinite supply of tea bags.

I love the contradictions of site work, that combination of meticulous labour and moral anarchy. The hours pass in pursuit of some infinitesimally small aim, the removal of microscopic specks of dirt from an object, say, or the application of tiny fragments of colour onto a paper surface with tweezers. It's an exercise in such extreme care that afterwards the world seems to give you permission to be reckless. People in my line of work are often drinkers and smokers, no strangers to a joint or a tab. When the pressure's on to finish, normal rules and timetables go out of the window. We work all the hours we can, until the light goes, or energy gives out – and there are times when people don't even make it home, but sleep in their vans, or under blankets on the floor, like festival-goers or besotted lovers. There are dangers associated with that unreal state; it's too easy to neglect the payment of bills, the looming dentist appointments, a marriage drifting off course (some people would say it's the perfect place to be when your marriage is drifting off course). The demands of the job absorb the mind fully, and when the day finally ends, there are compensations in the form of drink or sex. It's a social microcosm, like a hospital, I suppose, or a university.

Seen through the mist of an early-spring morning, the arrangement of tents pitched on the lawn at Turney House called to mind a military hospital close to the front line. This was where the damaged objects had been brought immediately after the fire. The sodden carpets had been laid out to dry in a marquee erected in front of the house. The stuffed animals in their glass cases had stood sentry on the lawn, growling in the firelight. Now we surgeons had arrived to begin the patch-up job, with our gloves and scalpels, our drinking rituals and our hard-won self-importance.

As a child sitting on Granny Pea's knee, sucking my right thumb and using the other hand to grip her earlobe – a habitual pose – I had once seen a news item about a Tudor mansion that was going to be lifted off its foundations and moved downhill because the owners wanted a change of view. I remember being fascinated by the story, though Granny Pea's verdict had been that 'some people have more money than sense'. This restoration under way at Turney felt like a similar piece of whimsy, but enormously more complex – the mother of all jigsaw puzzles, with at least a third of the pieces missing.

'It's like one of those explosions in reverse they show on TV,' I said to my cousin Natalie when she dropped round one evening to bring me some single portions hived off meals she had cooked for the family. 'You know, when you see everything flying back into its proper place? Only it's going to take about three years. Then everything will look exactly as it was.'

'Nobody will even know there was a fire?'

'That's the idea.'

'Blimey. All that effort just to go back to square one. Is it worth it?'

'Depends what you mean by "worth it".'

My cousin, solidly planted on the kitchen linoleum in skinny jeans that didn't suit her, blinked with a fear of having said the wrong thing.

'It's worth preserving things that are special,' I went on. 'You have to honour what went before. Otherwise there's no understanding.'

'But I mean you're there all hours. I thought Europe was clamping down on that. Some directive or other.'

'It's always been that way, Nat. I can't see it changing. Anyway, there's a lot of kudos in working on a job like this.' I could hear how weak that sounded, even though it was the conservator's mantra, as though kudos made up for never being able to afford a mortgage or a foreign holiday.

'Well, don't let the bastards grind you down. Look after yourself,' she said and endearingly bit her lower lip.

'You're always so protective, Nat, and I'm supposed to be the older one.'

'Never mind "supposed to be". You basically are.'

'And you really didn't need to do this.' I pointed at the stack of individual portions with which my cousin seemed to be sealing my single status though I knew she didn't mean it that way: we had both been brought up to regard Tupperware boxes as an expression of love.

'I wanted to. I've got a nurturing personality,' said Natalie.

'I'm sure, but –'

'I mean officially. People were sending round one of those Internet surveys and I came up as "nurturing".' She smiled. 'So shut up and be grateful.'

As Phase Two got under way, Turney marshalled its forces, established its pecking order and settled into a working rhythm oiled by jokes and stereotypes. Every site needs its clutch of pranksters and fall guys. There's always a favourite dance move and a favourite song to be hummed, whistled or wailed in a form of tuneless imploration. The team of specialist carpenters from Liverpool were stars of a running gag – they were making the staircase and weeks over schedule. The prohibition on screws – not invented in Georgian times – was a source of endless double entendres. The tally of injuries so far ran to a dozen sprains, two broken arms and one crushed vertebra.

Meanwhile the garden had disappeared under an encampment of tents and knocked-up workshops and sheds. Two long greenhouses had been requisitioned for carvers, gilders and stonemasons. The orangery was home to a team of plasterers. The old stables, which usually housed Turney's famous cafe, had been made over to Frieda and me for our intimate surgery. This was where the twelve panels of wallpaper – flayed by firemen from the walls as fire devoured the Rose Room – were delivered from storage in their paper bandages, still smelling sweetly of smoke and burned adhesives.

We spent our first two days on site leaning over the panels of salvaged paper, classifying the damage, identifying the areas that were going to be patched, and those that would need to be remade altogether. We worked in quiet restitution, brushing the surpaper with sable brushes or using a suction pipe which could be brought down close to the paper for micro-cleaning. The new paper was going to be made in two colours, one to match the wallpaper that was exposed, another for the areas that had been protected from the light because they were covered by paintings and the great Cranhook mirror, which had hung in the same place, over the mantelpiece, for 150 years. Other parts would be darkened by hand or deliberately rubbed away to recreate areas of wear and tear, for example around the fireplace where generations of people had leaned against the walls, pontificating on the issues of the day. The paintings and the mirror were going back to the same positions they had occupied before the fire, so the paper under them would never be seen, but it was Alexandra Marchant's wish that things look right, even when there was nobody to see them. She had said that she would 'hate to know that the colour underneath was wrong'. That it 'makes no historic sense' to have some sections of the room out of kilter with others. Even if she couldn't see it, she wanted to know that it was as it had always been. 'If we're going to do this, let's do it properly. Everything has to be exactly as it was the day before the fire.'

A rough-edged energy defined the garden. One of the gilders (they were both women, angelically pretty) complained that it was a macho environment, but I liked the shouting and radio battles, that sense of a tension barely held in check. It was a good contrast to the tidy solitude of the studio Frieda and I shared in east London. Calm prevailed because it must with so many fragile elements around, but every now and then tempers burst out in a rush of shouting and swearing. A boiler suit and hobnail boots seemed to embolden the wearer, while also making everyone else in a boiler suit and hobnail boots look like an aggressor. The rows were usually about something inconsequential like a boiling kettle or a missing cable. Frieda and I watched the sparring parties from the window in our stable. If the plasterers were the worst-tempered, perhaps it was because they had the hardest job. In the large marquee – where the carpets and curtains had first been brought to dry – they were attempting to recreate the library ceiling. Most of the plasterwork at Turney had been smashed to pieces when the ceilings fell down either during the fire or the following day, but four days after it was completely extinguished, a cartouche had been salvaged from the library with barely a mark on it. It survived only because it had fallen onto a cushioning pile of debris. That scene was now the centre piece of a giant puzzle. Dionysus reclined, bewildered, while pot-bellied ladies fed him grapes. Vines were going to radiate out from the cartouche and the hanging bunches of grapes would be moulded by hand, in situ, as the plaster dried. The team of four men and one woman were having to relearn a forgotten art, working plaster decoration by hand, without recourse to moulds. Every now and then one of them emerged from the tent to kick a stump of wood they had placed outside the tent for this very purpose. Two of the men I knew from previous jobs on other houses and it was comfortable to slip into old rivalries and flirtations, to sense that the door was open to more, that things could happen. It felt good.

In another tent the carvers were laying out pieces of panelling, fitting new pieces as they were finished into old ones. The new oak, some of which had been donated by the Queen, had been stored together with the old for a year, so that the two different woods would mature together and not be antagonists when they were finally joined. When I told her that, Natalie had spluttered on the end of the phone. 'Why does the Queen donate *anything* to them? That is the kind of thing that actually makes my blood boil. It's like nothing's changed, there's still this secret network of aristocrats and old alliances.'

At lunch and tea breaks the tension broke out in laughter and pratfalls, smutty jokes and wedgies. Some of the older ones did the crossword, puzzling collectively over cryptic clues.

'Bazooka? Enzymes? Hazards?'

'Perhaps the z is wrong.'

The debris of fire-damaged houses used to be shovelled into skips and carted off to rubbish dumps, but Turney was practising new conservation techniques based on the concept of 'ethical stewardship'. That meant every shard and smithereen must be saved and as little as possible recreated. If an object was mostly remade from its own original elements it couldn't be dismissed as 'repro' – a dirty word in historical circles – but was still deemed 'authentic' – a very good word. Days after the fire, ropes had been strung across each room to create a grid. Debris was collected and put into dustbins bearing the same grid references. More than three thousand bins were filled with charred and ashen remains, then each bin sorted by hand in a technique developed by police forensic specialists while working at the scene of IRA bombings. All the debris had been loaded onto a conveyor belt for inspection by student archaeologists who spent several thousand hours cataloguing every burned and charred remnant, sorting them into the constituent parts of different items that had come to dust within each grid. In this black, sticky netherworld everything could be something else. After hours on the job some of the sorters complained of heritage fatigue. Was the unidentified lump in hand a piece of cherub, a chunk of gilt frame? Was it part of an urn or a marble mantelpiece, cornicing or casement? And it was never good enough to dismiss something as dust. What kind of dust was it and of what provenance, what consistency? Anything that couldn't be positively identified was sent to the bottom of the garden to be stored in a polytunnel that was like an archaeologist's research project: lying on bakers' trays were tens of thousands of unidentified fragments, row upon row of items that could count as evidence towards a domestic life long gone.

There were days we worked fourteen hours, and all of us were underpaid. The Marchants tried to defuse the building resentment with an unending supply of tea and biscuits. A corner of the old kitchen in the servants' quarters had been made over to us, with a kettle and a microwave and above it a noticeboard covered with photographs from the time of the rescue effort, spurring everyone towards a heroism that had been here once and could be attained again. The effort of those early days had been shaped into an inspiring story. There were photographs of the volunteers who had spent weeks sorting pieces of crud gurning into the camera, crossing their eyes, sticking out pierced tongues. 'Anyone know what century THIS came from?' said a note above a photo of a woman holding up beside her face – with predictable disgust – a blackened melted square on which the letters 'Abba' could just be discerned. The vinyl had fused with the cardboard and many other ungodly fusions had taken place at Turney, between stone and paint, enamel and wood. Even a carver and a plasterer got it together once, behind the polytunnel. Another snapshot showed one of the electricians squatting down, exposing a wedge of hairy arse. Somebody had drawn an arrow pointing into the cleavage and added the words 'Finally located: the last piece of the Turney Chandelier!' And there was a photograph of three runners finishing the London Marathon, red and sweating under their powdered Georgian wigs with 'By Jove! I'm running for Turney' emblazoned on their vests.

A few days after we had started working at Turney, Alexandra Marchant ventured into the garden, wearing a crisp white shirt with navy-blue capri pants, cut at the calf to reveal graceful ankles and the requisite dolphin tattoo. Her hair, loose around her shoulders, had been blow-dried at a salon and her look was accessorised by two boys, trotting behind her in jeans and surfer-dude T-shirts. In fact, their clothes weren't so different from any other boys their age, but the hair-flicking, the languid confidence, gave this pair a look of wealthy scions. The older boy had a loose athletic stride while the younger one surged forward in bursts, putting his head down and charging like a bull. More than once he collided with a much older man, who walked ahead of the group with a halting step. The man had no option each time but to catch this child in the soft expanse below his belt.

'Tea break!' cried Alexandra Marchant. 'Down tools!' On an upturned crate she set down a tray on which there was a cake and a jug of some summery drink with fruit in it and sprigs of mint. She seemed nervous as she looped a few strands of hair behind her ear, exposing a diamond earring. The garden was no longer the Marchants' natural territory now that this land had been ceded to us workers, toiling in our overalls and boots. Her boys skittered around the doors of different workshops, inviting the workers to come out for cake – but not everybody was charmed by the Honourable Marchants; some of them looked irritated by the summons. These days the garden was a more complicated place than Capability Brown ever intended.

Frieda and I went with the others to stand around the cake which had the number 500 iced on it. 'Your birthday is it, Lady Marchant?' asked Bob, casting facetious glances up at the sky, the un-Barbadian sky. She slapped his arm with the back of her hand, then made a speech about how she couldn't believe we had all come so far and how she really just wanted to take this opportunity to thank everybody, that every single person had a part to play and every single person was appreciated. Hungrily she looked around the gathering, wanting to meet each set of eyes and, although some people were amenable to the contact, others deliberately seemed to make their gaze unavailable. Her speech was greeted with a half-hearted cheer, then a group of the more biddable workers posed with Alexandra Marchant for a photograph and she took up the knife and made as though to stab the cake, prompting a warmer response of laughter, before finding a more natural arrangement and smiling into the lens. The blade glinted under her red nails as she made the first cut.

'Like Lady Macbeth,' whispered Frieda as we went back to our stable workshop. We had finished our preliminary cleaning of the papers and I wanted to show her the photographs of the Rose Room wallpaper before we packed up for the day. As I took them out of their envelope and laid them on the worktop in front of her, she was still looking out of the window, as though at a framed picture of the people milling about outside.

'Look at the poor husband,' said Frieda, tutting.

'I hadn't realised he was so old.'

'He's about seventy, but not in good health, I believe. Drinks and smokes.'

There was a lopsidedness about Lord Marchant that could be down to drink, I thought. He seemed to stand at an angle to the ground, an unnatural disparity of the shoulders pulling him to one side, his hands clasped awkwardly in front of him. Alexandra Marchant, moving to speak to her husband, held onto one of his arms and pulled on it, treating it as a kind of handrail as she levered him down to gain access to his chewed-looking ear. Lord Marchant listened to whatever his wife was saying with a crumbling smile. I remembered the image of him tearing around Turney in his little racing car. He seemed less like an adjunct in his wife's restoration plan than an obstacle to it, someone who had grown used to being pulled and prodded and yet was somehow always in the way.

'So, show me what you've got,' said Frieda. She put on the glasses that usually hung on a chain made of tortoiseshell plastic links – the kind of object that becomes so identified with its owner that you love it disproportionately – and studied the pictures in front of her with a frown. It was a frequent complaint of hers that people had lost the habit of looking. In art galleries they would rather film or photograph paintings than study them. 'Nobody wants to pause,' she'd say. 'Everyone must keep moving. People have become more interested in recording their lives than in living them.' When I had first gone to work for her, Frieda took me on a 'horror tour' of paintings in the National Gallery, pointing out examples of overzealous restoration. 'They clean off the shading and they take away half the expression, and then it's too late.' Now she produced a magnifying glass and scrutinised the photos with a learned and slightly whiskery pout. I waited beside her, watching and waiting for revelation to bloom in her expression: my reward for good detective work. Decades of smiling and frowning had cross-hatched her cheeks and forehead with fine lines. Thirty years of smoking had puckered her upper lip, but Frieda's face, round and mischievous in the childhood photographs she had once shown me over tea at her house, still retained a girlish air; her eyes were bright with enquiry and her hair, although it was grey now, was still cut in a wiry bob that required clips and grips to keep it off her face.

'Yes, you are right,' she said with a slow smile. 'I can see some halo effect in this area, though we can't be sure that the original paper is still underneath – it could have left its imprint and then deteriorated, leaving only the ghost. Who's going to break the news to Lady Macbeth?' The tortoiseshell links rattled as she took off her glasses and turned to me. 'She won't like this, you know.'

'I know. We need to be absolutely sure there's something there before we say anything.'

'Let's leave it until Monday. We've done enough today. I think all your hard work deserves a drink.'

'I'd love to, Frieda, but I've arranged to go and meet Chris.'

'Oh,' she said, raising her eyebrows. 'You're definitely going to need a drink then.'

At six o'clock that evening I made my way into central London at the same moment that workers were leaving it, streaming across the river and away from the office blocks as though in flight from a disaster. After four long, intense days at Turney I seemed to come blinking back into the modern world, dazed by the speed of everything, the rich colours and variety of people. Women on phones, in trainers, strained their seams with the speed of their advance, the day's four-inch heels tucked into handbags that were large and expensive enough to have their own names: 'Birkin' or 'Alexa'.

The men were on phones too, wrapping up business – 'No chance to engage this week, I'm afraid' – striding together in companionable manliness.

'And after that,' said one man to another, 'he booked into his favourite hotel, had the best dinner of his life, then went up to the roof terrace and jumped off it.'

'Jesus,' said the other. 'No job ought to matter that much.'

'*Nothing* ought to matter that much.'

The evening sun cast a honeyed light on the unpromising buildings that lined the river, especially prizing the windows, so that some of the facades looked as though they were lined with bars of melting gold. Among so much spangled promise, a vegetarian cafe in a church crypt seemed like an odd venue for a meeting, and my guess was that Chris had selected it deliberately, as a kind of reprimand. We were meeting, but not with the aim of enjoying ourselves and before sitting down to eat we would have to line up for our food and water like convicts. I stood in the queue behind my husband, waiting for my vegetarian lasagne to be dished up, contemplating the reproachful monolith of his back. For years I had slept with my body pressed against this back, and now I didn't even dare place my hand against his shoulder.

'It's all kicking off at work,' I said, when Chris briefly turned my way to receive the plate of food being passed to him under the glass counter. He showed no sign of having heard me, leaving my anecdote to evaporate over the hotplate.

We found a table and I put my plate onto it, while Chris kept his plate and glass on the tray, creating a demarcated territory in front of him that gave the impression he didn't plan to stay long. Sadness descended on our table, marooning us from the great wash of Christian love lapping around us. On the wall were posters about goodness and kindness; the other customers were mostly women, whose goodness and kindness showed in the breadth of their hips, the generous drapery of scarves and loose tops. There were a few men, elderly in the main, in whom it was clear that testosterone had finished its work. The women smiled at one another, or turned their kindness on the people clearing away, who accepted the largesse with a kind of weariness. They looked as if they had been saved from the street and were learning to feel comfortable with their new security.

'How's work?' I asked.

'Good. Busy. You?' Chris glanced up with a look of professional enquiry. His eyes tipped down on their outside corners, giving all of his expressions a touch of hangdog that appealed to a protective instinct in women – something I had always noticed more than he had. His brow bone closely followed that curve and long lines framed his mouth like a set of brackets, as though his mouth were something significant that the rest of his face had forgotten to mention. The first time we had kissed we stood for two hours in a doorway of the Student Union, my hands under his jacket around his waist and thinking that I was getting under his skin, when all along I had only been under his jacket. Sitting opposite him now, I felt I hardly knew him and it made me fear for humanity, that we retain so little carnal knowledge, that somebody loved becomes a stranger so quickly.

There were symmetry and melancholy in my husband's face. Even when he laughed, for example when we used to go out to dinner with friends, it was with a kind of restraint, as though that moment of release, however joyful, couldn't reach a deeper sadness. My fingers wanted to trace his brow bone, but I wasn't sure that it was still mine to touch. I hated to think that I bore any responsibility for making him sad.

'We've found a mystery in the room we're working on,' I said, 'you know at that house in Roehampton. It looks like there's something hidden under the Victorian paper. It could be an original Georgian design, something really special.' It came close to gabbling, this false cheer I'd struck on.

Chris stirred very slightly, eliciting a creak from his leather jacket, and smiled at my enthusiasm, but said nothing. I don't know why I had expected a fuller response. I shouldn't baulk at the characteristics that had attracted me to him in the first place. It had been the economy of his reactions that drew me to him, coming as I did from a family where people's personalities were loudly proclaimed, even daubed across their eyelids. I had always liked the way his character was tucked away under jackets and good-quality shirts. The first time I had visited his student digs – we were both twenty at the time – and spotted his drawings for engineering projects, I recognised a kindred spirit. We were both perfectionists. We both had felt that it was important to defend seriousness in an environment that celebrated everything ephemeral, although we probably never dared say so in front of people our age. I wanted to rescue worthwhile things that had been lost or damaged; he wanted to make worthwhile things that would last long into the future. He had needed me – at least for a long time it felt that way – to bring him out of himself and I had thought it was impressive to be quiet. It looked less like moral strength now and and more like inscrutability.

'So.' Ridiculous to be sitting with a person I knew so well and unable to think of anything to say. 'The jacket's new?'

He glanced at his sleeve, as though to remind himself of what he was wearing.

'Yes,' he agreed, then, defensively, 'It's not a midlife crisis jacket.'

'Did I even say –'

'I got it in a sale. It's useful for work. We've got to the point with Crossrail where we're sometimes outside. And this summer.'

'I know: the rain.'

'The rain. Jesus Christ.'

Talking about the weather seemed to relieve some of the tension. He sat back in his chair and the movement provoked a plaintive creak from his jacket. But his discomfort was still so palpable that I wondered if people sitting at the next table could feel it. He was like a man contained within lines. It would be better, I thought, if he burst out and said something – anything – however hurtful; I'd rather have that than this awkwardness. I wanted to say that it wasn't that bad. Life goes on, people readjust. Nothing ought to matter that much.

'Look.' I reached across the table and lightly touched his hand. 'I'm sorry if I wasn't better at things.'

Under my hand, his fist rose from the table in bony notches, the gaps between his knuckles themselves a finger's width. I remembered the patient work of those hands on my own body, back in the days before pregnancy was the only object of sex. I knew the course of the veins, up along his sinewy arms, over the bicep that always surprised me when it rose on his flexed upper arm. His body had seemed to me more about a fluidity of line than muscle groups. Perhaps that was our problem: Chris was such a coherent whole that I didn't know where to merge in. We never made our lines blur, we didn't melt into one another in the way ordained by pop songs or romantic fiction. Right now, his hand, under mine, was a completely separate entity. My touch didn't mould him.

'Better how?' he queried.

'Better at marriage, at motherhood.'

'To be fair, Ros, you didn't try them. You carried on as usual. Being married never signified more to you than a ring on your finger – not even that.' He glanced at the awkward nexus of our hands, at my ringless finger.

'I've never worn a ring at work. You know that,' I said. 'The last thing I want is to lose it in a pot of glue!' But I withdrew my hand all the same, recognising that there had been a kind of complacency in this gesture.

'Anyway, why would you put so much stock in a symbol? I *knew* I was married.' I fixed him with what was intended as an unblinking gaze, then spoiled it by blinking and disconcerted myself by saying 'was'. Chris said nothing, but the cast of his mouth suggested scepticism. There had been a couple of flings at work he didn't know about and a more serious affair that I think he did suspect, but he never mentioned it. It didn't last long: a few months, the duration of a job. In our line of work twelve-hour days are so normal it was easy to find excuses not to be at home. Perhaps things would have been different if he had confronted me. He should have done that, I thought, turning myself into the aggrieved party with a neat flick of perspective. I hadn't been serious about the other man, just looking for a reaction: something to prove that our relationship was the real thing, and the other one a sham. It was Chris who had been negligent, in his refusal to notice what was going on.

Now here he was, unimpeachable in his leather jacket. It would look mean-spirited in this loving milieu, with the ladies smiling at everyone and the bounty of cakes, for me to put the blame his way.

'Look,' he said, frowning at his lasagne, 'I didn't ask you to come here so we could talk about who was wrong and who was right.'

'I know. The German prints . . .'

'Well, and everything else. I think we need to speed things up. Reach some kind of resolution. We're in a limbo.' He watched me sink my head in my hands and said, 'Ros, you were the one who wanted to leave.'

'Not *leave* – I never said that. Go *away* for a bit. We've been over this before. I didn't see that there was a choice, Chris. Things had got so heated. I thought limbo was exactly what was required for a while. What we needed.'

'I never felt I needed it.'

'But I thought we did. We. And I, me. It wasn't only about you.'

'You're saying I'm selfish?'

'No! You're deliberately –'

'OK.'

'You're deliberately misunderstanding –'

'OK. Never mind. But I don't think a state of limbo can go on forever.' He set his hands side down to the table, parallel to the tray, making a frame around the rectangle.

God, the semantics again. The refuge of bureaucrats. 'It wouldn't, would it, by definition. It's a pause. A hiatus. Something like this takes time. We need to learn how to put ourselves back together again. That can't be done in a matter of weeks.'

'Do you *want* to put us back together again?' he asked with a suspicious gathering of his eyebrows.

'Yes! I think so.' Actually, at that moment, I really didn't. 'Well, that's what I'm trying to work out. It's why I need some time.' It was weird, I was thinking, to go off and buy a leather jacket. Out of character. It didn't seem like something he would do. Perhaps he'd thought it would make him attractive to other women. Perhaps he considered himself on the market again. Should I be putting myself out there?

'That was a very heavy sigh.'

'I've just got so, so much to do at the moment.'

'You've always got so, so much to do,' Chris said with a laugh that irritatingly skirted the boundary of a chuckle.

'Oh, come on. Don't talk as if you weren't busy too. This isn't about me neglecting the homestead. Or is that what it is really? You would rather I had just been there as a wife and a mother.'

'Don't be stupid. Of course I wouldn't.'

'Stupid. Wow, that's a bit –'

'I mean it's a stupid thing to say. I never made out you

should be a domestic slave. I just wanted –' He shook his head, defeated.

'You got so hung up on the kids thing. It was like an obsession.' I knew that was a low blow: to accuse a person of being obsessive was a way to pull the muscle from his argument before he'd had a chance to flex it. 'It was frightening. It's supposed to be the woman that gets broody, not the man.'

'That's not true, and anyway – come on, don't cry.' There was a sigh of leather as he reached over to administer fatherly pats to the side of my elbow. I congratulated myself on this small victory: luring him away from his territory and over to my side of the table.

'Everything is happening at once. Packing up GP's house, work.' I wiped my eyes with the heels of my hands, feeling salt tighten the skin on my temples. 'How *were* we at the beginning, Chris? How was I? Have I changed? You see, I don't feel that I did change. I honestly don't feel that I'm different to how I was.'

'No, you're right. You didn't change. But people should. That's the point: we change as time goes on. We change together. Evolve, I suppose.'

'Ah. I hadn't realised we were part of a Darwinian experiment. That explains everything. It's a pity nobody told me that earlier on.'

'Don't get bitter about it,' he said, which was rich, coming from him.

'You know, I think I'm going to head off,' I said, because there was a sour familiarity to this exchange that was too depressing and if I was going to cry I would rather do it alone, at home. 'We'll speak soon, right?'

Standing by the table, I touched his shoulder, and Chris said 'Sure', but made no move to stand, or kiss me goodbye, only looking up as I started to walk away. 'I'll give you a call next week,' he said.

'I think if you haven't been a happy child yourself, it's harder to imagine making your own child happy,' I said to Natalie that Saturday as we were getting ready for lunch at her house. 'Chris thought that not trying harder for children meant I didn't want him enough. It wasn't that. Perhaps I just didn't see that there was anything in my own experience worth repeating.'

My cousin was unloading the dishwasher, treating this – as she did most activities and people too – as a chore that needed to be discharged in double time. It surprised me when we went out together how often I struggled to match the speed of her short, strong legs. I was standing beside her, at the granite-topped counter of the kitchen 'island' and holding on to Sadie who was ten months old, as she irresistibly offered her toes to be played with.

'This little piggy . . .' I'd started the game half a dozen times, but Sadie always dissolved in fits of laughter before we could take the piggy to market.

'It wouldn't just be perpetuating you but him,' said Natalie, swinging up with an armful of bowls from the lower rack, pink with her exertion. 'Perhaps he thought you didn't think *he* was worth perpetuating. That's a complicated way of putting it but –' She swung down into the dishwasher again and came up with eight identical square white plates. Each time she came up she was pinker and more pungent. 'You know?'

'Kind of. Well, no, not exactly. So who was round for dinner last night?'

'People we got to know in antenatal class. Just really lovely, nice people. Three couples. We wrapped it up early. Everyone was gone by eleven! Everyone's tired. We're all in the same boat.' She beamed, and gave a shrug. She was happy in that boat, her smug mothership, and I didn't begrudge her happiness.

'This little piggy went to . . .'

'To go back to what you were saying. I understand why that would make Chris feel rejected. A child is like the ultimate expression of one person's love for another, isn't it? But I understand your position too. They aren't easy decisions to make, are they, Sadie-ma-lady?'

My cousin had an irritating habit, since having the baby, of referring every world event or idea back to her experience of motherhood, as if little Sadie were a prism through which all life might be seen anew and with a degree of wisdom unavailable to the childless. Far from knocking her confidence – as people sometimes said it did – motherhood had made Natalie immensely self-assured. The advertisements of her complacency were all around, from the silver necklace with little charms bearing Sadie's fingerprints to the colourful handprints that decorated whole sets of mugs and plates, but you could also read it in her wearily important gait, the sigh with which she collapsed at the end of the 'bedtime routine'. At least if the child ever went missing the police would have a full set of prints, I thought, studying the homely spread of my cousin's corduroy-clad bottom as she bent over the dishwasher.

'This little . . .' I began, but Sadie was now so primed for laughter that she couldn't let her toes be touched at all. Instead she removed the temptation, picking up her foot and inserting all the little piggies in her mouth. 'Look at you, Miss Flexibility!' I felt the warm bulge of her thigh filling my hand as she sat on the counter, a plump, laughing Buddha, naked apart from her nappy. You could have eaten her up, this gorgeous child, and yes, I would have liked one the same; if children could be ordered, I'd order up one like this.

'Nat, do you remember when they used to put us to bed together at Alma Street? They topped and tailed us?'

Natalie, who had moved to the table on the other side of the island and was laying places for lunch, looked up with a smiling frown of puzzlement.

'Just – yes, very vaguely. Perhaps once or twice.'

'It happened lots of times! Don't you remember? I certainly do, waking up with your foot on my face. Your parents used to come over for dinner, and –'

'This would have been . . .'

'Mainly after Dad died, but before that too. I mean, a few times.' I shocked myself, the way I brazenly dropped 'Dad' into the middle of a sentence as though it were any old sound, humdrum, rather than a word I almost never spoke aloud.

'Your memory's a lot better than mine,' said Natalie levelly. 'Could you bring her over?' She lifted her arms towards us.

I gripped the baby under her arms and Sadie leaned into

me allowing a smooth transfer from counter to hip. She was at an age when it still made sense to be helpful – the dogged refusals, the tears and fury, were a year or two away. I kissed the baby's head and walked with her towards the table.

'What do you remember about my dad?' I was unassailable now, tossing out this word with no fear for the consequences.

'You mean – in what respect?'

'In any respect. Whatever you've got.'

She looked up with a nervous smile. 'What's brought this on, Ros?'

'I don't know. Everything that's happening, I suppose, with Chris and Granny, and the house. It's like I've arrived at this point in my life where I need to get the past straight before I can get on with the future. So I can move on, you know?'

The choice of words was more for Natalie's benefit than my own. 'Moving on' was one of her expressions, pilfered from the personal-development books that filled her sitting-room shelves.

Natalie was holding a fork in one hand and a spoon in the other, looking down at them uncertainly, as though she had hoped to play them as entertainment and now found herself wrongly equipped. After a few seconds she shook her head at them.

'There's nothing concrete, Ros. He's a hazy figure to me, at the periphery of parties, that kind of thing. I don't remember any specifics.' She looked from my face to the baby's, and I had the sense that she thought I was withholding Sadie in return for information. 'He smoked roll-ups, didn't he? He had a contraption that you put everything into and – didn't he? Or am I making this up? He used to stand near the door and lean and blow the smoke away from us out of the room, you know? I remember that, because in those days most people didn't care. They smoked anywhere. Right in your face. Pass her over?'

'Here.' It wasn't really enough of a ransom but I could believe my cousin didn't remember more, given how little I remembered myself. The baby travelled unresisting through the air above the table, her torso and legs dangling like a cat's.

'You see, I didn't even know that,' I said. It grieved me a little, Natalie's ownership of a memory that ought to belong to me.

'Yeah, but I mean, we were what, five, six? Your impressions of people at that age come down to silly details, don't they? Especially adults. You remember someone's beard, someone's watch. Then when you try to see the face – there's nothing. I mean, can you ever remember what somebody's eyes look like? We spend all day looking right into them, even,' she laughed, 'professing undying love and whatever, but I'd be hard-pressed to tell you what colour Andrew's eyes are, for instance.'

'All I've got is one photograph.'

'I know,' she said, nodding quickly. She didn't want her plans for this big day waylaid by emotional displays.

It was on my dressing table, a picture taken on a boat trip during my parents' honeymoon in Cornwall. My father smiled into the wind, his hair blowing across his forehead. My mother was pregnant by then and he looked like a young man squaring up to a responsibility. There was warmth in his eyes, but a hesitancy in the set of his mouth and the gathered eyebrows. It could have been nothing more than the nervous reaction of a northern European startled by sunshine – except that my mother, who must have taken the photograph, was the object of his gaze. There were a few other pictures of him in my grandmother's albums but in those he was either turning away from the camera or occupied a shadowy background, or the Kodak colours had become concentrated in an abstract representation of the 1970s generally rather than a true depiction of people and events. Whenever I tried to picture my father it was this version from the boat that came to mind. Even though I was used to manipulating images on a computer, turning a design through 360 degrees in order to study the workings of a pattern, I couldn't reimagine my father's face in any other context. He was always smiling and windswept.

'I know this sounds melodramatic but – it's as if this is my last chance to remember him. Sooner or later we'll sell Granny's house and then that link with him will be gone. At the moment the only thing I have of him is the knowledge that we've both been under the same roof. When the house goes I won't even have that. It'll all be lost.'

'Talk to your mother, Ros,' said Natalie, and when she saw my expression she remonstrated, 'It shouldn't be that hard! You could ask her today.'

'No, not when we're supposed to be celebrating Granny's birthday. It doesn't feel like the right time. I'd hate to have some massive –'

Natalie had walked round to my side of the table and

now laid her hand on my arm. Sadie mimicked the gesture, patting the top of my head. 'Don't ask her in front of everyone. Ask her afterwards. Make an arrangement to meet another day and really talk about this. Christ, Ros, it's important. Like you said, you need to move on.' Then, glancing at the kitchen clock, she said, 'Shit, they're going to be here soon. Do you mind getting some more stuff – another baguette and maybe olives?'

I picked up my bag and walked down to the delicatessen, past the common which had been a place to avoid in my childhood, somewhere for fishing and fighting, and nowadays the focus of an intense fitness effort. Most times of the day you could see women working out there with a personal trainer, shadow-boxing, swinging kettle bells or walking purposefully with ski poles. Some of the young mothers went running with their prams, their babies reduced to fitness accessories, clinging on to the coverlets. It annoyed me, the way a neighbourhood can be handed over to a new occupancy and the old residents have no say in the matter. In ten years we had lost our greengrocer, two bakeries, two fishmongers and an old-fashioned Ladies Outfitters and seen them replaced with boutiques or restaurants. One half of the high street was not yet gentrified, however, and there were still some old shops where you could buy yam and plantain, where a chair was provided for the old black ladies who wanted to sit down to chew over the day's gossip. Lena's spice store stocked every conceivable jarred condiment. The two Sikh brothers who ran it stood in front of shelves of jars like apothecaries in orange turbans. Next door, at the convenience store, Mrs Akash would go to her own kitchen to bring you coriander, if you only needed a little and were a good customer. But in return she expected you to hear out the story of her children's academic success. 'Daughters: independent schools. Son: independent school. Son is dentist now. Girls are doctors.' They were still on the high street – the Akashes, the Patels, the Kapoors – but they were making plans to leave, preparing to shut up shop and go south to Tooting, Streatham and Merton.

By the time I came back the party from Ravenslea had arrived: Natalie's husband Andrew and Mariel and John, plus my mother. It had taken three of them to collect Granny Pea from the home, get her into Andrew's Land Rover and then into a wheelchair. Now, decanted into a chair at the top of the table and secured with cushions, she presided over the family in a lopsided tribute to the old days.

'Drink?' said Andrew, popping up from behind the island and coming forward to kiss me.

'God yes,' I said, putting the shopping down on the counter. 'Bring it on.'

'Bring it on!' Andrew growled back, tigerish despite the evidence of his weedy physiognomy.

The others had already taken their places at the table, where Granny Pea, planted like a sapling in too little soil, was subsiding to her left. Seeing me approach, she made a great effort at righting herself in the chair and I met her halfway, kissing her cheek and clasping her shoulders which seemed shockingly narrow in comparison to her swaddled legs, so solid and monumental you could imagine ivy creeping in from the garden and encircling them, climbing upwards until it met the solemn edifice of her face. Next I bent to kiss Mariel, then had to execute a difficult stretch across the table to reach my mother, a manouevre she did nothing to make easier. From John I received a kind of angry salute, intended to draw attention to the awkwardness of his installation between the wall and Granny Pea. They were already communicating in semaphores and insinuations, I thought, as families always do, so much more rumbling beneath the surface than is ever expressed aloud. At Mariel's bidding, I sat next to GP while she moved to be beside the baby.

'She is good at feeding herself, isn't she?' said my aunt, drawing the table's focus onto Sadie who was employing a deft pincer movement to pick up individual grains of sweetcorn.

'Sadie is actually in the ninety-ninth centile for fine motor skills,' said Natalie, who was bringing a bowl of salad to the table. 'She had a test with the health visitor yesterday.' My cousin's nonchalance betrayed her secret, glowing joy. I wondered if she had been able to keep this information from the antenatal-group friends who had come for dinner the night before, if she had planned not to mention Sadie's superiority then blurted it out over the pudding, if they had all driven home worrying about their own babies' fine motor skills.

Talk of babies kept the mothers at the table happily engaged, while the rest of us chatted stiffly, avoiding any talk of the economy out of consideration for Andrew, the banker in our midst. Natalie's parents had been shocked when she first moved in with him. If we stood for anything as a family, it was for the public sector; my Polish grand-father had been a shop steward. In this twenty-first-century landscape of shifting affinities, our certainties were melting away. At Andrew's bank dozens of people had been fired in one week and made to carry their possessions off the premises in cardboard boxes. He had expected to join them, and for a time there had been calamitous talk about not being able to save up for school fees and the mortgage. He had survived the cull, though – to everyone's surprise – and in these times mere survival was a mark of success. Normal service had been resumed, but the recession required that everybody pay lip-service to the notion of giving things up and Natalie sometimes spoke gravely of cancelling her weekly organic vegetable box.

Pudding arrived, a fruit tart that was burned around its edges and sunken under the weight of its maker's ambition. Natalie deposited it in front of her mother with a clatter of disappointment. I felt for her, knowing how much it meant to my cousin to have all the elements of an occasion like this perfect and building towards a picture of family life that was both harmonious and effortlessly sophisticated, like the one presented in the professional family photographs around the house. Uncle John suggested we raise our glasses to toast Granny Pea who assented with a nod that sent her lurching sideways almost onto John's shoulder. He righted her and moved a little away and Mariel, after serving her mother, set the tart on a journey around the table. When it reached my mother she declined then, tremulous in the way of a woman who wants to appear desirable and unworldly, she asked John to explain something of the work his physics department was doing on the Higgs Boson. 'If you think I'll understand it.'

'It's about finding the missing piece, really, isn't it?' said Mariel, looking hopefully at her husband.

John, instantly annoyed, folded himself up, strapping his arms across his chest as though belting up for a journey into the stratosphere. 'Not really,' he said crossly.

'But isn't there an element of that?' asked Andrew eagerly. 'The Higgs Boson particle is the final piece to fall into the pattern? The element that will make sense of life, the universe and everything?'

'A question of symmetry is certainly at the heart of it, Andrew,' said John, more generously. 'We used to think that everything in the universe was part of a pattern. Now we're starting to see that human life and perfect symmetry may actually be incompatible. A universe in perfect balance would cancel itself out. So it seems that the laws of science needed to be broken for the world to exist.'

'So *im*perfection is the key?' said Andrew.

'Yes. It's what we call the "paradox of symmetry". The discovery of the Higgs Boson validates the Standard Model of particle physics, which we've been using to explain the workings of the universe for decades and of course that's reassuring. But there are still many questions to answer – about dark matter and dark energy for instance.' He sighed, and with his index finger pressed on the tines of his fork, one after another. 'I'm afraid we don't have all the answers yet, not by any means.'

'Oh dear!' cried Sadie at the other end of the table and everybody laughed, charmed by the timing of her intervention.

'She's dropped a little piece of sweetcorn,' explained Natalie, blushing with pride. 'She hates any kind of mess.'

Sadie was leaning out of her high chair with a determination that drew her torso parallel to the floor as she scrutinised the ground, pointing at the grain of corn. 'No, darling, it's dirty,' Natalie chided.

'Dirty,' Sadie agreed and sat back in her chair, but seconds later she was overcome by a distress that swung her back to inspect the floor, arms windmilling.

'Sadie!' said Natalie. 'Don't worry about that! Look, there's plenty more sweetcorn on your plate.' The entreaty only upset Sadie more. Her mouth turned down at the corners and her eyes communicated a dread of being completely misunderstood.

'She's tired,' Natalie said, first to her mother and then, as an announcement, to the table. 'She's tired. Otherwise she wouldn't do this.'

'Poor lamb,' said Granny Pea.

'Why don't you take her for a sleep, darling?' said Mariel. Natalie, who was already upset that her lunch had not met the standard she set herself, took this suggestion as a crowning criticism.

'OK, why don't I do that? I *was* going to let her have a little bit of cake to celebrate Granny's birthday but if you think it's better to send her off to bed, then fine. Just don't blame me if she cries for the next hour. Thanks for getting her overexcited before lunch, by the way, Ros.'

'I don't really think I did!' I protested, as my cousin swept out of the room dangling Sadie – who smelled sour now and had gone scarlet with screaming – by the armpits. I wondered why families did this, investing so much in the idea of a happy occasion that they made it impossible to attain.

'I'm sure you didn't, darling,' said Mariel, patting my leg. 'Anyway, Sadie's done awfully well. These occasions are tiring for little ones. You're proud, Mum, aren't you, of your lovely great-granddaughter?'

'Oh yes, love,' said Granny Pea, chewing with a ruminative motion of her lower jaw, close enough now to lay her head on John's shoulder if he hadn't kept twitching it.

'It's a pity she's only got the one!' cried my mother. 'But perhaps Natalie will give her a brother or sister.'

'The subtext being . . .' I looked steadily across the table at my mother, feeling for a moment that I loathed her. Iris returned my gaze with a youthful insolence.

'There's no subtext, Ros. What do you mean?'

'You sit there pretending to make these innocent remarks which you know are hurtful –'

'For heaven's sake, Ros – I've no idea what you're talking about. Obviously I think it's a shame that you and Chris never produced, but it turned out for the best in the end, didn't it? It wouldn't have been right to bring children into a relationship that couldn't last.'

Beside me Mariel started quietly clucking, making alterations to the arrangement of her cutlery and napkin.

'Better not to go there, Mum, when you don't really know the full story,' I said and my mother, who seemed about to make a retort, looked away, her bluster dissipating in blameless, pettish shrugs.

'I think the tart would benefit from a little cream,' announced Mariel, getting up from the table.

'I won't have any more, Mariel,' I said. 'I should probably go. I've got stuff to do at home before Monday.' If I wasn't enjoying a situation, I decided, I was old enough to take myself out of it. In years past I would have had to sit and endure my mother's gloating insinuations, the delight she took in praising other people's offspring above her own. There was no need for that now: I was free to leave. I stood up and began to push my chair away from the table.

'Sit down, sit down, sit down!' they all said and I felt hands on me, reaching across the table and wrapping around my arms like creepers, climbing up to pull me down, and to leave at that point would have looked petty. So I stayed.

In bed that night I lay awake for more than an hour revisiting moments in my life when a decision had been made that might have gone another way. Chris had thought, at one time, of taking up a job offer in Canada, an idea we decided not to pursue partly because his mother was ill but also because Frieda had made me a partner in her firm. I hadn't wanted to give up the position – in retrospect had I been selfish? Perhaps a new job and a change of scene would have halted the spiral of discontent we set in motion by staying in London and not following our friends into parenthood. Or, say we had stayed here but bought a house instead of continuing to rent? We could have afforded a mortgage on a house but Chris was always saying that it made no sense to buy at the height of the market and then – when prices went higher still – that the housing bubble was sure to burst at any moment and we would reap the benefit. We had both enjoyed living centrally, but a house in the suburbs with a garden would have made a proper home for us with room for people to stay and, if not children, then maybe pets, chickens – who knew? The housing bubble hadn't burst, though, just ours, our bubble. And what if I had agreed to try IVF, at least for six months, or a year? If not for myself, then for Chris, who would have made a good father. Perhaps I would have been a better mother than I thought. I could never see it – myself as a mother – but you shouldn't expect to see all prospects before you travel towards them. A leap of faith can yield greater rewards than the best-laid plans, I thought, turning into my pillow. Of all the questions this was the one I couldn't bear to dwell on. I didn't want not having children to become the defining tragedy of my life.

FOUR

Turney House when I returned to it on the Monday morning was a scene of futuristic entropy, the cathedral to a devastating new religion. The noise of giant heaters in the basement filled the spaces with a nasty buzz. Figures loomed out of dust clouds, dressed like astronauts in protective gear. It was possible to imagine some science-fiction scenario in which the old order had been wiped out, leaving a ravaged exoskeleton to be cleansed and rehabilitated for use by a new breed of occupant. And it was intoxicating, this idea that everything can be undone and remade as it ought to be.

The Turney project might well be a giant folly, a monument to greed, a symbol of a society that couldn't bear to be deprived of anything. But there was also something irresistible about a philosophy that said nothing need ever be permanently lost – and not only because it meant that Frieda and I would never be short of work. In two or three years' time the house would look the same as it had the day before the fire but now with the new rationale that it was *meant* to be this way, that nothing was an accident of light, or damage or time, or the whims of restorers or the experiments of DIY enthusiasts. Two conservators from a firm of specialist gilders were spending a year restoring the Cranhook mirror, not to its original state, but to its condition after 150 years of damage, deterioration and bad restoration. Every change that had been made in the past, no matter how unsympathetic or wrong-headed, was being meticulously recreated in their Camden workshop. And we could do this, I thought, remake all the good and the bad, with our experience, our world-famous techniques. We were artists of recreation.

Without taking off my jacket or putting down my coffee I walked through the house, looking in to see what was happening in the different rooms. In the library two women in breathing apparatus and full bodysuits were applying chemical putty to the stone fireplace, keeping the curious at bay with a 'HAZARD' sign at the door. In the dining room specialist ceramicists were studying a tray of remnants together with photographs and plans. They were working on a Japanese urn that had once stood on the landing above the hall and exploded in the heat of the inferno at Turney's core. The breed of specialists who circulated among Britain's ancestral homes seemed happy to be reunited every few months over water-damaged silks, infested timbers or scalded stone, and to share horror stories from recent conservation jobs. Sometimes you overheard them swapping specialist gossip with a relish that would be unintelligible to anyone outside their discipline.

'Then we found that an oily distemper had been applied *on top of the wood and under the paint!*'

'Ouch!'

Away from the noise and in its further reaches, the

house was a field of echoes, as though in the final hours of a party at which a few stragglers lingered. Bursts of laughter rang out from distant halls. The voice of someone on a mobile phone, pacing between rooms, came and went in waves.

In the garden, radios and arguments filled the space with human noise and the atmosphere was more normal: it just felt like another overwrought workspace. Frieda was already in the old stable and, when I had finished my coffee, we collected our tools and took them up to the house.

In the Rose Room we assembled our scaffold, and stood on it to remove the mouldings and the picture rail. First we pulled out the rusted nails, gently easing away sections of board to prevent paper or plasterwork coming away in areas where the wall had been distorted by damp. The wood was warped and some of the tiny L-shaped nails were so corroded that they crumbled to dust when we pulled them free.

Deep skirting boards had been added to the Rose Room when it was updated in the 1860s and the spaces behind them were packed with paper and plaster. In places the uneven floorboards gaped from the skirting and more fire debris had been forced into the gaps. The pulp behind the wood was wet and smelled acrid, but none of it would be discarded; it was all going to be bagged up and labelled. Some poor sod in a lab was going to examine everything for historic merit.

After the skirting, we started on the door frames. Standing on a stepladder, I eased off the architraves framing the doorway to the front hall. These were the areas in which the workers of previous centuries most often left a record of their presence because there was no reason to hide or gloss over it: nothing was going to show. I had found signatures, doodles and thumbprints pushed into the plaster before now. Once I uncovered an obscene sketch of a master by his apprentice, dating from the early nineteenth century. We photographed and preserved the sketch before covering it again. That temptation to leave some record of your presence in an inaccessible spot must be universal; in the roof space at Turney, five sets of handprints had been found in the plaster, recording the eighteenth-century builders, one set very small, perhaps belonging a child. The area between the roof beams had been packed with oyster shells, oysters being a poor man's food in eighteenth-century England and shells a cheap insulator. I've always found these secret signs from past lives inexplicably heartening, though it is hard to say why a letter discovered beneath the boards of an old house counts for more than one preserved and boxed up in an archive. Perhaps it is because we don't fully believe in people from the past unless we can catch them unawares, seizing on the ephemera they never meant to leave behind. To trust in an era before our own requires constant, surprising evidence: the Roman coin dug up in a garden, the royal tomb under a car park, the silken fragment caught on a nail. An intellectual appreciation of history is no match for the gut pleasure of coming across real bones, real possessions. And if you are first on the scene of a discovery you get to handle the object before it loses its currency and submits itself as a relic to the present day.

In Canterbury Cathedral, Uncle John had once taken

Natalie and me to see the stone steps that had been scooped out in their middle by the knees of centuries of pilgrims. He made us sit down and touch the grooves, conjuring the presence of those real men and women who had made them, thousands of people dissolved now into the air. At first the steps were only moulded stone: it took some practice to learn how to detect the presence of people in their absence. But nowadays I am absolutely persuaded of that ghostly presence; I can believe that materials have a memory and sometimes, working at a wall in a room alone, I have felt the silence behind me resonate with the presence of its long-dead occupants – not ghosts exactly, but something like a pulse in the air, a warming of the atmosphere such that I don't dare to turn round in case I see someone, though perhaps it would be worse to turn round and see no one.

'OK, I think I've got something here,' I said, the words muffled by my mask. 'This is definitely something.'

Frieda, standing at the bottom of the ladder, averted her face from a scattering of plaster and dust. A ragged scrap of vivid green showed through the grimy overlay. I lifted my mask to blow away some of the dust, touching the paper gently with my finger. Specks of green dust came away on my gloves.

'Looks like it's full of arsenic.'

'You're sure it's not mould? Be very careful, Ros.'

'It looks like an emerald green.'

'But it's too early, isn't it? More likely to be Scheele's. For goodness' sake make sure your mask is properly fixed.'

'Yes, I think it is Scheele's. It's beautiful, Frieda. The colours on it are so bright. This paper could have been put there yesterday.'

'It's amazing how different a covered paper is to one that's been exposed. Light makes everything a paler version of itself.' And with a rueful laugh she said, 'Even us.'

I took a scalpel out of my pocket and scratched at the blackened paper until a few flakes fell away and the green looked like breaking through again. Then I had to suppress an urge to laugh and cry all at once because to see something that has been buried for 150 years re-emerge from its shroud is the next best thing to time travel. It is the secret drug of conservators, archaeologists and restorers, the reason we look so nonplussed in photographs and documentaries. We know that we are working patiently towards a moment of exquisite revelation: it is only a matter of time.

Frieda and I knew all the pigments as well as the insects, plants and poisons that were used to create them. We mixed some of our own pigments in the studio, but we had never made a colour as vivid as this. I felt my eyes tightening with emotion. 'I think there's more there, maybe a lot more. I don't know though. Come up and see.'

At four o'clock I climbed the back staircase to the first floor with mixed feelings of excitement and apprehension. It seemed to leach from the brickwork, some dread of wrongdoing being the legacy of all the maids and man-servants who had hurried up and down these stairs over the centuries, carrying wigs and chamber pots, trying not to spill aristocratic urine on their only set of work clothes. I wanted everyone to be as excited by our discovery as Frieda and I were. I was hungry because we had worked all day with no break for lunch and the physical hunger felt like an actual craving for approval.

On the first floor I glanced into the Marchants' private sitting room, the only room to have been completely refurbished since the fire. 'We may not be living here, but we need somewhere to perch,' Alexandra had reasoned. The photographs that used to be dotted around downstairs had been reconvened on top of the restored piano: Lord Marchant meeting the Queen; Lady Marchant hugging her husband at a party, hugging her children on a boat, hugging the dog on a lawn. She was good at hugging.

Through another inconspicuous door the back staircase wound up again to the top floor which had once been the servants' quarters and was these days the centre of operations for the architect's team. Their brightly lit office was a bureaucratic satellite sitting on top of a yawning hollow. There was no specific charge about this room identifying it as the base for a historic project. It still had bare boards rather than a carpet, but otherwise it looked like any modern office. A shifting group of seven men and three women was installed here around ergonomic desks and on chairs that swooped backwards and forwards, tipping the occupant out for some spontaneous brainstorming or gossip, then back in for closer inspection of the job in hand. Computer-assisted drawings flickered on some of the screens. The original eighteenth-century plans had been digitally enhanced, geotagged and sprung into new life. The screensaver on one terminal showed photographs of different aspects of the Turney House project on a slide-show, each grainy image powered in seconds from vanishing point to full-screen. For a few seconds a collapsed lintel, a section of broken fretwork or carbonised wood became compelling drama; the task of making it good looked impossible, or would be so if not for the reassuring imprimatur of the architect's firm logo across the corner of every image. Hodder and Linton would fix things. That was what they were here to do, and they had brought the accoutrements of office life with them to Turney: a coffee machine, a work experience girl to operate it, a swear box and a mascot – somebody's cuddly toy wearing an Arsenal scarf. The Marchants had reciprocated with their own workplace joke: displayed in the fireplace was a chamber pot said to have been used by Lady Isabella herself, decorated with garlands of flowers on the outside and fitted inside with a small three-dimensional bust of Napoleon, so that every time Lady Isabella emptied her bladder she could souse the enemy of Albion. Lady Isabella's pisspot was one of the miraculous survivors of the second floor. On the day of the fire it had fallen twenty feet through the collapsing ceiling of the library, landing on heaped debris.

I walked towards the meeting room hoping for a trans-formation in confidence. It was at times like these that I worried about differences in education and background. Everyone at Turney was on first-name terms and there was a presumption of equal footing that concealed – or so I feared – hidden rules about observing social rank. Perhaps I should be tugging some metaphorical forelock. At least I had the advantage of coming fresh from the battlefield with news of a victory. The scrap of vivid green wallpaper was in my ziplock bag now, trapped like an etherised butterfly.

The Restoration Committee met in a small room adjacent to the office. When Turney reopened, and as part of an agreement reached with the Arts Council to improve the Outreach programme, this room was going to be designated a 'resource centre'. Already it had been fitted with a long beech table with a punctured row of holes awaiting the cables of computer terminals. The plan was to create a hub, a hive of research where visitors could zoom in on particular aspects of the house, its contents and the restoration programme. They would be able to look up, for instance, the Qing Wucai vase, trace its journey from China in the eighteenth century and cross-reference with similar pieces in other collections. When I arrived in the doorway, half a dozen people were sitting in the room, regular meeting-goers who knew how to bring to the table exactly the right mix of attention and disregard. Alexandra and Roger were at the table's far end and I recognised Fiona, Turney's part-time curator, who suffered from either frequent colds or perhaps hayfever and whose red eyes gave her a look of being indefinitely grief-stricken. It took me a moment to place the man sitting on Alexandra's left: he was one of the marathon runners from the photograph in the kitchen. Alexandra introduced him as 'Sebastian, my bro', emphasising 'bro' as though the abbreviation signalled something amusing and secret about their bond. 'He's helping us here for six months, on secondment from his exciting life.' The last two words, like 'bro', got their own jaunty inflection.

Sebastian grimaced and made a protest about his life not really being as exciting as all that, but everything about his appearance argued against the protest. 'I want to help get Turney shipshape,' he offered, an expression that sounded a bit fogeyish for him, bringing to mind sailing holidays and regattas, muscled thighs sliding back and forth in rowing boats. He was tall, square-shouldered, but otherwise lightly built with an athletic physique, and his skin wore the kind of expensive glow that is usually acquired on a skiing trip. Alexandra Marchant turned sideways to look at him, drawing the curtain of hair across her expression. Sebastian smiled into the private space.

There was a shuffling of papers, and of bodies on chairs, a generalised rustling that built towards a quiet crescendo, whereupon Roger welcomed everyone to the meeting and said that he would like to kick things off with a recap of the previous agenda and for fifteen minutes the talk was of logic models, evaluation tools, joint tracking and shared prioritisation strategies, obtuse phrases that nevertheless must have meant something because now and then they prompted the project manager, David, to frown, or to reach for his breast pocket onto which were clipped three pens in different colours, badges of his status and organisational savvy. Sitting next to him the work experience girl pouted seriously. I wondered if they were sleeping together. Out in the garden people regarded the management team as the enemy, and with good reason, I couldn't help thinking. Their air of jaded self-importance suggested they thought they were the real artisans at work here, as if software counted for more than hardware and they could rebuild Turney House with a few nicely drawn flow charts.

When this was done, Roger turned to me, one of his

eyebrows cocked in a gesture of enigmatic welcome. 'Ros. You're going to bring us up to speed on developments in the Rose Room?'

I cleared my throat and fumbled for the ziplock bag. 'Yes, well, we found a scrap of the original eighteenth-century paper this morning, under one of the architraves. I thought people might like to see?'

'Yes, please – let's all have a look!'

I passed the ziplock bag to the architect who put on his glasses with a look of concentrated application. He must have been called on to examine very small pieces of evidence hundreds of times over the last year and an expression of devout interest was second nature.

'Significant?' asked the architect, looking at me over the top of his glasses.

'We think it is,' I said, hoping to strike a confident note without being pushy. I wanted everyone to be as interested in the paper as I was but I also knew of colleagues who had damaged a cause by fighting too hard for it. 'We wondered if this could be the paper Lady Isabella refers to in her journal, when she talks about commissioning some paper from a Mr Houseman.'

'"I have this day ordered a pretty pattern from Mr Houseman which I intend for the principal bedroom,"' quoted Fiona with a tight smile. 'But that was the *principal bedroom*.'

'Yes, but –' I hadn't expected quotations – 'we were wondering – it's only a theory – if Lady Isabella could have been confused when she mentioned Houseman. She may actually have been referring to Gabriel Huysman, a printer who was active at that time. She said she intended it for the bedroom, but perhaps she changed her mind, or this is a second paper commissioned from the same man.'

'I think "intend" really has a stronger meaning than that in the eighteenth century,' said Fiona, whose eyes rolled upwards when she was speaking, the eyelids fluttering fast over them. The more seriously she felt about something the faster the fluttering. 'She means that she has ordered the paper for the express purpose of papering the bedroom. It's not likely she would change her mind about something like that. They're two totally different rooms.'

'What was in the principal bedroom?' asked Sebastian. 'I actually can't remember now.'

'A Chinese silk. Totally fucked,' murmured Alexandra, putting her head in her hands and ploughing the red nails into her blonde pelt.

'Is it pronounced Hiceman or Hoosman?' asked David, the project manager, whose eyes were about 20 per cent bigger when seen through his glasses. The enlargement gave him an air of astonished innocence. Sudden movements made his eyes seem to swivel in their rectangular frames.

'Couldn't she have made a mistake about the name? I mean people do,' said Alexandra Marchant, re-emerging from the cradle of her fingers. 'There are places in the diary where she seems to confuse the names of her own children.'

'We've all been there,' said the architect with a snigger.

'More to the point,' said the project manager, 'is there any record of a Houseman?'

Fiona's wrists rested on the table and she rolled the pads

of her thumb and index finger together in a gesture that was innocuous yet somehow repellent.

'Huysman is a really interesting character,' I said. 'He died in his forties, possibly as a result of arsenic poisoning, and his designs are rare. His wife and his children worked in the paper trade too. They used to go out collecting scraps of linen around the East End then mixing them with water from the Thames to make a mulch.' I wanted to recruit the group to my cause, wanted them to see the printer, his wife and his flea-ridden children traipsing beside the Thames with their bucket of sloppy rags, their hands red and peeling from contact with the toxic pigments.

'So a pretty colourful family,' said Roger with an encouraging smile that showed pronounced canines. His wrists were hairy under his shirt-cuffs and he looked like a werewolf in the very early stages of transmogrification, a minute or two after midnight, with the furring, the howling and the bone-breaking still to come.

'You know a lot about him,' said Sebastian.

'He is known,' I said, perhaps too emphatically, 'at least in the wallpaper community. Not many names have survived from that time, but Huysman's designs are very distinctive. Sometimes he added colour to his papers by hand, to avoid paying extra tax on the printing.'

The *wallpaper community*? I made my colleagues sound like a special-interest group, the sort of people who sent representatives to *Newsnight* with chippy complaints about a lack of opportunities. Come to think of it, they were like that. 'Also, this paper seems to have been coloured with Scheele's, which was only invented in 1775, so that makes it significant, historically. Even if you didn't want to keep it here, I think the Victoria and Albert would definitely want it for their archive.'

Sebastian sighed audibly. 'You mean we actually have a duty to preserve it? How annoying. What does everyone think? Should we be looking into this?'

'It's a nice story, a nice theory,' said the architect, 'but what if the paper isn't one of his? We can't make the evidence fit the theory just because he's an interesting character.'

The scrap of paper was still circulating the table, a tiny remnant demanding interpretation and threatening to exceed its claim on everyone's patience. It had reached the work experience girl now, who looked at it and blinked three times. Somewhere she had picked up that steady blinking could look like a form of intellectual reaction.

'It's surprisingly bright,' said David, when he got it back. 'No?' Again he shot the question over the top of his glasses. 'Almost garish, wouldn't you say?'

Arsehole, I was thinking, but I said: 'People tend to think Georgian colours were subdued and tasteful, but that's only because they've faded. In fact bright colours and gold were popular because rooms were lit by candle-light, so the pattern needed to be noticeable. Green was a very popular choice.'

'So to brass tacks,' said Sebastian. 'How long will it take to uncover this old wallpaper and establish its date and who made it?'

'Depending on how much there is – two or three days? We have to be a bit careful because this pigment contains arsenic. That's why it wasn't used after the nineteenth century.'

Alexandra Marchant pouted and shook her hair, flipping it behind her shoulders with a hand each side of her neck. 'Well, I suppose that settles the question. Unfortunately we haven't got the time or the money. We can't add three days onto the time that has been granted to Frieda and Ros. The plasterers want in, the electricians want in. And then what about removing it? How long would that take? Bearing in mind that this stuff is highly poisonous.'

'That could be a longer process. It depends on what adhesives were used, how firmly stuck onto the wall it is. You know – a flour-and-water paste is hard to remove whereas some animal glues release better.' I paused, suddenly finding the room airless and too full of people, and blew up through my hair. 'It's very hard to say without doing some more investigation.'

'You're not really selling this to me, Ros!' Alexandra said.

'I'm just trying to be honest,' I said. 'I mean, if you're asking my opinion I think you should definitely do this. I think it would be amazing to uncover some of the original decoration.'

'And if it's a question of money, the money can be found,' said Sebastian.

'Really?' cried Alexandra. 'Where are you going to find it, Sebastian? I don't think there's time to squeeze in another marathon!'

'So we've got the Heritage Lottery Fund, the World Monument Fund, English Heritage, the American Friends of Turney House . . .' Sebastian's tone of voice suggested this languid enumeration could go on indefinitely, that he chose to end it there only because he couldn't be bothered to keep name-checking the many funds at his disposal.

Alexandra turned to him, the blonde hair-curtain shimmering with rattled incomprehension. 'But all of those grants are allocated.'

'No they're not,' said Sebastian curtly. 'I mean, in broad terms they are, but we made sure to build some latitude into all the grant applications. In each case we kept the approved purposes as broad as possible so that there was flexibility in directing things one way or another, precisely to cover this sort of development.'

'Oh,' said Alexandra, 'I didn't realise we'd been so clever.'

'Did I say "we"? I meant "I",' said Sebastian with a giant yawn that arrived at every part of him and loosened him generally. He moved his head from one side to the other, easing out the tendons, and everyone in the room seemed to feel a vicarious benefit. The project manager took off his glasses and pushed back in his chair, resting one knee on the table. The work experience girl arched sensuously away from the table, flexing her spine. I saw how they were all held in a physical relation to one another, and that if there was antipathy it was the result of too many meetings like this, squabbling over minute pieces of evidence or questions of historical authenticity the wider relevance of which was vanishingly small.

'Well, funds or no funds, we have to decide if this is an avenue we want to pursue. However tempting it is to diverge from the plan.'

'Please!' said David with an exasperated laugh. 'Please – no diverging from the plan!' He raked his fingers through hair that was dishevelled and flecked with grey. 'Let's not get sidetracked!'

Alexandra turned to Fiona, who was sitting two seats away from her, on the other side of Sebastian. 'What in your view would be the worth of trying to preserve and analyse this paper?'

Her eyes rolled up, her eyelids started to flutter. 'The question we have to ask ourselves is what is the heritage worth of the paper. Whether or not it is a heritage item.'

'That doesn't *mean* anything,' said Sebastian with a surprising contempt. He let the words spill over his shoulder, sliding his gaze along the table to the area in front of Fiona instead of turning to meet her eye. 'Anything can be heritage. This cup of tea is heritage. My sister's husband could be described as a "heritage item".'

'Unhelpful, Seb,' remonstrated Alexandra.

Fiona produced a handkerchief from her sleeve and dabbed peevishly at her nose.

'What I feel,' said Sebastian, 'is that we don't want this house to take us over, but at the same time we shouldn't feel daunted when new evidence comes to light.'

'Fighting talk,' said Roger with a broad smile.

'Thanks, Rog. Actually, I'd say it calls for a drink,' said Sebastian, although his sister, open-mouthed, had been about to raise another point. 'Let's go down the pub?' – at which relieved laughter rippled around the table. People looked at their watches and agreed with a cheerful surprise that it was past five and therefore legitimate to stop working.

'OK,' said Alexandra Marchant. 'You win.' She closed the file on her desk with a defeat-conceding wallop.

'Sorry,' Sebastian said and squeezed his sister's shoulder as everyone began to get up from the table. 'Did I rather take matters out of your hands just then?'

'You always do, bastard,' she said with a hard laugh. 'I think you forget that I'm supposed to be in charge.'

'Oh, oh, oh.' He gathered her into him and she pressed her face against his chest like a child, even making a child's glum pout, though since Sebastian wouldn't be able to see it, I wasn't sure for whose benefit this was. I smiled a little, in case it was for mine.

They were tactile, this brother and sister, and as they walked away from the table wrapped around each other, I wondered if that was the legacy of childhood roistering in expensive surroundings. My own mother had barely touched me at all when I was a child, limiting her affection to kisses applied directly to my forehead. She had liked to look smart for work and had a horror of sticky hands or cheeks. When I was small she avoided picking me up, for fear of spoiling her clothes, and avoided helping me in the bath for fear of chipping her nails. Her strategy, come to think of it, was parenthood by avoidance. If I tried to put my arms around her, Iris used to catch my wrists to hold my hands away from her clothes. That must have been one of the reasons why I used to crawl into Granny Pea's bed at night. GP, especially soft without her teeth or corset, was all contact.

I gathered up my ziplock bag, phone and notebook and followed the others to the office next door, where the architect's team were readying themselves in the way of departing professionals, collecting their coats and cycle helmets and bundling notes into messenger bags.

'Are you going to join us?' said Sebastian. 'What's up?'

'I just wanted to let Frieda know we were leaving,' I said, frowning at my mobile. 'It's not going, though.'

'Signal's crap here for some reason,' said Sebastian, taking the mobile from me and striding away towards the window with it held high above his head as though leading a group of tourists towards a classical ruin. I began by following him, but he was weaving among the desks and it would look silly to copy him. Instead, looking for a diversion, I stopped beside a noticeboard covered in photographs.

'There, it's gone,' said Sebastian, striding back towards me. 'These are some of the photographs we're using for the book,' he said. 'About the restoration of Turney. Did you know a book was planned? And there's going to be a documentary too. I expect someone will turn up to wave a camera in your face at some point.'

The photographs showed Alexandra Marchant looking sombre but alluring in a hard hat; some female volunteers standing beside the singed curtains which were spread out on the lawn; archaeology students sifting through trays of rubble. In a much sunnier setting a group of doughty senior citizens was shown standing together and smiling into the camera. All of them wore trousers and trainers and T-shirts that read 'By Jove! We Love Turney!'. Some of the women raised teacups; behind them the men looked proud and proprietorial. One had placed an enormous hand on his wife's shoulder. Two were wearing Stetsons.

'Who are they?' I asked.

'Ah,' said Sebastian archly. 'These are the American

Friends of Turney House.' Somewhere behind us, the work experience girl sniggered. 'I don't know why people always *laugh* whenever the American Friends are mentioned,' said Sebastian, pretending indignation.

'Well, there is something funny about them, but we shouldn't laugh,' said Alexandra, walking over from her desk. She put a hand on my arm and whispered: 'They've given us shitloads of money.'

'You should really think up a better label for them,' said the architect, loud and languid, rolling out on his wheeled chair with his hands clasped behind his head. "Our Adored American Friends" or "Best Friends Forever". I mean if it's going to translate into more money.'

'We could just call it a "special relationship",' said Sebastian.

'We do tell them we love them,' protested Alexandra, 'often. We've made them all Lifetime Friends.'

'How do they even know about you?' I asked.

Alexandra flicked her hair behind her and looked out of the window at a distant spot above my shoulder. 'They were on a tour of English historic houses, the summer before the fire, and we hosted a tea for them here. It was a perfect afternoon. We sat in the Rose Garden. We ate cucumber sandwiches. Some of them overdid the Pimm's. Didn't we have a sing-song, Seb?'

'There were a few songs around the piano, I seem to remember.'

'And they just –' she shook her head, conveying her helplessness to put into words some remarkable experience of alchemy – 'they just felt a real *connection* with the place. Then the fire happened a few months after. The house was still fresh in their minds and I think they were all devastated. They took us on as a bit of a cause.'

'They're Texans,' said Sebastian in a stage whisper behind his hand.

'Which sort of explains everything, though it shouldn't?' said Alexandra, employing her upward inflection. 'One should never presume that people have deep pockets, just because of where they're from.'

'You're quite right. So long as they have deep pockets, we don't care where they are from.' Sebastian eased back his shoulders, working some complicated musculature beneath the shirt.

At the garden door we waited for Frieda to join us and then the group passed through the portal, back into a twenty-first-century London street where the speed and noise of everything seemed magnified after the minutely slow pace of a day spent handling particles of debris. A bus careered by us, empty and bound for the depot, carrying the ghosts of passengers in greasy smudges along its windows. A speeding car blared out a piece of rap that bent in the air as it passed, threatening violence on hos and bitches. We moved through the darkening evening in flapping coats and oversized work clothes, time travellers adrift in the modern world. The local pub, which was older even than Turney, was negotiating a similar dislocation. Inside, under bulging ceilings and low timbers, a much taller clientele than was ever envisaged in the eighteenth century strained to fit into the available headroom.

At the bar Sebastian said: 'Turney's unreal, isn't it? You spend the day fixating on things which seem crucially important. It's only when you come out into the real world that you see how completely irrelevant all of it is.'

I was shrugging off my coat, wondering if I could find a space for it and my bag on the floor between my feet. 'The real world?'

'Yes – the real world is blighted by war, recession, famines, tsunamis. The Middle East is exploding. Meanwhile, we have spent the day trying to find an authentic plaster recipe for the dining-room ceiling. And I mean, six or eight people poring over these fucking massive eighteenth-century tomes . . .'

His hands in the air in front of him wildly exaggerated the size of the tomes. Laughter smattered his face with red, as though somebody had flung a bout of hilarity at him.

'Well, somebody has to uphold civilisation . . .' I said, laughing too.

'. . . these eighteenth-century plastering tomes to find exactly the right recipes. So we know it's lime, sand and animal hair, but the right kind of lime isn't mined in this country any more . . .' He touched my hand and, although it was theatre, the contact made my skin shiver inside my sleeve. 'Then there's the hair. Is it cow or goat? We tried both, then we found a recipe that said it must be goat, a *particular kind* of goat. And that particular kind of goat, as it turns out, isn't bred in this country. I mean . . .' Sebastian shook his head, as if all of the possible ramifications were too outlandish to pursue. 'It's so – esoteric.' His face closed around the unexpected seriousness of this word and he looked, for a moment, genuinely perplexed.

I was nodding and laughing because he was right: it was

absurd and I had experienced the frustrations of this kind of work and read more than one ancient recipe book myself. Years ago Frieda and I even taught ourselves to carve mahogany woodblocks from a seventeenth-century manual. The problem with conservation was that it was defined by the era in which it was carried out, as well as the one it hoped to recreate, and subject to the whims and fashions of both times. Part of the job was knowing where to draw the line, though usually the budget drew it for you.

Absently dipping his finger in a puddle of spilled beer, Sebastian said, 'Here we are trying to make a dining-room ceiling which is exactly the same as the original dining-room ceiling but it can't ever be exactly the same because its components are different. The goats are from a different century, the lime isn't English, there isn't the same build-up of dust, or smoke. The permutations are endless. I don't know how we can make it exactly how it was the day before the fire.'

'Welcome to my world,' I said. 'You can't make it exactly. In the end it always has to be a compromise. You'll go mad if you get too hung up on the details. You're going to have to let go of that.'

He leaned on the bar, took his pint from the landlord and passed me mine. 'That's the trouble. My sister doesn't like letting go. She hates compromises.'

'Then you need to make more friends in Texas,' I said with a smile. 'So where did you get the goat hair from in the end?'

'Afghanistan, where they probably need it much more than we do. Hey, look, let's grab those seats by the window.' He glanced over towards the rest of our party to give them the nod but in that moment a group of women intervened at the bar, separating us from the others, and we found ourselves sharing a table with five women on a hen night, bulging out of strappy dresses and straining miniskirts. We were squashed up against each other, embattled by noise and bare flesh. Sebastian asked about my work; I told him about it and he listened with an expression combining puzzlement with approval – not an unusual response, in my experience. People usually thought that it was good to preserve things, but that paper was an odd candidate for preservation. I plied him with some persuasive anecdotes which he accompanied with well-trained movements of mouth and eyebrow. His hands resting on his legs were bigger than I would have expected from his frame. The knuckles were purposeful. The finger-nails had pronounced half-moons.

'Frieda's authenticity shtick,' he said, 'that people have to be told what's original and what's been reproduced. I'm not sure I get it. People like a bit of smoke and mirrors. They don't come to Turney to get a history lecture. They don't want to know what life was really like in the eight-eenth century, they want the Sunday-serial version.'

'It's about distinguishing the real from the fake,' I said, leaning into him to be heard above the music – which had suddenly increased in volume – and the shrieks of the women. 'Telling the true story and not letting people be tricked. Restoration should always be visible to those who want to see it. We like to say it should be "there and not there".'

'"There and *not there*"?'

'There and not there, yes. That's our motto. Don't laugh!'

'I'm sorry – only, as a motto it's not quite up there with "Who Dares Wins" or "Just Do It" . . .'

'Yeah, OK . . . All it means is that nothing's hidden. Our restoration work doesn't stand out, but it's there for anybody who wants to see it. If they don't want to they're free to keep on deceiving themselves. It's not a new idea. William Morris said it was immoral to confuse people about what's old or new.' But it was difficult to talk about morals and integrity with someone you didn't know when the woman sitting opposite was pretending to suck off a chocolate penis.

Sebastian made a caricature of serious contemplation, sticking out his lower lip like a sulky child.

'Most people would wonder why it matters in the end, if it's cow hair or goat hair holding the ceiling together. It's the same ceiling, basically. It's still going to look pretty.' He shrugged and sat back against the seat, grazing my shoulder as he lifted his glass. 'But it's your job, I get that.'

'What about you? What do you do, when you aren't rescuing houses in distress?'

'I organise fun for people who don't know how to create it themselves.' He fixed me with a solemn gaze that after a few seconds let in a sly smile. 'Events management. You know, parties, music festivals, corporate events. Spontaneity, with the risk taken out. You create an environment where people feel free, as if anything can happen. It can't of course. It's an illusion. We're just better at disguising the security nowadays. And everyone is better at pretending not to know they're being watched.

They understand that Big Brother is watching. They've decided not to mind.'

He glanced through the window in a brisk motion that seemed to dismiss himself and his work. Outside a double-decker, fully loaded, braked with a lurch that threw all the standing parties backwards. The doors opened and wan faces debouched onto the street. They could have been delivered to support Sebastian's thesis because they looked like people who had forgotten how to create fun for themselves, if they had ever owned this information in the first place.

'It's what people want now,' he said, still looking through the window, seeming to speak to no one in particular. 'Fun without the danger, as if you can control everything. It isn't possible to make everything safe, not without taking away people's freedom. But it turns out that people are more interested in being safe than being free. We live in a regimented age. Cameras – you know – everywhere. There's nowhere to escape to any more.'

I often heard my uncle fulminating on a similar theme. 'Orwell couldn't have predicted it' was one of his favourite phrases.

A pub spotlight, spliced into the old beam, shone on Sebastian's high cheekbones and the freckles that had been scattered with a free hand over his nose, cheeks and temples. The random distribution of melanin was like a marker of upper-class nonconformity, giving him the look of a Boy's Own adventurer or public-school tearaway. What may have started off as a polite side parting had been disordered during the course of a day spent puzzling over plaster recipes. The spotlight caught different parts of his pupils, revealing a cast in one that seemed to guard against arrogance.

The music from a speaker opposite felt trained right on us. It was getting harder to speak and be heard. Sebastian reached into his breast pocket and brought out a white plastic tube on which it surprised me to see him take several quick sucks, releasing a whiff of peppermint.

'Sorry about this,' he said. He had to speak right into my ear to be heard over the music. 'I've tried patches, gum. If this doesn't work the next step is hypnosis. There's no fun in smoking any more if you've got to go outside every time.'

One of the women burst into laughter, deep and gravelly. 'You're a fucking cow!' she said, slapping her friend.

Sebastian leaned into me, and I felt the pressure of his arm against the length of my own. He smelled of sandalwood with an undertow of plaster dust. 'Now if she'd said "you're a fucking *goat*", I'd definitely be interested.'

FIVE

The Schiller and Freeman studio was in Shoreditch, in a row of workshops that had been built 150 years earlier and since then had mostly been used by tradesmen – blacksmiths and bakers, metal merchants and carpenters. After the street fell into disrepair the council had acquired all thirty units, making them available to small businesses on low rents.

Frieda and I opened a bottle of champagne the day a sign painter emblazoned our names across the front of the studio. I remember feeling sick with the thrill of it: I had never dreamed that I would put my name to anything. In some ways, though, Chris was even prouder. I may have struck our friends as the sunnier partner during the years of our relationship, but my heart was secretly freighted with gloom. Chris, though outwardly quiet, was more willing to believe in the rightness of things, that if something was deserved, it would come to pass. Our sign might be there for decades, he said, a business handed down through the generations. Perhaps one day it would read 'Freeman and Daughter'. I remember laughing and saying give me a chance to have a daughter first.

Our community of self-starters included a bike-repair

service and a 'trashion' studio where clothes and accessories were made out of 'upcycled' and 'repurposed'
materials. There were designers and artists, including a
woman who made jewellery out of recycled bottle lids
and another who made corsets with conical breasts.
Three studios were rented to furniture makers and up-
holsterers who worked on their larger pieces outside
when the weather allowed it. Among all the tenants there
was a friendly solidarity that drew us outdoors, to work,
eat lunch, smoke or turn our faces to the sun when it
rose above the buildings on the other side of the road.
In the summer months a tang of urine sharpened the air,
with sour top notes on Monday mornings (there were
five or six pubs in the surrounding streets and our alley
was a convenient place to empty your bladder). That
didn't stop the tenants from prettifying our shared space
with plant pots and improvised artworks. For the last
five years we had even been organising a summer party.
We celebrated the royal wedding with a tea party so
dripping in gaudy decoration and lashings of traditional
confectionery that the question of whether this was
a sincere tribute or a parody of national pride was neatly
sidestepped.

But the council had cut its subsidy the previous year,
and with rents on the rise, some of our neighbours were
moving out. The corset woman left early one morning,
carrying her startled mannequins across the cobbles to a
friend's van. The bottle-top jeweller was these days
working out of a flat in Stoke Newington.

They weren't the only casualties of the recession, which
was biting harder in the East End than other parts of

London. The Beautylicious Hair Salon, full of stylists one Friday, purveying funky hairstyles to London's black professionals, was empty twenty-four hours later, closed down with so little warning that you could still see plugged-in hair irons lying on the counters. The bailiff's note stuck on its door looked like a mean refutation of all the joy that used to be dispensed here, but these were straitened times. For that reason, although we had at one stage planned to look for a larger studio, Frieda and I had decided to stay where we were for another year at least. The room was small for our needs, but you couldn't be precious about space in London: this was a city where it was now possible to pay a million pounds to live in a converted garage.

If I had time in the mornings, I got off the Tube at Bank then walked the last twenty minutes to the studio. The City was nowadays so noisy it was hard to believe that there were people here charged with such important work as how to save the Euro zone, or repair deficits that ran into trillions. Didn't they need a bit of quiet to work that sort of stuff out? On Bishopsgate it was possible to stop and watch the construction in progress, through a hole the size of a large flat-screen television. What you saw on the other side of the hoardings was a city of mud under the rule of men in hi-vis jackets and hard hats and the occasional turban. The archaeologists had already been in and out, sent away with a clutch of Roman coins and broken amphorae. Now this area belonged to earth-movers that marauded over the space, flattening the stumps of old brickwork or the odd abortive sapling. Gigantic cranes and tunnelling equipment were sinking pilings into the clay, twenty thousand feet below sea level as global construction companies built higher than had ever before been attempted in London, and lower too. The quest to be ultimate had in no way been chastened by the economic crisis.

From one street to the next, the atmosphere fully changed: you got sucked through an urban wormhole from the global financial hub right into the cor blimey heart of the East End, with market traders calling you darling, and chuggers the only people who still dared to be flirtatious. Outside Dirty Dick's pub drunks who had either started early or not yet gone to bed could be found singing about their own dicks, with late commuters dashing past from Liverpool Street Station. I picked up a coffee and entered the quieter streets of Shoreditch, though this area wasn't free of demolitions either. Round the corner from our studio they were knocking down a church and community centre. Walls that once protected staircases and corridors had been ripped away, and now these private spaces hung in the air with nowhere to go, doorways leading nowhere. The words 'Jesus Said I am the Way, the Truth and the Life' were attached to a tower that was any minute going to fall victim to the wrecking ball. I wished they could have let us in there, Frieda and me, with our tools and our ziplock bags. I would have recorded everything and taken away samples; I hated to see the old neighbourhood vanishing, buildings that had looked so solid reduced to piles of dust and mangled rods. It seemed to make a mockery of other people's stories. All around us old things were being torn down while we alone – it seemed to me – were trying to piece old things together again.

What a relief to get to work, takeaway coffee in hand, and submit to the comparative calm of the Schiller and Freeman studio and the absorbing world of historic decor. Our space was L-shaped with skylights all the way along its longest part and under them a table that occupied the main body of the room, where we did most of our work. This was where the forensic operation that had begun more than a year ago on conveyor belts at Turney House and continued in the old stable was entering its next phase. Lengths of paper from the Rose Room were laid out on the table and we were salvaging the good, cutting out the bad and making new paper to match the old.

Our studio was quiet and cool. For most of the working day we could count on light from the north, which is truer than the yellowy southern sun. When that was not enough we had daylight lamps which could be angled right over our work, as well as light boxes to illumine the paper from underneath. No mark or tear was ever going to escape such a blazing interrogation. Knowing that different sorts of light reveal different imperfections, I used a more sophisticated version here of the method I had tried on the dining table at home – experimenting with light sources, turning the lamp on and off, the light box on and off, scanning for tiny marks or patches of fugitive colour, no matter how small. This sort of scrutiny quickly exhausts itself; somehow the obsession makes you blind – you're looking so hard for imperfection that you can't see it. Every so often I had to stand back, take a breath and remind myself of the brief. If the front looked good and the colours were stable, the job was done. There was always a temptation to over-deliver, though, mending even tears that weren't going to show out of a misguided perfectionism, or as a way to ingratiate yourself with the client in the hope of more work. When you're self-employed it makes sense to keep lining up the commissions. There was such a thing as too much perfection, though, and usually the object wasn't to return a length of paper as pristine as the day it was made, but one on which the 'bad' marks had been differentiated from the 'good' ones, the historic blots singled out for special treatment among the commonplace stains that were going to be removed. Some clients needed themselves to be reminded of this distinction. We in the trade loved exchanging horror stories about rich cretins with no understanding of the value of damage. There was the man who bought Disraeli's battered old leather sofa and wanted it completely reupholstered. It had to be explained to him that rips and stains count as historical evidence. Who would banish Lord Nelson's blood, Clinton's semen? Who would send the Turin Shroud for a deep clean? After the ban on smoking in public places was introduced, Schiller and Freeman had been contracted to work on the Smoking Room in the House of Commons. The brief then was to remove a thick layer of dirt that had turned the surface of an early-Victorian wallpaper into something yellowing and narcotic. But in the end the work we did was superficial, all parties agreeing that it would be a kind of heresy to expunge the smoke from Harold Wilson's pipe or Winston Churchill's cigar. Somebody had argued that these microscopic particles of carbonaceous matter were a by-product of brilliant thought and therefore a part of the building's story. When damage could be attributed to a celebrated person or event then it wasn't damage at all, but heritage. Nobody wanted to jeopardise 'the patina of authenticity'. Patina, for some, was another way to say Englishness.

But there was always a difficulty in deciding which damage was good and which bad. In the case of Pugin's rose paper, Frieda and I were asked to remove all traces of singeing, scorching and soot, but no marks that would have been visible the day before the fire. In the early twentieth century there had been a set of silvery chairs in the Rose Room, and although the chairs themselves had long since disappeared, the marks made when they were pushed up against the walls for ladies waiting to dance were still in evidence on the panels of paper that survived the fire. These silvered indentations were going to be preserved and reproduced in the new areas of paper. 'It breaks my heart almost,' Alexandra Marchant had said, 'to think of those poor girls sitting and waiting to see if anyone would ask them to dance. Each of these marks stands for a girl. We can't erase them.'

Cleaning the papers was a matter of brushes, vacuum and then water. A robust paper could be left to soak in the free-standing bath we kept at the other end of the studio. Anything with less stable pigments had to be treated more cautiously on the spray box which was positioned at one end of our work table so that lengths of paper could be fed directly over it. Gently the marks were sprayed with water and alcohol, in a ratio that allowed the water to be taken up more evenly.

Once the new paper was ready, I was going to patch in the replacement pieces by tracing over the ragged lines of the damaged paper on a piece of Melinex. Then I would copy those same lines onto the new paper, scoring and cutting it with a needle to create a mend invisible to the naked eye. It never crossed my mind, until a friend once suggested it, that this wasn't truly 'creative' work. I was satisfied to think that I was mending something that had brought happiness and meaning to other people's lives. In fact it was more than a satisfaction: there was a pleasure in the idea that I was joining my work to that of a much earlier hand, corroborating an idea that had occurred to someone two hundred years ago and was still good. It moved me to think that the mechanics of pattern, which began as a by-product of weaving or stitching six thousand years ago, had changed so little. The repeating motifs that were so familiar – zigzags and chequerboards, the guilloche, the Celtic knot, the swastika – had been found in Egyptian tombs, on Roman buildings and in the illuminated manuscripts of Early English monasteries. Now they were part of a timeless language, a universal lexicon encompassing the sacred, the infamous and everything in between, and from which there were infinite points of departure.

'We learn how to be human by doing the same things, over and over again,' Frieda had said to me once, soon after I first went to work for her. 'Everything we learn is by repetition, from potty training to times tables. The behaviour that is rewarded is repeated. The behaviour that has no reward is discarded. That's how our brains learn to look for patterns, and they will always look, even when everything around us seems random.'

Eighteenth-century patterns were the ones I liked working on best with their exuberant colours, wild fronds and feathers, their imagined fruits. It would have taken an anonymous printer in an East End studio a year to carve some of the designs that covered the walls of a fashionable drawing room. And it was poignant to come across tiny indications of those distant lives: the places where a line was fudged, or colour was painted in by hand. Sometimes, bending over my work, I could become so immersed in its details that it startled me to hear the kettle being switched on, or to see Frieda climbing onto her stool with a Victorian sash pole to open the skylight and release a bee. It was like waking from a dream of the past to a fabric of modern noise: the call to prayer from the East London Mosque, the schoolchildren running past the studio window, a background of sirens, aeroplanes and smartphones.

'What do you make of Alexandra Marchant?' asked Frieda, out of nowhere.

I was using a stencil to copy Pugin's design onto the new paper. Pausing at the tip of a curling frond, I stepped back from the table to look at my work. 'I don't know. She's dazzling, but she seems to switch it on and off. You think you've got her full attention and then . . .'

'She freezes you out,' Frieda agreed, adding, without looking up from the table, 'She's clearly sleeping with Roger.'

'That's quite a leap!'

'That grin he has. It says everything.'

'Oh, come on. He's just like that. You read too much into things,' I said, remembering the whorls of dark hair on Roger's hands as I bent over Pugin's thrusting blooms. 'I like him. I like the way he's always saying "by all means".'

'I bet he is. "By all means, darling Alexandra! By all means!"'

'Frieda . . .'

'What about the brother? Did I tell you he's coming by later to look at our work so far?'

'Is he? OK. He seems all right. Why, what do you think?'

'Oh, I just think he's one of those public-school boys. Arrogant, you know, pleased with himself. I don't rate him much.'

'That's a bit damning. It's not a crime. Look at our government.'

'Exactly. It is a kind of English criminality, I think. A kind of perversion.'

Frieda's views, while never conventional, seemed to acquire a particular stringency when we were working in the studio. Her house in Camberwell was an artistic jumble of Persian carpets, dog-eared journals and books. The crockery came from incomplete sets collected at car boot sales. Her husband had been an artist and some of the paintings they owned were by his better-known contemporaries. Surrounded by the warm clutter of her own home, Frieda was an indulgent conversationalist, willing to believe in people's good natures, but the cool regimentation of our workspace and the pressure of deadlines seemed to play to her prejudices. Tracing the circles and swirls of concentric designs could lead us into contentious territory; capital punishment, immigration and education were among the hot topics that got an airing in our studio. Frieda was a defender of liberal values, but every so often she flared up, taking surprising umbrage against people who had too many children or lived on junk food.

'So – should they close down all the public schools?' I asked.

'No, of course not. They have to continue to exist to give a function to those magnificent old buildings. It's like bullfighting in Spain. One doesn't like to think of the bullrings standing empty, serving no purpose. So bulls must still be sent to the slaughter, and English children to boarding school. There's not very much difference.'

'You're too dry for your own good sometimes.'

Frieda laughed, set down her tools and went to switch on the kettle. 'The truth is that this project makes me angry.' Since she had never mastered an open 'a' vowel sound, there wasn't much difference for Frieda between 'angry' and 'hungry'.

'What's different about it? It's just a job.'

'They are trying to put Humpty-Dumpty together again. It will take them years and they will be left with a lovely fake. It may look the same as it did before the fire, but it will feel wrong. Atmosphere isn't something that can be made, instantly, just like that. You can't recreate the process of light striking the same area of paper every day for 150 years unless you take 150 years over the job.'

When I didn't reply she said, 'You don't agree?'

'Well, you can approximate it . . .'

'But that's not the same.'

'I don't know. This job certainly feels like it's going to take 150 years sometimes.' I sighed and stepped back from the table. 'I just think it's more complicated than that.

Turney House is their home and it's their business too –
their livelihood. They can't *not* restore it. I agree that they
are a bit arsey, though.'

'Not something I said!'

'You would have done, Frieda, if you'd known the
word.'

We both laughed, knowing that antipathy towards the
client was a part of the process, that it tended to grow in
proportion to the length and awkwardness of the job.

'So what's happening with Chris?' said Frieda, pouring
coffee from the cafetière into two cups and bringing them
over to my side of the room.

The question exposed me – I hadn't expected to talk
about Chris – and having stepped away from the table I
couldn't hide my face in my work. Instead I studied my
nails, first resort of the anxious. 'I don't know. We've been
apart a long time now. It's hard to see how you work your
way back from that.'

'A few months isn't very long, in the greater scheme.'
She drank from the cup, fanning her upper lip as though
anticipating a scalding. 'Do you miss him?'

'Yes,' I said, but the tears I felt coming were like a
compulsive reaction unrelated to anything I was actually
feeling. I looked up at the window, hoping they could be
reabsorbed. 'Actually maybe not. What I miss is how he
used to be. Not what he became more recently.'

Frieda set down her cup and put her hand on my arm,
ending any hope of composure: the tears flooded out.

'He said that people change, you're supposed to change.
That I didn't change in the right way or – I don't know!'
I was laughing and crying at the same time with nowhere

to wipe my nose but my sleeve. 'We're going round in circles.'

'You think he would still like to try?'

'Yes.'

'And you?'

'That's what I don't know. Maybe it was selfish to leave. He didn't want me to go. We could have staggered on somehow.'

She frowned, leaning back as though to bring my face into focus. 'What do you need to find – what do you need to know before you can decide?'

'What's real. What's truly still there and what's – a matter of convenience.'

'Convenience? That's not a good word. It makes me think of public lavatories.'

'What I mean is –' I wiped my eyes hard, pressing them with the heels of my hands – 'if you're going to be with someone it should be because he's the only one you could ever have been with, that there's something unrepeatable about it. I don't know if that's the way I feel about Chris. I'm fond of him. Is that enough? I feel like what we have should be unique, not just – *nice* or good.'

Frieda studied me for a moment. 'It's asking a lot,' she said, but it sounded less like a reprimand than an acknowledgement that this was something that could be asked, if you were bold and prepared to risk disappointment. 'But you shouldn't underrate fondness. It's more than a lot of people have. In the end maybe it counts for more.'

'What about you and Jack?'

'We didn't have so many expectations. In those days if you couldn't have something, you couldn't have it. You weren't expected to go off and fix whatever was wrong – wrinkles, or infertility, or low moods. Anyway, you know what I think about the babies and so on,' she said. 'Your body belongs to you and nobody else. It was your choice to make.'

'I suppose his body was involved too.'

'Only for a few minutes!' Her laughter spun into the air as she walked back round the table. 'And what about all that poking and probing you would have gone through to have an IVF baby? And perhaps then the disappointment of not getting anywhere. And the cost of it all. And the heartbreak.'

That word choked me up – it conjured a physical damage that was so different to all the other kinds of damage we were used to seeing and evaluating in this cool, functional room. Hearing my own predicament laid bare brought back feelings that had lost their heat in the time Chris and I had been apart. There were so many things about our life together I had been missing, these last few months. Now I remembered, with a rush of indignation, the powerlessness, the anger I had felt at the insinuation that my infertility was a fault I should strive to correct, rather than an accident of fate that was sad but didn't have to be tragic.

There was comfort in working, in following a line. But it was no good if you couldn't keep a calm head. And once Frieda had left for her dentist appointment, I put my tools and overall to one side and went to ask a friend in another studio for a cigarette. Then I sat outside on one of our old fretted chairs, smoking and crying in a continuous process that was consoling because it made a kind of rhythmic sense. The words of the man crossing the bridge at Embankment came back to me with a quality of revelation. *Nothing ought to matter that much.* You can't have everything in life and what you can't have shouldn't be so important. Not to care: that could be a panacea. I should try to care less.

A man appeared at the end of the lane walking towards me with a patrician saunter that looked almost provocative in our working community. I squinted at it for a few seconds before recognising the figure as Sebastian, then, swearing under my breath and hurriedly stubbing out the cigarette, I wiped away my tears and tried to smooth composure into my face and my hair, without success, clearly, because his pace slowed as he got closer and it was obvious that he could see something was wrong.

'Hello,' he said. 'Weren't you expecting me? Frieda said any time after twelve.'

'She told me and I instantly forgot.' I might as well make a virtue of my distress since I couldn't hide it. 'As you can see, it's been a bad day.' I spread my hands wide and said with a laugh: 'I appear to be getting divorced.'

'Shit, I'm really sorry,' Sebastian said, shaking his head and rocking back into the heels of his leather shoes as though physically knocked by my news. 'Look, I can come nearer the end of the week or –'

'No, it's fine. Honestly.' And because he had already half turned to go and I wanted him to stay, I put body into the lie. 'It's been on the cards for a while. Come in. I'll show you what we've done so far.'

Inside the studio I started straight away on a summary of the work to date – the pigment analysis, stencilling, the new paper that we were in the process of making. I showed Sebastian how the finest grade wool had been dyed in two colours to provide matches for the areas of paper that had been exposed to light and those that had been covered with paintings. I treated him to the 'royal tour' – our jokey allusion to the visit the Princess Royal had paid to these refurbished workshops when they were first opened. There was a photograph of Frieda taken with the princess that day that I transposed to a mug, both to commemorate the event and to rob it of gravitas. I showed him the stereoscopic microscope, how it could link to a computer and supply close-up images to the screen, and the portable X-ray diffraction machine. 'Crick and Watson used one of these to study the structure of DNA.'

Sebastian whistled under his breath. 'I didn't realise your work was so high-tech.'

Quietly he attended to the temperature control panel, the different-sized Japanese brushes hand-stitched with goat hair arrayed along one wall. 'Look, you have to feel how soft this is,' I said, drawing the brush across his cheekbone. 'And you know what? It really does matter that it's goat hair, and not cow.'

He smiled at me, and I had an ache to kiss him, a hunger that had come over me in the raw aftermath of my crying jag.

'These are our palette knives. We prepare them ourselves. We sand them down to get the right sharpness.'

'You use all of these?'

'No, not all the time, but we collect them. The good ones are hard to find and you always have favourites. I don't know why, really. Some tools just have particular associations. Jobs you did, or people you worked with. And then you don't like to let the old ones go – you know how it is, a woman and her tools . . .'

He smiled and nodded and at the pigment cupboard he stopped to study the jars, frowning at their printed labels.

'Dragon's blood. That's got to be something a marketing team came up with.'

'No, you're wrong,' I tutted. 'That goes back to the ancient Greeks.'

'What about viridian?'

'Chromium oxide dihydrate. Invented in Paris in 1859. Stable and non-toxic. The first really safe green.'

'OK. Impressed,' he said with a smile that flattened down the corners of his mouth.

'I know my pigments,' I said, primly, and it was true. I had observed the catalytic qualities of copper green, the effects on Prussian blue of alkaline ferricyanide. I knew that the pigment euxanthin was made from the urine of cows which had been fed mango leaves and was therefore irresistible to beetles. I had worked on illuminated manuscripts where every detail in Indian yellow had been nibbled away by silverfish, turning priceless pages into doilies.

Sebastian walked around the room, bestowing on everything an exaggerated attention, at the chin-stroking end of gravity. The safe for explosive materials, with its skull and crossbones, caught his eye and the long wooden arms, at the far end of the studio, over which were looped several trial lengths of the new papers, testers for colour. On a shelf were some of the woodblocks we had used in the past, carved pieces of cherrywood and mahogany, and beneath it a pinboard on which we stuck thank-you cards from customers or friends and ephemera to do with our work. There was the exhortation, from an eighteenth-century manual, 'to make ye flowers join'. A quote from Andy Warhol caught Sebastian's eye: '*I like boring things. I like things to be exactly the same, over and over again.*'

'That's good,' he said, smiling broadly for the first time and daring to leave his chin alone. 'Unconventional, nowadays. I mean we've come to expect constant change.'

He seemed about to expand on the sentiment, offering some philosophical rejoinder. When that didn't come I said, 'Yeah, we're not really about change, Frieda and me. We're all about the repetition. Doing the same thing over and over. Frieda thinks patterns soothe the brain. They're a subconscious reminder of the natural repetitions that govern life. When life pushes people towards disaster or chaos, pattern reassures them.'

'You think that's true?'

'Absolutely,' I said and then, nodding at the rose paper, 'Only this particular pattern doesn't seem to be soothing us much at the moment.'

He laughed. 'It is very red. Where is Frieda, by the way?'

'She's at the dentist having a crown mended. I had to talk her out of trying to stick it back on herself. Believe me, she was this close.'

'It would be a temptation, with so much glue around.'

There was a cloudburst of noise then, of car horns and shouting, and we hurried to the door. At the end of the alley an articulated lorry had tried to turn and got wedged.

'Hey – do you want to get some lunch?' said Sebastian.

The invitation surprised me. I made a feeble allusion to the sandwiches in my bag.

'I think you need someone to take you out. Come on – let's go to the Royal Club.'

'That sounds very smart.'

'Believe me,' he said, 'it really isn't.'

As it turned out, the Royal Club was the kind of place you would go to only if you knew about it. It was doubtful that a casual passer-by, however curious or hungry, would ever choose to step under the broken sign on Shoreditch High Street and climb the dirty staircase that twisted so sharply to the left that a person at street level could only dare imagine what kind of lurid establishment was waiting out of view. I climbed the stairs half wondering if I had been lured to a rooms-by-the-hour joint, half hoping that I had. Upstairs the atmosphere was more salubrious than expected. There were six tables, two of them taken by groups of men, some in salwar kameez and topi, others in jeans and nearly all religiously bearded. A door swung open as we walked past it, allowing glimpses of the kitchen and faces wreathed in steam from the boiling pots.

Sebastian made for one of the unoccupied tables and motioned me to take a seat without waiting for any word from the waiter who had followed us with a plate of poppadoms and selection of chutneys.

Our window looked down onto a fabric stall and, across the way, in a shop selling outfits for weddings, headless mannequins turned out their hands in Bollywood poses.

'My sister was saying you live in the house where you

were born,' said Sebastian, holding his poppadom up high and breaking it like a priest breaking a wafer.

'It's not exactly like that. I haven't been there ever since I was born. It's my grandmother's house and my parents were living there when they first got married because they were students and they didn't have any money. When I was about one, the three of us – me and my mother and father – moved to a flat in Earls Court.' I let the word 'father' go lightly, grazing the consonants. I found it hard to say, even when I was talking about other people's fathers, or fathers in the round, variously errant, absent or doting. Sometimes it was easier to incorporate the word into a sigh or a breath, make it ghostly.

'I moved back with my mother to my grandmother's when I was six and then for a while we were all over the place, until Mum finally realised it was just better to leave me there and stop pretending she knew how to be a parent.'

'Your father had –'

'Yeah, he was out of the picture. They split up.'

The lie wasn't intended to conceal my father's death – it was just an easier option than the truth. Runaway fathers were commonplace and a father who was a shit wouldn't divert the conversation the way a dead one would. I liked Sebastian. I had already imagined sleeping with him, in the way that I sometimes imagined sex with men I saw on the Tube when the trains slowed between tunnels and the lights went off, the brakes letting out a suggestive moan. Sex with Sebastian worked, as a mental image. There was a suggestive ease about the way he used his body. He seemed relaxed about physical contact – happy to lean into my space, pressing me to try things, even feeding me a piece of tandoori lamb from his own fork. His soft-collared shirt, in faded pink, staked no claim to masculinity and was, for that reason, manly. His collarbones pressed outwards and I could imagine putting my tongue into the dip between them, the sweet-salt taste of his skin. The other times we had met I had thought of him as somehow too posh to deal with the real world outside Turney, but away from that rarefied atmosphere, he seemed more normal. The Royal Club wasn't a place for toffs and clearly he had come here before because he ordered our food without reference to a menu, accompanying each of his suggestions with endorsements and exhortations that made the waiter smile, assenting modestly.

'So you lived with your grandmother from – when?'

'I was kind of coming and going for a few years,' I said, chewing the lamb. 'Then once I'd started at secondary school I stayed with her. I pretty much refused to see my mother any more. Or at least to see her all the time. Her and her rather weird assortment of boyfriends.'

'Oh really?'

'Let's just say she had interesting taste in men. They weren't what you'd call father figures. One was a bouncer. One was her landlord. They often seemed surprised to find out I existed, when she finally got round to telling them about me. Then I just got in the way. That's how it felt, anyway.'

He nodded and fixed me with a blinking intensity, as if this were much more interesting information than I knew it to be. He probably spent a lot of time pretending to be interested in Turney House contractors, inspecting our work and listening to us grumble – conservators were first-rate grumblers. He would have learned to feign an interest in the minutiae of our lives and histories. On the wall behind him there was only one picture, a photograph of pilgrims at the hajj, walking round the Kaaba Temple at Mecca. The photograph had been taken on a long exposure, so that the walking pilgrims were a frantic blur, while the onlookers were beatifically still. It looked as though the photographer meant to endorse one of these groups above the other but I couldn't tell whether it was the people who were moving or the people who were standing still.

'What's happening at Turney House today, then?'

He set his fork down, rolled his eyes. 'Have you heard of rot hounds?'

I laughed, raising a hand to cover my mouth. His physical confidence seemed to produce its opposite in me, making me coy. 'Go on. Tell me.'

'They're collies trained to sniff out dry rot. We let them loose in the basement this morning. They were tearing all over the place, wagging their tails.'

'Sweet – or –' Noticing his baleful expression I said, still laughing: 'Am I misreading this?'

'It's not sweet,' he said, though he was laughing too. 'Tail-wagging means they found something. So it's not good at all. Actually it's fucking disappointing, because we thought we'd got rid of all the damp and the fungi and whatever else.'

'How was that not picked up?' I said. 'You've been monitoring the basement for over a year.'

'God knows. We ran a million tests. Everything is temperature-controlled, radio-controlled. There are sensors in all the beams. Believe me, that place is like some high-tech laboratory disguised as a quaint old house. All the results were coming back clear. Then there was one that didn't tally with the others. I don't know – I didn't wait around to find out, to be honest, though I expect there's a message waiting for me.' He moved his hand towards his phone then seemed to think again, nudging it away across the Formica. 'You know, I'm not even going to look. There's nothing useful I can do today.'

'I suppose a year isn't that long for a building to dry out,' I reasoned. 'Hampton Court took two years.'

'Different scale. Different materials. All the experts agreed Turney was dry.'

'Didn't they say it was the equivalent of Niagara Falls falling on the house for seven seconds?'

'Water-based disasters always get compared to Niagara Falls. Have you noticed that? As if there were something epic and extraordinary about putting out fires.'

'It's cinematic, as an image. So what does it mean? What happens next?'

'The wood panelling, which we thought was sorted, will all have to come off again. It shouldn't affect your side of the house, though. The walls in the Rose Room are dry.'

'I like the idea of rot hounds, though. They should let them loose in the City and the House of Commons.'

He nodded, chewing fast. The nodding and chewing merged into an expression of furious agreement. 'Sniff out the cheats and frauds. Chase out all the bankers. Fantastic idea.'

Bankers were safe ground and we spent a few minutes in shared indignation at City bonuses, the lack of accountability, the scandal of national bailouts. Then Sebastian abruptly pushed his plate away, dismissing it as he had the smartphone.

'What I need now is a cigarette.' He looked around him in a puzzled way, then transferred his puzzlement onto me, as if this urge had come out of the blue and I might explain it to him. He struck me as someone who wasn't given to the patient development of inklings or ideas. He seemed not to need the thousand little pauses that cushion the conversations and exigencies of most people's day.

I said: 'Haven't you got your plastic whatever? Your thing?'

'My thing.' He pulled the inhalator out of his pocket and held it up in front of him, examining it with disgust, as though it were one of the unidentified objects plucked from the sodden debris at Turney.

'Shit. I need the real thing today, what with the bloody dogs and the . . . Ali,' he called, 'I don't suppose you've got any cigarettes?'

The waiter, who had been standing sentry at the swing door, glided towards us in a way that suggested he was very tired, very bored or so accustomed to this trajectory between kitchen and table that he could cover it with no effort. He was young, perhaps still a teenager, and single hairs poked at crazy angles through the soft skin at the side of his jaw and on his upper lip. On his unstarched white jacket there were faded turmeric stains. Ali took from his pocket a packet of duty-free Marlboros and knocked it against the heel of his other hand so that one cigarette rose above the cardboard parapet. All the while he watched Sebastian askance, every one of his actions seeming to occupy the liminal space between courtesy and contempt towards this man who was, I was beginning to think, a regular customer.

'Sorry, mate, but I need a light too,' said Sebastian, holding his eyes on Ali's as if they were plunging deeper into a mystery together. The cigarette, clamped between his lips, waggled up and down as he spoke.

Ali shook his head and sent his shoulders halfway towards a shrug, then he said, 'I have in kitchen.' He plucked the cigarette from Sebastian's mouth without waiting for it to be proffered and glided back to the swing door. When he returned, it was with the lit cigarette between his lips. He passed it to Sebastian, with no acknowledgement that that was an unusually intimate way to light a customer's cigarette. They were grazing the acceptable boundaries of health and safety here, I thought, not to mention good hostelry, but Sebastian accepted the cigarette with a wordless admiration. We exchanged covert smiles and I knew then that there was something between us, an alliance growing under the radar. This new information came as a soft pressure in the solar plexus, unfurling in a pleasurable way, and I caught myself smiling at the Formica tabletop. I wanted something to happen between us.

'But you have to go outside.' Ali was smiling too, as if he had also noted a change in our table's microclimate and was in on the complicity.

'Oh Christ, not here too. You're messing me around, right, Ali?'

'Not messing you,' protested Ali. 'It's the law.' He shrugged again with more conviction, still looking askance as if he did not care about the law, but would enjoy sending us outside anyway, especially now that a light drizzle was setting in. 'Here on roof is fine.'

'Will you come outside with me?' Sebastian said and as he stood up he took my hand, presuming that I would. We ducked through two low doorways, stepping across cranky floorboards to reach the flat roof of the Royal Club which jutted out like a podium into a service area hemmed in by other buildings. Opposite us was a ragged skyline of old tenement flats. The restaurant's kitchen protruded to our left where a man who looked like Ali's brother was standing washing pans at the sink. Ali and an older woman who could have been their mother were moving around behind him. A mop and bucket stood by the door. I imagined Ali drawing the mop across the stairs at night, never quite getting into the corners and not caring about that, or about the cracked sign that was such a poor advertisement for their restaurant. Sebastian passed me the cigarette and I became its third partaker, the hit of nicotine curling around the front of my brain, like those exotic fronds I had been stencilling in the studio. The view in front of us was giddily enhanced. Along a parapet above the top row of windows, two pigeons followed each other up and down, heads bobbing back and forth like comedians in a music-hall skit. It was back-stage London, a glimpse of the things that signified home for the largely immigrant residents; people who may have arrived perhaps only days or weeks ago from Dar es Salaam, Freetown or Quito, who by some miracle of human interaction, and such unifying media as television and food, schools and public transport, would find their place in the city and become part of the pattern. One of the windows opposite was covered by a flag of Brazil, the light from a bare bulb shining through it, showing up tears and ragged edges. In other windows sheets or blankets took the place of curtains, a statement of poverty or transience. On one window there was a Union Jack, cut out from a newspaper at the time of the World Cup, its fixer either too disappointed or deluded to bother removing it; a pair of trainers had been banished to a window ledge. Beside that another window opened and a woman in a salwar kameez leaned out to tip breadcrumbs from a packet out onto the patch of ground below. The pigeons that had been roosting above swooped down into the lot, solving the mystery of a white cascade of guano down that section of wall.

'So. When does the divorce come through?' asked Sebastian, taking the cigarette back from me. 'Or would you rather not talk about it?'

'It's fine, and the answer is that I don't know. We're not at that stage yet. It's still a separation.' Had I said that word before in relation to Chris and me? It sounded more like a culinary concept than a legal one. 'We're – what do they say? – considering our options?'

He looked sideways at me, sending the smoke out of the other side of his mouth. '"Taking time out"?'

I laughed. 'However you put it, it doesn't sound good.'

'It's all horribly familiar.'

'You too?'

'Yeah – not a marriage as such, but a long-term relationship that came unstuck. Not very pleasant at all. No kids though, so . . . What about you? Do you –'

'No.' I shook my head quickly. 'Luckily not. That would make things so much worse.'

'Well, look. Come round sometime if, you know, you'd like someone to talk to about it.'

'I don't know if I really want to talk about it, to be honest.' I took the cigarette back, letting our fingers touch in the transaction. 'But I'll come round. I'd like to do that.'

When I arrived at his flat that Saturday evening Sebastian opened the door with a worked-on panache, flicking his hair and motioning me inside then catching me, one hand on my waist, and kissing me on the cheek. He seemed more nervous than he had been at the restaurant and, again, his demeanour moved me towards its opposite so that I felt calmer than I would have expected as I walked on into the flat, unbuttoning my coat and looking around me. I had thought hard about what to wear, considering the relative merits of buttons and tie-wraps with a composure that would have shocked me if it had been some other woman who was so methodically preparing the ground for sex. 'What the hell,' I had said to myself as I stood in the centre of my gabled bedroom, looking at myself in the mirror that was attached to the back of the door. 'Who cares if he thinks I'm a slapper?'

Sebastian's flat was in a Victorian school building, one of several in the area that had been converted into luxury flats over the last ten years, and a deliberate attempt had been made to make the ex-school feel unschool-like. A kind of deconsecration had gone on, an effort to banish the dead hand of education as surely as God might be banished from a converted church. But God and head-mistresses are formidable presences and the space still felt institutional, for all that its centre had been rededicated to squashy sofas and deep pile rugs. The windows, ten feet high, were stern lozenges of light. On the wall where once there had doubtless been portraits of dismayed head teachers, there was now a giant pop-art canvas of a woman with tectonic nipples and muscular thighs that seemed aggressively out of place. Beneath her, a 1950s jukebox had been refashioned to hold an iPod, a tiny brain in a big, shiny body.

'I wouldn't have associated you with this,' I said, turning to Sebastian.

'Meaning?' He was standing at a counter in the gleaming kitchen area, fiddling with a gadget for cutting the foil on wine bottles, the kind of present that is given to the man 'who has everything'.

'I just assumed you were into old stuff.'

He laughed. 'I'm not into any kind of *stuff*. I hate *stuff*. This is background. It was all here when I moved in. I suppose they were trying to make it look like a Manhattan loft. Trying a bit too hard.' Looking around me, I saw that the room's vernacular was not what I had thought. At first glance it had looked like authentic fifties Americana. Now I saw that I hadn't read it the right way. The key was not authenticity but irony. It was less a reconstruction of fifties Americana than an ironic commentary on the *desire* to reconstruct fifties Americana. A kitschy joke about kitsch. The effect depended on getting the joke, but it was hard work establishing where the joke began and ended, at which point to engage a wry smile. It would be difficult ever to have a serious conversation in this room, I thought, to break the news of a bereavement or to consult a doctor about chlamydia. These were the kind of surroundings that demanded a perpetual sacrifice of earnestness and it surprised me that Sebastian could be bothered with such a pose. Even now, as he stood at the giant American fridge in the kitchen area, filling two glasses with chilled water, swearing mildly as crushed ice from the dispenser cascaded onto the floor, he was out of tune with his surroundings. I wondered why he had rented a flat that was fully furnished. Was it because he didn't have the patience to acquire furniture, pictures – stuff – himself? Could he literally not be bothered to go to a sofa shop, or –

'I didn't even ask you,' he said. 'Is red OK?'

'Yes,' I nodded. 'Yes, it's fine.'

Glasses on a tray. A dish of olives. The arrangement was such a time-honoured prelude to seduction it unnerved me. Sex was what I had come here for, but now that the journey towards it was under way I felt the beginnings of panic. I didn't remember how seductions worked, where foreplay began. Had it already begun – should I be stroking the stem of my wine glass and looking up at him through my fringe? Or could we have a normal conversation about carved finials and adhesives, then at some mutually recognisable sign switch to sex? I was so out of practice I couldn't even be sure of recognising such a sign when it came. Chris and I had been students when we met and in those days the only necessary seduction technique was a bottle of vodka and a great mix tape. My other liaisons had been opportunistic, powered by the thrill of secrecy and the difficulty of removing boiler suits.

His phone rang. 'Shit. Do you mind?' he said. 'I should take this.'

'No, of course not. Go ahead.'

He walked towards the windows, holding the phone to one ear and bringing his free hand up behind the other one to loosen out his collar, an emblematic gesture of the stressed entrepreneur, the fixer.

'Yeah, I know,' he said into the phone. 'Yes. I know . . . I know . . . I said . . . Well, is there any other way of looking at it? They can't expect to have it *all* their own way.' His hand dived down his back sweeping across his neck and shoulders. 'Well, that's the nature of the job, isn't it? If everybody insists on sticking to an eight-hour day we'll be finished sometime next century.'

He swung round to face me, grinning in a way that invited me to share his exasperation, but I knew what it was like to be at the mercy of employers who took 'flexible hours' to mean that all the flexibility was on their side and all the hours on yours. Sebastian was probably a bastard, I thought, not minding very much, at that moment, if he was.

'I don't know – I'll leave that one to you,' he said. 'It's a big ask.'

I walked over to look at the jukebox, angling my head in a way that flattered the line of my shoulder and neck. When he ended his call, it didn't surprise me to feel Sebastian's fingers, and then his lips on the skin of my shoulder. I allowed myself a few seconds' inaction before turning to kiss him back, at which point he took the wine glass from me in the manner of a 1970s schmooze-ball and we seemed to enter a world of ironic allusions. I didn't know what I was playing at – it was such a long time since I had been in this position – was I the vamp, the kitten, the sex goddess? Was I a 'natural woman'? Something about the scene didn't feel real. Even the tiger-skin rug I could feel under my back was a fake, a joke about tiger skins and the sort of people who have them. *No animals were harmed in the making of this rug.* The sex itself was punctuated with comic interludes including a dash for condoms which had Sebastian hiding his genitals with a pink angora cushion. And when he tried to remove my halter-neck top, biting the soft skin around my breast and armpit, he wormed his way under the strap and ended up wearing it himself. It was funny, it was good, but above all it was a relief to feel wanted for my body alone and not for my potential as a partner or a mother. 'Pure sex', people talk about, and 'meaningless sex', and I was never sure what they meant – surely the purer it is, the more meaningful? Well, this was it! A physical experience, emotionally blank, with no history, no future and – best of all – no need to offer any kind of commentary. Instead, in a wry tribute to the classic movie sex scenes, Sebastian fished into his jacket for his inhalator, took a puff on it and passed it to me. I sucked on the plastic mouthpiece, noting a sting at the back of my throat, followed by a chemical rush of nicotine and then the surprise of not producing any smoke. Not to exhale – it made me feel like a fraud.

'What do you think?' asked Sebastian, and when I

hesitated, and possibly began to blush, he clarified: 'I mean about the inhalator, not the sex.'

'It's OK, I suppose,' I said. 'I can't really see the point, though. Do people ever get addicted to these?'

'They get addicted and have to wean themselves off with real cigarettes. It's a vicious cycle.' He turned and smiled at me. 'I'm sure you can get addicted to anything if you try hard enough.'

SIX

Sebastian's body was engineered for expensive sports – his upper body honed by rowing and swimming, his legs by tennis and skiing. Sport had reconfigured him and he was, at this stage in his mid-thirties, a product of triumphs and accidents on the field. His shoulders were like polished newel caps, the skin tightened to a shine, but his left clavicle protruded at an odd angle, the result of a ruptured ligament sustained in a rugby match. The white striations fingering the top of his chest on the right side were stretch marks linking to his bowling arm. The metal pins in his left leg – as he explained to airport staff every time he passed through a scanner – were acquired after he broke his leg in two places while skiing. These are the bones of the ruling classes, I thought to myself, watching the ziggurat of ribs rise and fall with his breath as I lay next to him in bed and – drawing one finger along the line of his bicep – this is the arm of the whip hand. I thought of Uncle John ranting over Sunday lunches about the smug faces of Tory bastards who think they own the world, and smiled at the joke of myself as a class traitor.

I did feel guilty lying beside him, especially when I remembered Chris sitting in the vegetarian cafe, everything about his manner so painful and tight. But it had been good to be reminded that sex wasn't only a reproductive act. And there was a relief in knowing that our encounter wasn't going to lead anywhere: I didn't want it to. This was the best bit of a romance, when the connection was still flimsy and febrile and all physical contact had sexual overtones, when nobody felt the need to march out their emotions for inspection. It was the layering of expectations that was so deadening, the setting down of routines, the hand lazing on a partner's knee, the invitation to attend events as that four-legged entity, 'a couple'. Then the bulky ostentation of a 'relationship' rolled in, flattening everything with its timetables and duties. Nothing ever matched the enjoyment of the first few weeks, the first night. It was probably better, I thought, safer, to have work and friends as your guarantee of stability and pleasure. Have sex when the occasion arose and take pleasure in these rare moments of satisfaction. Because it did feel good to lie in a super-king-size bed in linen with such a high thread count that it stood up in creamy folds and peaks around my body, following my movements with an expensive susurration.

His bowling arm struck back and grabbed my thigh.

'Ouch!'

'Checking you were still here.'

'I'm here. Where would I have gone?'

He turned towards me, wheeling one shoulder over the other.

'I don't know. You might have slipped away. You might be one of those types who don't like to stay the night.'

'I think there's a name for women like that.'

'Last night was great,' he said, laying his hand along my cheek and looking into my eyes with an abashing sincerity. I'm not good at dealing with sincerity at such close quarters, especially not horizontally; I didn't know how to respond to this sincere appreciation of sex. So, 'Yes,' I agreed and then, 'Thank you,' and because that sounded so prudish I said quickly: 'You know I went to a school just like this?'

'Really?'

'It was a grammar school. After I left it merged with three other schools and now it's some massive comprehensive. The science wing alone is bigger than my whole school was. And the children you see coming out are massive as well. Everything's got bigger.'

'Grade inflation. Did you like school?'

'Yeah – eventually. Once I stopped fighting the system.'

'This is good. Tell me how you used to fight.' His hand moved over my shoulder and down to my ribcage and my skin responded with a rippling of goosebumps.

'We just went to ridiculous lengths for the sake of rebelling. We were always either rolling up our skirts to make them shorter, or rolling them down again if one of the senior staff was coming round the corner. And wearing make-up. God knows why when there weren't any boys around to impress, but you had to wear it, to show that you were fighting the system, even though it meant getting sent straight to the toilets to wash it off again. Anyway, somebody discovered transparent mascara, which seemed to solve the problem because then – even if the teachers couldn't see it – we *knew* we were breaking the rules and that was enough. There were these Pakistani twins, Meena and Leena, who used to pierce people's ears in the lavatories for 50p and –'

'What are you smiling at?'

'It's all coming back to me now.'

'Such as?'

'Just, how desperate we were to be desirable. To get a bit of male attention.'

'How desperate? Show me.'

I turned in to him, acquiescing in a game of knotted fingers, tangled limbs and sheets, and sex.

Afterwards he said, 'I hate to say this, but I actually have to get up.' I felt a defensive tightening in the area of his shoulder that lay under my cheek – a drawing in of sinews, a bony shifting of plates.

'What? It's the weekend!'

He eased my head off his chest, held my jaw in his hand for a moment and kissed me on the mouth before moving away, but even so I felt the withdrawal of his body as a miniature crisis. I had been lonely and Sebastian was easy company. We had got a bit drunk the night before, lying on the polyester tiger-skin rug, and I had ended up telling him that my father was dead. It hadn't been a convulsive revelation – no tears or hugs – but a natural contribution to a conversation about families and growing up. This morning I had woken up feeling relieved of an inchoate sorrow. I had put a name to a long-held grief (though, admittedly, 'Terence Donaghue' was not a noble name for grief). I didn't expect, or want, the blossoming of true love to follow, but an overpriced brunch with Sebastian in one of the zillion eateries nearby would have been a nice way to round off the weekend's romance. I turned onto my front, pressing into his body's imprint on the sheet. Sebastian, sitting on the edge of the bed, pulled on socks, the skin on his back crumpled after a night on Irish linen. 'Will you come with me?' he asked, in the same breezy tone he had asked me to come out onto the roof of the Royal Club.

'That depends where you're going,' I said. His warmth returned in the shape of a handprint on my back.

'I'm going to meet my sister for lunch. It's her birthday.'

'Oh my God,' I said into the mattress, speaking through layers of lambswool, cashmere and silk to the three thousand springs, each hand-stitched into individual pockets. 'Jesus Christ.'

The hand on my back gave me a shove. 'It's going to be chilled. Just her and Roger. Not a big deal.'

'*Chilled*?' I turned my head and lifted up a corner of the pillow to make a conduit for speech. 'If it isn't rude to ask, why is she celebrating her birthday with Roger and not Lord Marchant?' I couldn't help dressing his name with sarcasm. Talk of lords and ladies seemed to belong in the realm of nursery rhymes.

Sebastian's mouth twitched with amusement. 'I don't think she and Rafe are really together any more. They've got some kind of arrangement, I suppose. As for Roger – I don't know. I don't ask. He's married too, but he seems to manage to get a lot of time away. Perhaps he and his wife have an arrangement too.'

'All these arrangements – it sounds quite harmonious.'

'That's pushing it. Come on, it won't be for long. You'll enjoy it.'

'Won't she be surprised to see me there?'

'I'll text her. I'll say I was visiting you at the studio and I persuaded you to join us. You might get a chance to talk to her about that paper you want to uncover. Come on, we can be there in fifteen.'

Fifteen minutes? London knows how to punish that kind of hubris. By the time we reached the restaurant in Soho we were forty minutes late. Alexandra Marchant, sitting with Roger at a window table, marked the delay by not smiling or saying hello, while Roger proffered a smile so wide and white it hurt your teeth to look at it.

'OK, so I think your friends are here now!' called a young woman who came beaming to the table. Squatting beside us, in the style favoured by London waiters, she put her arms on the tabletop and rested her chin on her hands. 'Hi, guys,' she said, 'I'm Kasia and I'm going to tell you about your specials today!' There followed a recital of some dozen dishes, into each of which Kasia introduced a degree of physical theatre that sometimes required her to stand up and display a five-inch span of toned abdomen.

'Pig chicks?' queried Sebastian after the recital of specials was over. 'Is that piglets – or . . . ?'

'No. I explain to you,' said Kasia patiently. 'I am the chicks of the pig –' she squeezed her own cheeks with a little pout – 'I am braised and laid flet on a bed of mesh.' Her stomach traced a sensuous arc between her navel and the top of her jeans. The skin was taut and looked as though it would make a satisfying noise if you slapped it. After taking our order Kasia returned to the kitchen with a sexy sashay, a purple G-string pulled clear of her low-riders and a calligraphic tattoo spanning her hips.

Alexandra followed her departure with a look of scornful incredulity. 'You'd have thought at least a place like this would have English waiters. Does nobody English work anywhere any more? Have the natives of these islands become so fat and stupid and downtrodden they can't even get jobs as waiters?'

'Keep your voice down,' admonished Sebastian. 'She's nice. I don't know what your problem is.'

'My problem?' She glared at him. 'My problem is that in *my* country, nobody speaks *my* language any more. Everyone is foreign!' It sounded like round one of a ding-dong, but Sebastian stayed smiling in his corner. I guessed from their reaction that both the men were used to hearing this kind of invective from the mouth of Alexandra Marchant.

Roger's hand on the tablecloth scuttled crablike to where Alexandra's hand lay rigid and bejewelled. He lifted a little finger and gave her a warning nudge. Alexandra immediately withdrew her hand, leaving Roger's finger twitching for a second in the air.

'I also detest being referred to as a "guy",' muttered Alexandra.

'We should have let her know you prefer "Your Ladyship",' said Sebastian. 'Come on, darling, it's your birthday. Chillax.'

At a window in the building across the road some men and women in their twenties were gathered around a table inspecting images, laughing and flicking their hair out of their eyes.

'Packed in like sardines,' said Alexandra Marchant to nobody in particular. 'More and more of us all the time.

I wouldn't stay in London if I didn't have that millstone round my neck.'

We were left to guess whether 'millstone' referred to Turney House or Lord Marchant.

'At least it hasn't rained today,' said Roger brightly. 'After the week we've had I thought we'd never see an end to rain.'

'What's wrong?' said Sebastian, speaking at the curtain of hair.

Alexandra said nothing for a moment then muttered to Roger, 'You tell them.'

Roger, who had been about to unfold his napkin, now returned it to his plate. 'Ah,' he began, in Rogerly fashion, 'well, I think Alexandra is referring to the documentary series.'

'*Turney Inside Out*?' said Sebastian.

'There's been a hitch,' said Roger. 'And it looks like the project is on ice.'

'It's not on ice!' barked Alexandra. 'It's just not going to happen. It can't happen now.'

'Why?'

She glared at Sebastian, saying nothing. Then, turning back to the window, 'Rafe doesn't want to do it. He refuses to be involved.'

Sebastian said nothing for a few seconds and then, 'He's got previous, hasn't he?' He was eviscerating his bread roll, plucking out the soft inside like candyfloss. 'Rafe's never wanted to do any publicity. I'm surprised you thought he would this time, to be honest.'

Alexandra looked briefly confounded. 'Well, he said he would do it. Now he's in one of those moods. He won't do anything that could be helpful. Without the series, there's no book. The book was going to be a BBC tie-in. You can't have a tie-in if there's nothing to tie it to.'

'You can't do the series without him?' Sebastian asked. 'How would we explain that?'

Alexandra's eyes slid over my face with no lightening of her expression at all, so that I felt almost as if I hadn't been seen.

'It's more complicated than him just refusing to be in it,' she said, rearranging the cutlery in front of her. 'That would be fine – we could hide him away somewhere. But he would make it impossible. I know him. The BBC was already having second thoughts and this will be the death knell.'

'Why do they need to know?' asked Sebastian, then straight away, 'Why were they having second thoughts?'

'I don't know!' Alexandra glowered at him. 'Some executive thinks there are too many restoration programmes on TV.'

Sebastian, having excavated all of his bread roll, had made a start on the crust, tearing strips off it like someone who is hungry but must make his ration last. Laughter caught him out mid-swallow, and coughing on a crumb he said, 'You've got to admit that there has been a bit of a glut.'

'But for a reason – which is that people *love* them! What about the glut of soap operas or football? I don't hear any complaints about that. Because the BBC is so craven it won't do anything to upset the working classes.'

Sebastian stiffened at the anachronism; it was awkward to be with someone who alluded to class in a public place.

'Look,' he said, glancing around at the neighbouring tables, 'it was going to be a pain in the arse, anyway, having the film crew around.'

'It's not the fucking documentary I care about. It's the book. We could have made something really beautiful. Have you seen the one they did for *Downton*?'

'Of course. I surf more stately home porn than a Russian billionaire. It swamps my inbox. People who want me to stage music festivals at their castle so they can afford to mend the roof. Every lord and lady in the land needs more money. They always do, don't they? There's never enough.'

Alexandra sat back in her seat with folded arms. Finally she said, 'Well, then you'll know it would have made us a lot of money at a time when we can't make money out of anything else. You realise what next weekend is?'

Sebastian shook his head and Roger leaned forward with jolly eyebrows. 'It's the May bank holiday,' he said. 'The weekend when the British run like lemmings to their nearest stately home.'

'The tills will be ringing at Chatsworth, Blenheim, Knole,' said Alexandra. 'And Turney's closed. And will stay closed for another two years at least.'

'Is the May bank holiday really that big a deal?' Sebastian had finished the roll now but licked his finger and collected the crumbs off his plate with its moistened tip.

'Oh yes,' said Roger, with an inward whistle that denoted both the importance of the weekend and a quiet surprise at Sebastian's ignorance of it.

'It was always our biggest weekend of the year,' said Alexandra, adding crossly, 'Are you starving or something?'

'No breakfast,' explained Sebastian and he called across the room to Kasia: 'Could we get some more bread? And some olives and maybe nuts?'

'I can bring you guys some nibbles to share?' Kasia called back, as though friends sharing nibbles were an exciting new concept she herself had devised.

'Excellent! Thanks.'

'Well, it's everyone's biggest weekend,' continued Roger. 'You're looking at a nearly two-million-pound spend on catering alone.'

'On tea and cakes?!'

'Yes, yes,' said Roger, nodding vigorously. 'If you like. Yes, absolutely. To put it in perspective, nearly ten million people visited historic houses last year. They spent £5.4 billion. Tourism is practically 10 per cent of the British GDP.' Roger held his hand out flat in front of him like a cake slice, raising up soft layers of argument. The hairs running along the side of his hand lay neatly together like stitches. 'In this country heritage is our strongest product driver, our USP. Let's face it – what else have we got? Manufacturing's dead and buried. Financial services are going down the drain.'

'So as a country we have nothing to offer, except our past,' said Sebastian. 'Bit depressing really.'

'Not at all,' said Roger, who seemed constitutionally incapable of gloom. 'The great thing about the past is that there's plenty of it. It can't run out! And heritage is the one sector that is not seeing a slump. It's booming in fact.'

'Tut, tut, Roger,' said Sebastian. 'Not the H-word. Not in front of the ladies.'

Roger's smile lost some of its wattage and he drew his

hands away from the table before clocking the joke then laughing as his cheeks coloured. 'Yes, but you see heritage – if you'll forgive me, ladies – is something the British really *know* how to do. When it comes to pageantry and tradition we're world leaders. We're ranked fourth in the world for built heritage. So all we have to do at Turney is keep ahead of the game. If you restore it, they will come!' he said and his own joke made him hiccup and laugh simultaneously, an awkward confluence he tried to conceal in a cough.

'What you need to do now is find ways to use the grounds while the house is still off-limits,' said Sebastian. 'Once all the workshops are out of the way.'

'You mean we have to host a rock festival?' said Alexandra miserably.

'No, it's totally the wrong venue,' said Sebastian. 'You'd never get permission.'

'Opera?' suggested Roger with a smile. 'Operetta?'

Sebastian shook his head. 'Chilli,' he said.

'Chilli?'

'Chilli festivals are massive at the moment. Or chocolate. Or rare-breed meats, regional cheese. Artisanal food is big. Obviously with meat and cheese people need refrigeration, so you have to have generators.'

'There are all kinds of revenue streams worth investigating,' said Roger. 'What would you say to appearing live on a webcam, Ros?'

Since I hadn't been contributing to the conversation, the question caught me off-guard. I pictured student dominatrices operating in the ghoulish light of their computer screens from bedrooms that still bore poignant witness to

Snoopy or Winnie-the-Pooh. 'I'm probably being stupid – I don't see how that would generate money.'

'Every time someone donates twenty quid, you strip off another layer,' said Sebastian, 'I mean another layer of wallpaper, obviously.' Everybody laughed at this, even Alexandra, and I felt heat rising in my cheeks.

'No, no, no, no, no, Heaven forfend!' said Roger, extending his hands in a rescue gesture. 'The idea is that on the Turney website people would be able to watch some of the restoration process as it occurs. Believe me, the public appetite for this kind of thing is gigantic. It's not a fund-raising exercise per se. It's just a way of making people feel interested, involved. It's about creating stake-holders. And yes, if that inspires them to make a donation or become a Friend, then, you know, fantastic.'

'I don't know,' I said. 'I'm not sure how I'd deal with being on camera all the time.'

Roger was preparing some emollient response but then Kasia arrived at the table with our food. 'OK, guys, I *think* we are ready,' she said, treating this dining experience as a communal effort in which all of us had responsibili-ties. In front of Sebastian and me she placed two large dishes, at the centre of which was a tiny, artful pile of food, a tangle of onions and sliced green beans masking a disc of mashed potato. Three slivers of meat sat on top of the arrangement. It must have been a small cheek, I thought, feeling sorry for the pig. The red-wine reduction was more like an abstraction – a few flecks dotted around the plate's perimeter.

The restaurant, which called itself a 'dining room', was a small operation, just ten tables on the first floor of a

Georgian house. Once it would have been a merchant's sitting room and the room still had its original dark panelling and a fireplace in which a flame-effect gas fire had been installed, providing instant atmosphere safely on winter days. On the walls were framed prints of eighteenth-century caricatures by Gillray of plump aristocrats speaking in bubbles that floated upwards like gassy eruptions. The one above our table was of George III and Queen Charlotte receiving the news of the death of Sweden's king while sitting together on a double lavatory. 'What! What! What! Shot! Shot! Shot!' This place made a virtue of its shabby furnishings – tables that wobbled and chairs with subsiding seats were part of the attraction along with waiters who could offer more in the way of style and interesting conversation than expertise. The clientele was clever and ruffled – media types rather than bankers – and presumed to be above such bourgeois conceits. They didn't mind if the food was late or if they snagged their hosiery on the chairs; it was part of the charm.

Kasia came back with the other dishes, a tuna Niçoise for Alexandra and lamb shanks for Roger. 'So if someone now can find me a place for the nibbles,' she said, wanting everyone to play their part – but with the table being so small and the plates big it wasn't easy to find extra space. Insinuating one toned hip between Roger and Alexandra, Kasia leaned over the table, her breasts floating towards us like twin jet engines, as she prepared to land the wooden platter on a narrow strip of table.

'It's a bit late for that now,' snapped Alexandra.

'Oh?' Kasia, still hovering above the table, turned to look at Alexandra over her right shoulder. 'Did you decide you don't want your nibbles?' I noticed that the skin stretched over her hip was mottled above the jeans and there was inky writing on it, too. *Ad Astra*, it said, in a dainty script, with three little stars above it.

'Well, we *would* have liked our *nibbles*,' began Alexandra with cruel precision, 'while we were waiting for our food. But now our food has come – do you see? – we don't need to *nibble* any more, because we can actually begin to *eat*. You see the difference?'

Kasia coloured and without saying anything began her retreat, reversing platter, breasts and hips back through the space between Roger and Alexandra. She was going to call Alexandra a bitch the minute she got back into the kitchen; her lips were already pinched around the word, ready to spit it out in front of the cooks. Then Sebastian protested.

'Well, actually I would still like it!'

'Sebastian,' remonstrated Alexandra, 'she's brought it too late. We're onto our meal now.'

'I don't know about you, but I'm hungry enough to eat everything on this table and probably on everybody else's too. Just put it down, Kasia. Thanks.'

'No problem.' Kasia eased forward again.

'Seb!' said Alexandra with an exasperated laugh. 'Sorry, but! This is *my* birthday, *my* lunch, *my* rules. And *I* say it's too late.' She put up a hand and pushed aside the platter which had begun to advance once more towards the middle of the table and was now close to her shoulder. This small action was decisive enough to unbalance the platter on which one of the bowls toppled over, tumbling olives onto Alexandra's white cotton shirt.

'Oh shit,' said Sebastian.

For a few seconds Alexandra said nothing, but drew herself back from the table in silent horror, her arms raised awkwardly up at her sides, as though a puppeteer had control of her elbows. Kasia, with hot apologies, tried to retrieve the olives, picking at Alexandra's shirt in a way that could only make things worse. Alexandra swatted her away.

'You idiot!' she said, and then she shouted: 'That's a new fucking shirt! I want the manager here right now!'

There was a hiatus in which the other diners either stopped talking or made low murmurs of disapproval. Kasia stepped back, trembling, then retreated to the bar where a colleague, alerted to customer grievance by a change in tempo on the restaurant floor, had already come out of the kitchen. The skin on Kasia's back seemed to cringe as she walked away, the calligraphic tattoo shrinking from her hips. She didn't bother with the sashay.

'For Christ's sake, Alexandra,' said Sebastian, scraping back his chair, 'what makes you think it's acceptable to speak to people like that?'

'You stay. I'll go and talk to her,' said Roger. 'I'll explain it's a difficult time.' He got up and wove a stolid path through the tables, his jacket flaps ruched from contact with the chair.

'I can't believe you did that,' Sebastian hissed across the table. 'She goes on Twitter now and wrecks your reputation in five minutes. All that good publicity you're worried about goes out the window.'

'Fuck that.' She swiped at his arm, catching his cuff, so incensed that the whites of her eyes completely encircled their cobalt-blue irises. 'I'm in the *wrong* about this? Excuse me for expecting her to do her job properly!' Her upper lip curled back from her straightened, whitened teeth.

Sebastian snatched his arm away. 'It's not good enough. You're not lady of the manor here.'

Alexandra shrank, shaking, back into her chair. If there was any way for her to make a graceful descent from such a pinnacle of anger, Roger was the man to facilitate it, and he did his best for the remainder of our meal, with mellifluous conversation, small amounts of alcohol, and regular, reassuring physical contact. Alexandra allowed her shirt to be dabbed with a wet cloth and agreed that no lasting damage was done and the incident was best forgotten.

I couldn't forget it though – I'd never before seen such a display of petulance. It wasn't so much Alexandra's arrogance that shocked me but her sense of entitlement. What must it be like, I wondered, to feel so sure that you are right, that you deserve to be given so much?

Uncle John's face, seen through the square hatch of my grandmother's loft, had the whimsical look of a computer-generated elf as viewed by a giant, his ears and hairy eyebrows exaggerated for comic effect. 'Pass the boxes down,' he said impatiently. 'Then we can get everything out and sort through it in the sitting room. It will be easier than trying to do it up there.'

'Do you think?' I had been sent up to the loft because I was the most comfortable with heights, but looking around me at the cardboard boxes, I felt vertigo anyway, brought on by the thought of what we were about to do, dismantling the life of a person who was still alive, who might have been asked for an opinion except that it could be so laborious talking to Granny Pea these days. There were times when she followed the conversation fairly well, or at least we could keep her in the running, like a band of horsemen corralling a riderless horse. At other times even an observation about it being a fine day led us into wild territory and we might as easily find ourselves dissecting the love life of Doris Day as discussing the dangers of coal mining. My grandmother, whose life had been a model of literalism and common sense, was becoming a surrealist in her eighty-sixth year. We had no choice but to be her acolytes.

'Perhaps you were right when you said we should leave this for another time.'

'Well, we're here now,' said John irritably. Then Natalie came blinking into the same square, her face echoing the father's impatient brow, the resolute mouth from which disdain was only ever a flicker away.

'Is it very, very dusty up there?' she asked, perhaps hoping that a note of sympathy absolved her of a duty to join me.

'Yes! It's an actual proper loft – must be the last un-converted one in the neighbourhood.'

'That won't last long, once it's sold,' said John bitterly.

Here and there shafts of light struck through gaps in the tiles, giving the scene a cinematic quality that seemed to make some facile point about the pathos of passing time. Under the eaves lay the tiny body of a house martin, its head and beak still a perfect creation, while the flesh of its body was coming undone, shrinking into the tiny bones.

I had a spatial picture of myself standing at the top of the house with the walls stripped away. In front were the two streets leading down to the high street, where the butcher was, and the newsagent, and the chip shop where Mrs Andropolous used to cuddle me by the deep-fat fryer. Behind me was a patch of wasteland on the other side of which stood the Victorian prison. I used to lie awake in bed at night and frighten myself with thoughts of the prisoners sawing through the bars. In my imagination they'd be proper jailbirds with arrows on their uniforms, like the ones I'd seen in comics. Sometimes the prison guards, all of them overweight, walked back from the high street past our house with their great bunches of keys and packages of chips it surprised me to see they had got from Mrs Andropolous: I didn't see how she could exist in both our worlds. The wind, blowing from the south, carried the noise of trains chuntering through the night and the house locked into the rhythm of my grandmother's snoring and the ticking of the carriage clock downstairs punctuated by the wild cries of foxes mating among the rubbish bins. More than once a vixen's screams had been enough to drive me to the bedroom next door where Granny Pea accommodated me to her bosom. My grandmother was sympathetic to these night-frights, understanding that my father's death had made me overly anxious: if a parent can disappear completely, not just from the physical landscape, but from conversation, from all records, then the door is open to every other kind of disaster. She had to reassure me, often, that things were going to be all right. 'Shh now,' she would say, patting the side of my head, and I would grab onto her earlobe, stick my thumb in my mouth and go back to sleep.

'Are you still with us, Ros?' called John from the landing. 'We've got work to do here!'

'Sorry. How do we handle this? Do I start passing things down?'

'Yes, that would be the best approach.'

Squatting down by the hatch, I said, 'Is it OK to be getting rid of everything, do you think? I mean, what if Granny actually does move back home?'

'I think that's very unlikely,' said John. 'She seems set on a course towards –' he paused; you don't idly invoke the death of someone who is still alive – 'increasing infirmity.' He looked down at his shoes, showing me a circle of pink scalp from which the hairs were in jagged retreat.

'I know. But it feels wrong to get rid of things that belong to somebody who's still around and might want them.'

'We're not getting rid of everything,' said Natalie. 'Just seeing what there is and doing some sorting. Think of it as streamlining? It doesn't hurt. I mean, she won't know.'

'That doesn't make me feel better!'

Natalie shrugged. 'She'll be relieved, I'd have thought.'

Now Sadie crawled into view and looked up, her face shining like a moon against the blue carpet. 'Dirty,' she said.

'That's right, darling!' said Natalie, stooping to swoop Sadie up and prodding her tummy. 'It's dirty, dirty, dirty! It's dirty, irty, wirty!' Sadie flung her arms around in wild excitement.

'Well, are we doing this or not?' said John.

'I'm on it.'

I started with the boxes that were closest to me, lifting them over to the opening, then passing them to John, whose arms, wiry and hairy, waved in the air. Some of the boxes were intriguingly light. I would have thought they were empty if it hadn't been for their sealed edges. Others were so heavy I had to nudge them over to the opening with my foot, the portentous clank of china sounding from inside. John had to come to the top of the ladder to receive those, with Natalie, beneath him, holding on to a lower rung with one hand and on to Sadie with the other.

'Keep a firm grip, Natalie,' called John, as though this ascent were taking him very far from terra firma.

'Now I know what families are for,' I said.

'Yes. When it comes down to it,' said John. 'Heavy lifting, in every sense.'

When I had passed down six or so boxes, about half of all that were in the loft, we went down to the front room to investigate their contents.

'Would you believe it: one whole box for *Reader's Digests*?' said Natalie. 'Do you remember these, Ros? She used to keep them in the cabinet, behind glass, like they were too precious to actually handle.'

'I don't think anyone ever did read them. She wouldn't even let us touch them! She thought it was enough to have them in the house. That the knowledge would magically transfer itself. She used to say to me –' I stopped and smiled at the sudden recollection.

'Go on!'

'She used to say: "I love watching you think. I can see the cogs turning."'

Natalie laughed. 'She did think it was an amazing thing to be clever. Do you remember how she was always going on about Roy Hattersley? "What brains the man has." And David Frost! "So intelligent and handsome."'

'Well, *she* was clever too. She just –'

'Didn't get the opportunities. No.'

It was touching to see the care with which everything had been put away. Baby clothes had been ironed and pressed between sheets of tissue paper. Tiny mittens and bootees were packed with lavender sachets. Natalie tutted that they were clothes that should have been passed to her, though it was doubtful that Sadie would ever have fitted into them. They seemed to have been made for the ethereal babies of another era. Natalie and I held them up between us, the christening gowns and bonnets, marvelling at the detail in the lacework.

'We can't get rid of any of these,' I said.

'No way.' She was folding a baby's blanket, using her chin to pin down the middle while she joined the corners. 'I'm sure my mum can find somewhere to store them.'

'Storage is the thing. Storage is key.'

'Ros, look! The plate Granny used to put the Sunday joint on. It must have got broken and she had it fixed.' The dish was a piece of imitation delftware, attractive if not unusual. Metal staples had been used to fix the break that ran like a stitched scar from one end of the plate to the other.

'She took so much care of things,' I said. 'I mean, who bothers to get a plate mended these days? You just don't, do you?'

Natalie shook her head slowly. 'I wouldn't. You shouldn't in actual fact. The cracks harbour germs. It's different if something has sentimental value I suppose. People's possessions have all kinds of stories attached to them that we don't know about. Sometimes things can seem so precious, and you don't even know why.'

'The person goes, and then the story's lost.'

She nodded thoughtfully. 'Granny maybe loved this dish because it reminded her of all those family meals, our Sunday lunches.'

'Which always ended with someone having a row or storming off?'

'Well, no, they didn't. You're exaggerating.'

'Have you noticed? We're talking about her in the past tense.'

'We're not! We're talking about part of her life that's over, which isn't the same thing. I mean, she's not going to knock out any more roast dinners, is she? That's not the same as saying she's finished. Poor old Granny Pea.'

The moniker had once been intended to differentiate her from another grandmother, 'Granny T', who was Uncle John's mother. Of course Natalie and I, being very little, wantonly misunderstood the distinction, and our nickname for her soon acquired its own logic, because peas were so small and Granny Pea was so big, a bulwark against all disaster. When she was wearing a housecoat there was no knowing GP's true dimensions, and she had two of them: one for home and one for her cleaning job at the house of a wealthy family in Chelsea. The work one was smarter with blue-trimmed pockets which could be made to hold a few dusters and the odd aerosol. Inside it, my grandmother was solid and springy, held within wire brassieres and corsets that were strictly focused on containment rather than eroticism. Hurl any sort of adversity at her and you felt that she would bounce it off.

I don't believe that my grandmother ever worried about her size – rather she turned it to her advantage. If she had something complicated to carry, she used her voluminous bust as purchase. Even large objects, like a laundry basket, could be handled in this way, leaving one hand free for a cup of tea, which was something my grandmother carried with her most of the time. A stack of Tupperware boxes, which might contain shortbread, rock cakes or fancy leftovers from the house in Chelsea, could be accommodated between bosom and chin. It was her undoing, in the end, this mania for multitasking, because it was while carrying the laundry basket that she had slipped on the stairs, the first of a series of mishaps leading to several long spells in hospital and, finally, the care home.

I used to hate to think of my grandmother having a life outside our home, although I grudgingly accepted the claim of the rich folk in Chelsea. It made me nervous as a child to come home from school and find both the housecoats hanging up on the back of the kitchen door. To turn from the television and see my grandmother 'dressed for bingo' in a Viyella blouse with a brooch glinting on her bosom was to witness as unnerving a transformation as Superman's or Wonder Woman's on the TV shows Natalie and I loved watching at the weekend. Granny Pea's housecoat was as potent a symbol of world safety as Superman's cape and even though everybody knew that Clark Kent was still a hero on his civilian days, you couldn't help feeling that world security was compromised when he wasn't dressed for action, at least for the time that it took him to locate a phone box and change. And so it was with Granny Pea: she was more dependable in a housecoat.

'Ros, your phone is flashing and whirring and jumping about on the counter,' said John, coming in from the kitchen with mugs of tea on a tray. 'I don't dare pick it up in case it explodes.'

'I don't know why you pretend to be a Luddite, John,' I said, brushing past him, 'when you're actually a professor of particle physics.'

'It's all an act. You should know that by now,' Natalie shouted. I was already in the kitchen, picking up the phone.

'Hey, Sebastian, how are you?'

'I'm really well. How about you?' said the voice at the other end, unctuous in the way of a recent sexual intimate. It offended me a bit that Sebastian should introduce this seamy note into my grandmother's innocent kitchen. There was no reason why sleeping with someone should change the way you spoke.

'Yes, fine,' I said briskly. 'I'm sorting through some of my grandmother's things with my cousin and my uncle.'

'I tried to call you a few times last week.'

'I know. I'm sorry I missed your calls. The reception at the studio isn't great, plus we've just been really busy. You set us quite a tight deadline, remember?'

'Not me –'

'Well, your sister.'

'I thought maybe you were avoiding me. That the scene in the restaurant put you off.'

'No, it's not that!' I said, lying, though I wasn't altogether sure why I hadn't wanted to talk to Sebastian. I had liked sleeping with him, and would sleep with him again, I just didn't have much enthusiasm for the bits in between: the phoning and dating. Sex was enough, though I wasn't sure that it was ever acceptable for a woman to say this, even to a man who felt the same way.

'I wouldn't blame you if it had. My sister's mortified about what happened. She behaved really badly and she wanted me to apologise.'

'She wanted *you* to? How does that work?'

'Obviously she ought to herself, but she's embarrassed. It wasn't good. She knows that.'

'Well, she was probably very stressed, understandably, with everything that's going on.' Through the kitchen door I could see a robin struggling to get purchase on a feeder, pecking at the last few nuts. I had been looking after the garden but now I realised that I had been neglecting the birds, which had always been such a source of joy to my grandmother. However hard you try to do the right thing, guilt rushes in, storming the barricades.

'Kind of you to say so, and yeah, it's all getting to her a bit. Anyway, something good came out of it.'

'Oh?'

'After you'd gone, we talked about your mystery wallpaper and Alex agreed that you should go ahead and uncover it.'

'Seriously? How much of it?'

'As much as you can. That whole section of the wall if it's feasible. We can make the funds available, if you think it won't take more than a few days.'

'I might even be able to get it done in a day. It's hard to say for sure, but I don't mind putting in some extra hours.'

'Well, go ahead. You've got the green light.'

'She must really be feeling guilty!'

'Guess so. She's not usually like that. It was a bad day.'

'Don't worry about it. Anyway, it was fine. I had a good time. It was nice of you to ask me along.'

'It was a pleasure – and see you soon, right? I mean, if you want to.'

'Absolutely I do. Definitely. And – Sebastian?'

'Yes?'

'I really am sorry about not getting back to you before.'

John and Natalie had got absorbed in a collection of old board games in the front room and as I walked through the door I saw my uncle holding Sadie on his knee, their two sparsely haired heads bent together over some heirloom. I decided to give them all time alone and took my tea up to the loft, curious to see what was in the remaining boxes. This decluttering exercise was taking the form of a journey through my grandmother's life, a survey of her milestones and her unfulfilled ambitions. The china from our family dinners, the intellectual aspirations represented by the *Reader's Digest*s, the baby clothes passed down through the generations: all this was a moving enough testimony – but I almost cried aloud when I discovered the box of Christmas decorations that used to be brought down every year, including the plastic reindeer that I had felt so guilty about hating as my tastes outgrew my grandmother's. In another box were the remnants of her young married life: a Teasmade that may have been a wedding present, and appeared never to have been used; Bakelite containers that had been superseded by Tupperware but never thrown away. There was a mincer with a box of metal attachments and I remembered how it had sometimes been my job as a child to stand on a chair at the kitchen counter and push into it the pieces of mutton left over from Sunday's roast, turning the handle to grind out long worms of grey meat that would go into Monday's cottage pie and feeling a temptation to push in my own fingers and make worms of them too.

Another box rattled in a way that suggested it had been less carefully packed than the others. I moved it out from under the rafters and placed it beneath the single bare light bulb that hung from the loft's highest beam. The box had been well sealed, but the masking tape was old and dry and tore off with a sound that put me cheerfully in mind of birthdays and Christmas, until I pulled open the flaps and was assailed by a smell that went direct to whatever part of the hippocampus records fear. It was a sticky fragrance – a fusion of perfume and hairspray evoking the background smell of my worst childhood years, the times when we had been continually moving, either because my mother couldn't afford the rent or because she had found a new boyfriend and thought it would be nice for both of us to live with him. Inside the box were the contents of my mother's dressing table: a make-up bag into which foundation had spilled, jamming the zip; a lipstick, ground to a stump from force of application, and some half-finished pots of cream. The pots were repellent because I could still see where fingers had dug into the cream in a visceral record of the transfer of grease to skin.

My mother's belongings weren't the only ones in the box: there were men's things too. A bottle of aftershave. A man's watch. A leather wallet, loosening its seams. My father's things.

'Ros?' a voice called up from the landing.

'Chris!'

I scrambled over to the hatch and looked down to see my husband, perhaps soon to be my ex-husband, standing beneath.

'Hi – I didn't hear you –'

'Nat let me in. I just wanted to see you. To drop in for a few minutes. I hope that's all right. You seem to be raining on me, by the way.'

'Sorry.' I sat back out of view, wiping my eyes on the backs of my hands.

'What's happened? Can I come up? Is there room?'

'Yes,' I said. 'Come up. Please.'

And as he emerged through the hatch and came level with me, I felt my skin tighten in a shiver of relief. Chris with his sad, hooded eyes, his kind mouth, the austere arrangement of bones, was exactly the person I wanted to see.

'Hey?' he said, face full of concern. 'What's going on? What's happened?'

'Nothing really.' I shrugged. 'I didn't expect to see you.' Putting out my hand I stroked his arm in a lame gesture of welcome. 'What brings you south of the river?'

'Really it's just that I wanted to see you, to know that you were OK.'

'I'm not especially OK.'

'I see that. What's happened?'

'Life has happened. That's all. That's the problem though, isn't it? Life keeps happening, when sometimes you wish it would stop and give you a chance to catch your breath or work out what's going on. Then you could press a button and let it all start happening again.'

He leaned towards me, using his thumb to wipe away a mark or smudge on my cheek, then let his hand stay alongside my face, a warm cradle. He nodded. 'Yes. Life's shit that way.'

'And look what I found. Come over here.'

Chris had to stoop under the rafters as he picked his way across the floor. 'You're sorting through your grand-mother's stuff?'

'Yes, but this, as it turns out, is from my parents' flat. See?' I turned the box to show him the writing in marker pen: 'Newton Road'. 'They thought they were going to be happy there. They moved in. They were young, they had a child and they never dreamt of how everything was going to fall apart.' As I tried to calm my breathing it started coming in bursts, making motes of dust somersault in the air in front of me. I turned towards the rafters, not wanting John and Natalie to hear me downstairs. 'All these houses are full of people's dreams and plans. Street after street. People don't realise how dangerous it is to trust that everything will be all right. I can't bear to think of all the disappointments and the grief and the tragedies. It's such a waste of love and hope when everything always ends in death anyway. There was a woman on the radio this morning who lost her whole family in the tsunami.'

And it was this woman on the radio who undid me, not the trials of my own family. Chris saw the unbalancing wave and steadied me, folding me into his chest. To be in his arms again felt like a summary of all the other times he had held me, after disappointments and bad days at work or arguments with my mother, back in the days before bitterness and anger drove us apart. For a few seconds he said nothing as I sobbed and then: 'It's not a waste. It's what life is. Joy and pain all bundled together. The disappointments, the plans that don't work out aren't failures. There's no perfect way to be alive. Nobody gets it one hundred per cent right.'

I sobbed louder then because it was such a relief to be speaking to him properly about things that mattered. 'That's the thing, you see,' I said. 'I never got it. I never got that that was what life is. I'm wetting your shirt.'

'It doesn't matter.'

'We're a plan that didn't work out. Is that what you think?'

'No, I don't think that at all.' He shook his head with a deliberation that allowed it would be understandable for someone to come to that conclusion, even if he refuted it. 'I shouldn't have tried to fit you into a plan. Or come across that way.'

I shook my head against his chest, inadvertently wiping my nose at the same time. 'It wasn't your fault. I didn't give you everything. I was always holding something back. I was scared and I didn't know how to say it.'

'Hey –' he began, but I stopped him.

'Look, I want to show you something else.' Leaning away from him, I stooped to pick a book out of the box. 'I found this sketch pad with his name on the front.'

Chris took the book in his hands and ran a finger over

the biro indentation of my father's name. Opening the cover he looked at the first page, then paused before saying, 'It's a drawing of you. "Rosalind sleeping".'

'He was being kind,' I said with a sniff. 'I don't believe I ever looked that adorable.'

In fact it was the picture's inaccuracy that was moving because love had so obviously guided the artist's hand more than truth. The soft bulge of the cheek, long lashes and angelic curls were features you would want to see in your own sleeping child; perhaps you would be less indulgent with someone else's. It was the only evidence I had ever found of my father's love, and it filled me with a painful happiness.

'I bet you did, Ros. I can well believe that you did.'

'Why didn't she give me any of these things, Chris? I had a right to them. At the very least the sketch. I would have preserved it. And if I'd had his watch, I would have worn it. All these years I would have been wearing it and it would have been a connection. If I had known that these things were here – buried away for thirty years – I would have had something to hold on to. Something of his. Something to show that he was real, that he existed.'

He nodded, saying nothing, letting me hiccup my way through the soliloquy.

'Does she care so little about me? Does she think I –'

He put both his hands on my shoulders. 'She did this in a hurry, didn't she? She stuffed everything in a box and decided not to think about it. Why else would you keep an old lipstick and half a packet of tissues? It must have been too painful for her.'

I nodded and in my jeans pocket I found a scrap of

tissue on which to wipe my nose. 'You weren't coming to talk to me about Otto Dix, were you?'

'No'. He laughed. 'I wanted to see you. Otto Dix was only ever an excuse. Same goes for Paula Rego and John Bellany.'

'The Paula Rego is definitely mine.'

'You see, I knew you would say that.' He lifted my face into his gaze, appraising me with the same sobriety he might have offered a set of plans for Crossrail. I had always liked that about Chris, that he didn't try to dodge an awkward moment or nudge it towards levity.

'It doesn't seem right,' he said, 'us not being together. Being in different houses.'

'No.'

'Why don't you come home? Come back with me now – I've got the car, if there's stuff you want to bring.'

'When the time's right I will, but not now.' I covered his hands with mine. 'I don't feel ready yet. I need to finish this.'

And I think Chris understood that by 'this', I meant something more than clearing out my grandmother's attic.

SEVEN

Academics have identified nine agents of deterioration in a historic house. They are water, light, physical, chemical and biological damage, theft or loss, wrong relative humidity, wrong temperature and fire. The last of these is the most catastrophic because it brings so many other kinds of damage with it, but, over time, light is the insidious villain, robbing everything of its colour and bleaching the interest out of it. In the studio I've handled documents where nothing remains of the words except their indentation. The information isn't always lost though. Sometimes the ghosts are eloquent.

If it were possible, we would keep everything in the dark.

A few years before the fire Frieda and I joined a working party on how to assess light damage and limit it at Turney House. We recommended a maximum annual dose of 150,000 lux-hours. That is achievable if the rooms are kept in darkness whenever possible. Before the fire, the house used to be closed every year for three months after Christmas, and during that time the public rooms were shuttered and blinded and all the furniture was covered with dust sheets. The Marchants kept to their rooms upstairs and spent weekends at their cottage in

Somerset. Smaller objects were protected with bespoke coverings made of acid-free paper. The contents of the doll's house – ornaments, books, pots and pans no bigger than a fingernail – were individually wrapped and put away in boxes. It was strange, one of the cleaners remarked, to see how people coming to the house during those months instinctively dropped their voices on entering the darkened rooms, and more than one spoke of stepping into an underworld, or of somehow stepping out of time. At its most effective the conservation process is about precisely that: taking objects out of time and removing them from the ageing process. There are books and papers that I would lock away and never allow to be seen again if I had my way, but, as the saying goes, each man kills the thing he loves. It's not enough for us to know about the existence of the Magna Carta, we want to see it – the real thing, in raking light. A replica won't do because the object represents so much more than itself – it is our only tangible link to people of another age. We touch where they have touched. It's why a fingerprint or a smudge, a name scratched into the woodwork, means so much more than the perfect absence of the object's maker.

Today's visitors want access to these artefacts on their own terms and some of them refuse to accept that their enthusiasm takes a toll. Even a very low light can be damaging. The largest number of complaints made to volunteers working at Turney House, and logged in the day book, concerns the lack of light in the library. Lighting levels have to be kept low there, as the guides have often explained, to protect the spines of the books, and the priceless French Gobelin tapestries commissioned by Lady Isabella Marchant in 1805. Humidity and temperature also have to be controlled to prevent the books drying out and cracking. Over time, wrongly adjusted humidity can cause a bloom to creep across the surface of glass and more than a hundred different kinds of fungus to flourish in the air pockets behind cabinets or paintings. Mrs Winburne, the house manager, who had been overseeing the daily running of Turney House for fifteen years, used to say that she knew when there was too much moisture in the air because her hair began to curl. We may think that a historic house is dead; in fact it teems with life, from the microscopic level upwards, and the battle to keep everything in the right balance is unremitting. The only way to win is to give the house its own climate, safe from the volatile conditions that prevail outside. Global warming, flooding, storms and heatwaves have to stop at the door. That isn't all: each room needs its own microclimate – and even mini-microclimates, inside display cabinets or archives. The house must be an environmental fortress. Control is everything, but visitors don't need to be told the details. They would probably rather not know about the hygrometers and dosimeters, the wireless accelerometer and the seismograph measuring vibration on the staircase, the electronic data-logger and the computerised environmental controls hidden beneath the floor grilles.

That is the ideal, anyway, but looking after historic artefacts can only ever be an exercise in damage limitation. When a thousand people walk on the same stretch of floor or carpet, most of them turning at precisely the same moment to admire a view or gaze at a particular object, the damage caused is more brutal than anyone realises. It's not as if you can instruct the public in how to enjoy their heritage. You can direct them with requests not to touch, or to use flash photography. You can distract the children by giving them quizzes on clipboards, in the hope of occupying hands that might otherwise stray to delicate surfaces. You can politely relieve the adults of umbrellas and pushchairs. It isn't acceptable to make visitors take off their footwear and yet shoes, when they have thin heels, can do permanent damage to a wooden floor. Apparently the question of whether to rule against kitten heels did come up every now and then in meetings at Turney House, but the feeling had been that it would be asking too much. Alexandra Marchant's belief was that 'we shouldn't ban things'. The illusion had to stand: that this historic house was at the public's disposal, to appreciate as though it were a true representation of the way one particular family had lived through three centuries. Let the visitors feel like guests flattering themselves that in choosing a particular moment to pause, to admire a view or an object, they were showing a unique sensibility, when the truth was that thousands before had made the same choice. At Uppark House a silk covering on a chair was worn away by long lines of visitors brushing past it in coats. Each one of them, no doubt, certain that they were taking care – sensing the frisson between coat and chair and never imagining how harmful even that very slight contact was. There is no kind of contact that doesn't cause damage; even caring for an object can spoil it. Overpolishing, powerful vacuum cleaners, dusters that snag on inlaid surfaces – all of these have caused irreversible damage. Overzealous dusting can remove gilt from an antique frame – that's why our predecessors used a goose wing to lift the dust. The challenge in an old house is to control the rate of deterioration because stopping it is impossible: a house can't be preserved unchanged if large numbers of visitors are coming in – and if no visitors come it can't be preserved at all. So deterioration is also a sign of life. Everything has to deteriorate, but let it deteriorate gently, under the ministrations of professional conservators and a skilled amateur workforce.

Mrs Winburne headed the amateur team at Turney House. It was her job to instruct the cleaners and the volunteer guides, to oversee the interaction between people and objects. She taught the cleaners about new and old dirt. The first is an agent of deterioration and should be removed. The second is historically significant and must be preserved. Similarly, new graffiti is vandalism, but old graffiti may be culture. People are the main source of dust in historic houses, through the clothing fibres, skin and hair that they shed. They also bring in mud and grit on clothes, pushchairs and shoes. They leave fingerprints on metal, glass and wood, on textiles and wallpaper. Mrs Winburne regularly attended workshops on optimising visitor flow with minimum damage. 'Bunching' was when too many visitors were grouped together, often at the start of a tour. 'Dwell time' governed how long people could spend in each area. Upstairs in the nursery – home to the Victorian doll's house – dwell time often threatened to exceed the sustainable capacity of the room. For that reason a volunteer was always posted at the top of the stairs directing people away from the nursery if it was too full.

It was also Mrs Winburne's job to monitor the Problem Book, a log of all the day's incidents, from trip hazards and accidental damage to heart attacks or threatening behaviour.

There were no live-in staff at Turney any more. Mrs Winburne returned each day to a semi in Sheen, but she knew Turney as if it were her own home: all the codes and the settings, the locks and the gauges. 'She knows where the bodies are buried!' Lord Marchant liked to say and Alexandra Marchant had said she was part of Turney's mythology, which sounded like a clever way of saying she was old. People always said that she gave her all to Turney House and she looked like someone who was giving everything, her skin suckered straight onto the bone with no intermediate layer of fat. Hard-working sinews and veins ran over her arms. She didn't wear make-up or any hand creams that could interfere with the chemical balance of the surfaces under her care. She kept her hair short, as if to save even the energy that might be spent in having it longer, so that there was more lifeblood for Turney, this house which was sometimes a hive of industry or a school for swearing and always a theatre. It was Mrs Winburne who ushered the principal players and bit parts on and off the stage and cast an indulgent eye over all the gossip-mongering and japery. And it was Mrs Winburne who opened the door to me when I arrived at Turney House to begin removing the burned paper in the Rose Room.

'What's new, Mrs Winburne?' I asked, heaving my bag of tools over the threshold. Nobody called her 'Wendy', though Wendy Winburne was her name. 'Any scandals? Any murders?'

'Not as far as I know,' said Mrs Winburne with a smile. 'But the staircase is finished. Come and look.' She took me through to the front hall to admire the finials and tread ends with their intricate designs of a fruit believed to be the Jamaican ackee, a reference to Samuel Marchant's plantation in Jamaica. The carvings had been made by two brothers from Wisconsin, working from photographs and a few carbonised remnants salvaged from the debris.

The walls had also been painted in the front hall, with a flatted lead paint, a new mixture made specifically for Turney House to an eighteenth-century recipe. 'It's preaged,' explained Mrs Winburne, 'so that once it's on it won't continue to darken naturally with the passage of time. It's clever, what they can do.'

'They call it "accelerated ageing", which is what's happening to me,' said Alexandra Marchant appearing at the door of the Rose Room. 'The stress of this job will send me to an early grave! How are you, Ros?' She laid a hand on my arm and looked at me with placid affection, as though the scene at the restaurant two weeks ago had never taken place, and I wondered if she had in fact been as embarrassed as Sebastian made out, or if he had thought she ought to be. Before I could answer she continued: 'Mrs Winburne, remember that there's a group coming through the house later in the afternoon. From the Richmond Historical Society.'

'I hadn't forgotten. We're preparing a finger buffet and cakes,' said Mrs Winburne with a kind of startled indignation. Her eyes, moisture-laden, swivelled towards her feet.

'That's wonderful,' said Alexandra. 'And they need to de-shoe if they're going upstairs.'

'I've ordered disposable overshoes,' said Mrs Winburne with the tremulous conviction of a woman defending her integrity in court.

'Perfect,' said Alexandra. 'In fact, there's really no need for them to go upstairs after all. Oh, and please could you tell the guys working in the library to keep a lid on the swearing this afternoon? They can swear twice as much this morning if it helps – get it out of their system.'

'I'll pass the message on,' said Mrs Winburne.

'I suppose I'd better get started,' I said.

'Coffee or anything, dear?'

'I picked one up on the way. Thanks.'

With the hallway close to being finished, the Rose Room looked by comparison even more of an aching void, its walls still raw, its ceiling a plain plaster bed waiting for adornment. Through the window the bushes in the Rose Garden were ranged in stumpy rows. The garden beyond it was a sorry encampment with some of the improvised workshops empty or dismantled now and in the Deer Park the trees thrust their budding arms towards an unresponsive sky. I unravelled my toolkit and laid it ceremoniously on the workbench – my palette knives and brushes, my sponges and solutions. My radio, paint-splattered and dented from previous jobs, went on the end of the bench. The scaffolding platform Frieda and I had used when we were last here was still in the room and I rolled it back into position in front of the section of wall that was to the right of the fireplace. Then I went back out to the van, to fetch two work lamps. I put them in position and fixed the cables to the floor, tearing strips of masking tape off a roll and cutting the lengths with my teeth – I never could find scissors when I needed them. The lamps' positioning didn't look right and twice I changed it, sticking the cables down each time. With so many preparations, an hour had gone by before I was ready to start work. I began by cleaning the surface with a latex sponge, stroking it to lift off the loose, sooty residues. When removing wallpaper it is sometimes possible to take several layers off the wall together then separate them later in the studio; on a recent job, in an old coaching inn, Frieda and I had found a thick sandwich of papers, an inventory of decorative fashions dating back three hundred years. The size had broken down and insects were feeding on the starch in the paste – bugs, silverfish and mould between every layer. The bugs were merely disgusting but the spores could damage your lungs which was why it was important to wear a mask. In the Rose Room it wasn't going to be easy to separate the layers because acid leaching out of the paper underneath had broken down the glue, causing them to fuse together. I would have to get the top layer wet enough to weaken the underlying adhesives, so that I could then remove it with the palette knife – but not so wet that the paper beneath it weakened and tore. A hand-held steamer made the job easier, but it was still time-consuming and tedious work, especially as I had to keep climbing on and off the scaffolding, to make minor adjustments to the positioning of the platform, or to the lighting. Every time I moved one of the lights, the cable had to be fixed into its new position on the floor with masking tape, to comply with health and safety regulations.

At about eleven o'clock I heard voices in the hall and remembered that Mrs Winburne had mentioned that two experts from the Society for the Protection of Ancient Buildings were coming to visit and give their verdict on the new staircase. It had been a policy from the start to invite specialists in to inspect and advise on the myriad jobs taking place at Turney House. This wasn't only a way to tap expert advice, but also to steal the enemies' fire. Better to have Turney's critics air their feelings here than in the press.

'You can't deny that it is beautifully done. The brothers have excelled themselves,' Alexandra was saying.

'The craftsmanship is very good,' conceded a man whose sing-songy voice contained a note of menace. 'It doesn't alter the fact that this is a twenty-first-century staircase masquerading as an eighteenth-century one.'

'Masquerading is quite a strong way of putting it.' That was Roger speaking. I could hear his smile.

'Well then, let's call it a copy, if you prefer that.'

'It isn't a copy,' protested Alexandra. 'They didn't *copy* the old staircase, they put back what ought to be here, what made sense in terms of the history of the house.'

'But with some apparent modern overtones,' said the man mildly.

There was a pause I could hear being illustrated by Alexandra's frown, her imperious disbelief.

'What do you mean exactly?'

A pause again and then the man said, 'Well, I think – and I don't know if you would agree with this, Simon – but it looks to me as though the leaves of the fruits are marginally spikier than they were in the original carvings. Do you see?'

I heard the man approach the staircase, rustling over

the plastic sheeting, and imagined him pointing out some detail to the others, his dry curatorial hands hovering over the woodwork without touching it. 'The serration on the edges looks sharper than it was. It's admirably done, of course. Nobody disputes that these are first-class craftsmen.'

'It does look perhaps a bit spikier,' said the voice of his companion.

'It's almost as if the brothers have introduced into Samuel Marchant's design their own subtle commentary on his status as a slave owner. Rather clever, if so.'

'Oh really, I hardly think –' began Alexandra, but the first man's voice ballooned over hers.

'It may be a very subtle moderation, almost imperceptible, but these are the sort of differences we have to look out for with an eagle eye. You see how difficult it is to reproduce something entirely without alteration? It's nigh on impossible not to bring your own experience and beliefs into the equation. That's why we always argue that it is safer not to reproduce at all. A simple structure that made no period allusions would have been free of such interpretations.'

'We're not setting out to deceive anyone!' Alexandra said, with an angry laugh that rang out in the open space, glancing off the hard surfaces. 'Anyway, I refute your reading of the leaves.'

'As regards the whys and wherefores of the decision to replace the staircase, I think we have to accept that we have lost that argument,' said the one who was called Simon, sounding nasal and managerial. 'What we have here, for better or worse, is repro – a twenty-first-century staircase in the style of a Georgian one. The important thing now is that it be made clear to any visitors that this is not an original fitting. So the staircase shouldn't be made to look older than it is. There must not be any attempt to scar the wood or damage it to make it look old or worn.'

'We planned to use a dark wax on it,' said Roger. 'Would there be any objection to that?'

A pause, a moment of serious consideration. 'I can't see any objection to that.'

'Visitor traffic will aid the ageing process,' said the first man encouragingly. 'A couple of years of foot abrasion, of sweaty hands on the banister, it all helps. Everything needs a bit of scuffing up. A bit of patina.'

Patina. They handed the word around, let it roll off their tongues.

'That is if we ever get the punters back in,' said Alexandra with a broken laugh.

'I'm sure they'll come, in due course,' said the man. 'You're famous for your cafe after all, and the quality of your baking.'

'I believe it's fatally poisonous if wrongly prepared,' said his colleague, and when nobody responded he added, laughing softly, 'I mean the Jamaican ackee, of course, not your baking.'

By noon I had wetted the wall completely and attached a polythene sheet along its upper edge to cover it. Jumping down from the scaffold, I turned back to look at it. Close up the wall was a blackened mulch, smelling like a bonfire after heavy rain. When I took a few steps back, it looked like a macabre artwork inviting de-codification by gallery-goers.

I wandered into the hall – wanting to satisfy my own curiosity about the spikiness of the new leaves – then I continued into the dining room, where a team of plasterers were covering the ceiling with a cartoon for the mouldings they were going to make, recreating a 400-year-old process called 'pouncing', by which colour would be puffed through thousands of holes in the design onto the plaster bed. At the moment the ceiling was covered in a fluttering ocean of paper. Shapes had been drawn in sweeping blue lines that covered the surface, a tangle of vines and grapes, of maidens with flowing hair, and at its centre, Dionysus languorous and naked. I thought of my first visit here, when Uncle John had drawn down the points of the universe to this house at its centre.

Before the fire, the Turney Chandelier had hung in the middle of this room, and when the ceiling collapsed it had crashed onto the floor, smashing into thousands of pieces. Tiny bits of glass were propelled across the room and out of it, through the shattered windows and doorways. And of those fragments, three thousand and twelve pieces had been found and identified and were even now being re-assembled by glassworkers into another chandelier. Particles that would never be visible to the eye were going to be reincorporated to make it as close to authentic as was physically possible. So when it was finished, you would be able to say that, even if most of what you saw was new, the essence of the thing, the heart of it, was original.

Did it matter? Sometimes I struggled to believe that it did when there were so many other less expensive and more deserving candidates for grants and lottery money. At other times my romantic instincts got the better of my pragmatic ones and this house seemed such an unlikely survivor of its age that I would have fought to repair every bit of it, from the first kitchen flagstone to the last roof tile. So many historic buildings had been destroyed in the twentieth century: one thousand houses burned down or demolished in a hundred years. The archives bulged with stately casualties. Coleshill House burned down, like Turney, while the roof was being mended, and now only its four sets of gateposts remained. Agecroft House was taken down brick by brick in 1925 and sent to be re-assembled in Richmond, Virginia. Dawpool had needed extra dynamite in its demolition because of its 'immensely solid construction'. During the fire that destroyed Stoke Edith, the chauffeur and the gardener died while trying to rescue the maids, who had fled to safety along the rooftop. Lulworth Castle burned down in 1929 when electric wires fused. Some Girl Guides who were camping near by had helped in the salvage effort. And then there were the houses that escaped fire or dynamite but fell into a hopeless neglect, lying empty, stripped of their fittings and deteriorating at the hands of the local thieves and vandals. In the 1930s, an article in the *New York Times* remarked on the sad decline of Manresa House, in Roehampton, whose socialite owner could so rarely be counted on for dinner at home that six or seven times a week the meal laid out for him was left untouched and had to be eaten by the butler.

Back in the Rose Room, armed with another coffee, I lifted the polythene and slid the palette knife under the top layer of paper until it met the resistance of solidified animal glue, two centuries old. I began the process of wetting again, this time dousing the paper more heavily. After reattaching the polythene sheet I sat back on my heels picking at my nails before deciding I could more usefully spend the time sharpening my knives. For thirty minutes or so I sat in the back of the van with the doors open, re-edging blades on a sharpening stone. I ate my lunch, ham sandwiches and an orange, awkwardly leaning back on my elbows, my view full of Turney as it rose behind the mossy garden walls, turning cold shoulders on the twenty-first century. I wondered where I would be in a year's time and if I would be living with Chris or on my own. If we didn't get back together, perhaps he would find someone else and start a family. I could see him doing all the kid stuff – the swings and slides, the bikes, the kickabouts and tickling sessions. It would be wrong to deny him those pleasures, in which case maybe it was better to let him go now, while he was young enough to find someone else and start again.

People went in and out of the Rose Room as I worked there during the afternoon, some of whom I hardly noticed, though others made a statement of their presence by coming to stand right beside my scaffolding, staring up at me as though waiting for a wink or a bow from one of those human statues. Generally, I found it awkward to work with an audience, though I did appreciate the public's hunger to see behind the scenes. Since I had to work with my back to the room, thankfully I didn't have to engage as directly with visitors as other conservators who were sometimes expected to set up their tables in full view of the visitors and patiently explain each step in the process of repairing a vase or a plate. Stuff that. I was a jobbing conservator, not a visitor attraction. But when the historical party came shuffling into the Rose Room in their disposable overshoes, mid-afternoon, and ranged themselves behind me in an expectant semicircle, they seemed too large a group to ignore and so I did lift off my mask and come down from the scaffold to answer questions. I told them that the oldest paper I had ever seen was a sixteenth-century paper at Oxford University, that it was true that traces of arsenic had been found in Napoleon's hair, though it was unlikely that wallpaper was the cause of his death. No, I didn't worry too much about making mistakes because all the changes I made were reversible. No, the lights were not hot. Ever since the fire at Windsor Castle, which was started by a conservator's light, we had to work with cool LED bulbs. The faces were sceptical; experts were admired and mistrusted in equal measure. And there was always someone who wanted to prove he knew as much as you, maybe more.

'If you wanted to be *really* authentic you'd do all this work by natural light, and leave the fancy equipment at home,' said a man who, even as a smile of self-congratulation was spreading across his face, seemed to acknowledge his own powers of irritation by touching his tongue to his canine.

'True,' I said, and my animosity towards the man joined to an ache in the soles of my feet so that all I wanted was to go and sit down somewhere on my own. 'We're not that desperate to be authentic, just to show the paper how it was.'

'But won't it be out of keeping with the other rooms and furnishings?' asked a woman sharply. 'How will you put it in context?'

'No decision has been made yet about how the paper will be shown. We have to wait and see what we've got.'

'Miss Freeman – a cup of tea?' The voice came from the back of the group and I saw Sebastian's face appear among the historians. 'I think it's time for your break.'

'Oh,' I said, and glanced at an imaginary watch. 'Yes, I think you may be right.'

'Thanks for rescuing me,' I said, as we walked quickly down the corridors to the old kitchen where several fellow workers stood defensively around the biscuit plate, while another was heating up noodles in the microwave. 'There's a queue for the kettle,' one of them said.

'Actually let's go and sit in the Rose Garden,' Sebastian said, but the amateur historians were already there, blinking in the pale sun, holding plates of cake and sandwiches, so we continued past them, quickening our step through the garden and the Deer Park and down towards the river.

The Thames was narrow at this point, and at low tide it seemed to be wending its way through a foreign land-scape of stony ground covered in a fine, ceramic dust. Overhead, white clouds hurtled towards the horizon, one incongruous grey smudge travelling with them. On the other side of the river, further downstream, was another Georgian villa, a popular venue for weddings and confer-ences. For Alexandra Marchant it was an example of how commercial diversification can come at the expense of character and charm. In its grounds a mighty cedar of Lebanon cupped its crown to the sky like a satellite dish.

There were no boats on the river apart from a young woman sculling on a vessel that was so insubstantial she seemed to be skimming across the water's surface with no support in a miracle of weightlessness. A narrow strip of shore lined both sides of the river and on the beach immediately below me two mallards, a drake and a duck, were sleeping side by side on the stones, inches apart, their heads bent all the way back and tucked under their wings, each a homely reflection of the other.

'I tried to call you again,' Sebastian said with a look of puzzled amusement.

'Yes, I got your messages. And I'm sorry.' I shrugged. 'No excuses, really. It's just that –'

'You regret what happened?' Sebastian had a habit of looking hard into people's faces when he spoke to them, so that there was no mistaking his expectation or your own responsibility in meeting it. 'Because all you needed to do was say. I wouldn't have hassled you. I understand things are complicated, with your marriage and whatever.'

'I didn't regret it! I *wanted* it to happen. I had it all planned out.'

'Really?'

'Yes!' I laughed, with a gasp of surprise at the recollection of my own gall. 'Put on my best underwear. Got my hair cut, even.'

He let out a burst of laughter – 'So you were using me for my body?' – sliding his elbow along the wall towards mine.

'Sorry. Does that make you feel dirty?'

'Obviously on one level I'm flattered. On another I'm deeply offended. I must have been a disappointment.'

'No, it's not that.' I turned to face him but then Sebastian turned too, squaring us in a closer contact than I had intended. He put his hands on my waist and would have kissed me – and I would have kissed him back. But I saw the river bending out of view behind him, and foresaw a possibility of my life meandering into a future built on short measures, short relationships and solitude. 'I don't want to start a new thing when I still don't know what's happening to the old thing. Sorry if that sounds vague. I just want to do what's right – not be unfair to you.'

He shrugged. 'I would have coped. It's OK, though. I get it. I won't push you. Look, look.' He brought his hands up to my shoulders and turned me away from him, symbolically it seemed to me, to face upstream. 'See that guy over there?'

Following his gaze I saw on the opposite bank a man in his mid-thirties, dressed in black, crouching beside the water, apparently washing something.

'Yes. What's he up to? Looks like he's washing a knife.'

'He lives there beside the river, in a tent.'

'Where?'

'See the wall further up the bank? It's in trees behind there. He's been camping out for more than a month. I've seen him a few times. I don't know whether you feel sorry for someone like that or envy him.'

'Sorry, I'd have thought, but it depends on his reasons for doing it.'

'He's homeless, I think.'

'Why would you envy him then?'

'For all we know he might be intentionally homeless. So he's free from obligations, jobs, emails, people, all the crap . . .'

'Hard to believe many people would choose to live in a tent long-term. And you've still got to eat.'

'Nobody's going to starve in a place like London. You just need to know where to look. I bet you can eat like a king out of the dustbins in any neighbourhood. Every high street is lined with places to eat, all of them throwing away, what – about a third of their food every night?'

'So you're tempted by the lifestyle?'

He paused for a moment, thinking about it. 'Aspects of it, definitely.' Then he straightened up and took a step back, as though physically detaching himself from our liaison. 'Actually I'm thinking I might travel for a while, when I'm finished here.'

'Really – new horizons?'

'Yeah, a bit. What about you?'

'No, I'm the opposite. I want a home.' I surprised myself with the statement. This wasn't something I had consciously felt before. Working in a big empty house, sleeping in a small empty house and living out of a suitcase had made me yearn for the comforts of a well-cushioned sofa, a modern kitchen and somebody to read the Sunday papers with. 'Maybe I'm getting old.'

'Age is neither here nor there,' he said.

'You think?'

Back in the Rose Room the knife wouldn't yet move smoothly under the paper, but I could feel the beginning of pliancy on my blade. One last spray should do it. I added alcohol to the water to strengthen the underlying paper and keep it from becoming too saturated. I put on the radio, lay back on the platform and listened to the news, losing my gaze in the white plaster bed of the ceiling above. After a time it struck me that the house had gone very quiet. The plasterers had gone home. Lights cast onto the lawn suggested that there were still people working in the office two floors above. It was six hours now since I had applied the first lot of water and this time when I worked under the paper with my palette knife, the top layer started lifting clean away. 'Finally,' I said to myself. I switched the radio station from talking to singing and turned up the volume, let music fill up the space. Now I began to peel away the blackened dripping outer skin with both hands. Within minutes I was rewarded with a tranche of the room's original paper, the scheme chosen by Isabella, the young wife of Samuel Marchant. Covered over for 150 years, the colours had held their lustre; the design was strikingly modern: a green ground printed with grey circles containing orange cogged wheels, each one finished by hand and, in its flaws and slubs, subtly different from the last. I was sure now that this was the work of Gabriel Huysman.

My breathing sounded heavy and historic through the mask. I felt like someone stepping into eighteenth-century London, alighting among its rioters and revellers, its enlightenment thinkers and scientists. I touched it, could feel it in the grainy green powder on my fingertips: London's toxic air, the ambition and audacity of its moneymakers, its businessmen and highwaymen, its venal priests and politicians. It was a city on the make, a city racked by questions of faith, fearful of revolution. A city of invention. And while the wealthy had an escape route to homes like this along the river, that journey to the outskirts also entailed hazards. London's highwaymen were the celebrities of their day, one so famously brazen that he pinned letters on the doors of rich gentlemen requesting they never leave home without a gold watch and at least ten guineas. Hounslow Heath was the most dangerous patch of land in Europe. None of that deterred the rich from building their mansions along the Thames. Why should it when money was rolling in from the sugar plantations and into the coffers of families like the Marchants, whose new villa in Roehampton was the subject of envious chatter everywhere? They had even followed the example of their good friend Horace Walpole, opening their house to curious day trippers. This room, this very wallpaper, had been the backdrop to conversations about the Catholic ascendancy, the revolution in France, the loss of the American colonies, slavery. It was beguiling and infuriating, that unbridgeable divide, less than a millimetre thick, between my life and the one under my fingers. I wished with a child's fervour that I could make Turney's first inhabitants live for a few minutes, conjuring their presence so that when I turned round, there they would be: Lord and Lady Marchant in their powdered wigs with the children, and in the shadows, the servants and kitchen staff. What a stunt that would be: to bring the dead back to life, even for a few minutes, and hear them speak again.

The dripping black Victorian overlay was falling away in my hands and within two hours I had completed the lower part of the wall and was back on the scaffolding, working at the upper half, at the centre of a pool of light.

By now I had lost track of the time and when I lifted my mask – rubbing my liberated nose and mouth – and turned round to squint into the further reaches of the room, it shocked me to see how dark it was. The room was as empty as ever; the areas beyond the compass of my working light looked monochrome and beleaguered, a daunting space to have at your back. Through the windows the light was fading and the trees resembled a printed pattern on muted fabric. The house had fallen quiet, and without the radios and the shouting of my colleagues, I felt the beginnings of apprehension. Where had the time gone? I wasn't even sure how long I had been standing on the platform, or when I had turned the radio off. Then I turned back to the wall, and was delighted all over again by a fresh sight of the paper, vivid in front of me. I imagined the whole room covered in this modern but delicate pattern, the movement of shadows that would have been produced by flickering candlelight as men and women walked through it in their silks and wigs. So much green though. The Marchants' lungs must have been coated with arsenic. They had come here to escape the pollution of London and made themselves an even more poisonous refuge. Perhaps it was arsenic that had killed Isabella in her forties, not tuberculosis.

It was all mine, this moment of revelation, and sweeter for that. To have guessed at a piece of evidence, argued for it and found it; to have followed a trail of ghosts to a remnant of living history: there is no greater satisfaction in our line of work. It's like being spoken to across the centuries by a clear, true voice. I took off my mask and sat on the floor, filling my gaze with Huysman's work. After a few minutes of relishing my victory, though, I was wishing there was someone to share it with. Frieda would see it with me tomorrow, but by then there would be people around and noise, and it wouldn't feel so special. I could hardly drag her out to Roehampton at this time in the evening to see it. I put down my knife and stretched my stiffened fingers, then reached into my pocket, the instinct of an ex-smoker, and found my phone. For a moment I stared at this object in my hand, dazed by its garish luminosity, then I called up Chris's number and wrote: *I miss you. Let's see each other soon, Rxx.*

'So it's done?' Natalie sounded breathless on the phone. In the background I could hear Sadie shouting 'Mine! Mine!'

'It's done, finally. It took hours. I spent all of Sunday on it.'

'Wahey!'

'Don't do that. You sound like one of those creepy DJs.'

'Now then, now then. What does Lady Whatsit say?'

'Best part of twelve hours actually. Oh, she said, "It's stunning blah blah blah, so original blah blah blah, reminds me of an Orla Kiely handbag blah blah –"'

'She didn't!'

'I'm afraid she did.'

'You have to send me a picture instantly. Let go of that, Sadie. Let *go*. Not yours. *Not. Yours.*'

'I won't be there today. I'm going into town.' In fact the bus I was on had come to a juddering stop and the driver had descended onto the pavement, hitching his trousers up over a rear that seemed long ago to have surrendered shape to the demands of the job. With the air of a man heading for a tea break he disappeared into an anonymous door on which the initials of the bus company were printed in exquisitely small letters, as though to avoid drawing the attention of angry passengers. It seemed that there was no replacement driver ready to take over. 'Shit. Just what I need.'

'What?'

'Nothing. Just feel like I've been on this bus forever.'

'Are you all right, Ros? I worry about you. You looked upset after Chris came round the other day.'

'Not upset. Emotional,' I said, directing myself to the window and everyone outside it. 'You don't need to worry about me, honestly. Things are fine.'

It had been disheartening, though, to stand like a weather girl in front of my wall – I did think of it as *my* wall now – indicating to my audience the areas where movement in the underlying plaster had caused abrasions, the pockets of damage, reassuring them that the overall picture was very good, while Alexandra Marchant looked on with an expression of amused scepticism. Frieda had made the odd supportive remark, but what I had needed was a stream of them.

'The colours are so vibrant,' she had said. 'Scheele's green and this orange. What is that?'

'We'll need to have that analysed. It's too early to be cadmium. If you look at it through a magnifier you can actually see the grains of paint. These here are tiny alterations made by hand to disguise the fact that the papers don't join that well. These stains, here and here, are caused by water. This could be a candle burn. There are some tears, caused by movements in the plaster underneath, but surprisingly few, all things considered.'

At that point Alexandra Marchant, who had been listening and nodding during my exposition, tilted her head and made the sort of glum face of pretend sympathy you would offer a child who wasn't going to be allowed an anticipated treat.

'It's wonderful, Ros, but we obviously can't keep it,' and then with a tragic sigh, 'lovely as it is! It doesn't fit with the rest of the room.'

I had anticipated this and was ready with my responses. 'We can conceal it behind a panel. Then visitors get to see what the room would have been like at two different points in its history. You'd have the Victorian decor as it was, but people could slide this wall away to see the original. We've done that in a room before, haven't we, Frieda?'

'Yes,' Frieda said, but flatly, it seemed to me, without real conviction.

'God, we really don't want to start encouraging people to slide panels! I can already foresee the disasters. Damage to the material. Children losing fingers –'

'Well then, don't let them, but conserve this paper anyway, under the new one? You could show it – I don't know – on special occasions. It's a small area and tucked away.'

'No, Ros. I don't want to start getting into different eras and secrets and layers, attractive as that concept might be to someone in your line of work. We've settled on the character of this room. What you see is what you get. No magic doors or secret panels or – Besides, you've said yourself that these colours are toxic.'

'But, I mean, there's Perspex –'

'No, I hate that. And it's another layer, another complication –'

I couldn't help clicking my tongue in annoyance. Poison seemed like a sideshow, a minor distraction. 'There are ways of dealing with these things,' I said.

'Look, I'm really glad we did this,' Alexandra said, with her hands in front of her, fingers splayed as though ready to play a noisy piano piece. 'We'll photograph it. We'll include it in our exhibition about the fire. We'll have it in the book. But it can't stay.'

'When it's in such good condition, and so beautiful,' I said plaintively, pathetically. 'It would be a crime –'

'Ros,' said Frieda, 'this kind of work always involves compromises. You know that.' I heard the warning edge in her tone and ignored it.

'I do, obviously, but we've got something here that's worth fighting for. This is authentic. This paper is the real thing. The stuff we're making to go on top, I mean, it's nice, but at the end of the day it's a copy.'

'Well, if I'd known that was how you felt!' began Alexandra, and Frieda said 'Ros' again, but the words were out of my mouth anyway.

'It's pastiche, basically.'

In the van afterwards, Frieda sat with both hands on the wheel, not making any move towards starting the engine. Turney House loured at us through the windscreen.

'Well, are we going?' I said, and then, 'I don't know why you're angry. I was only telling the truth.'

'Why does this paper matter so much to you?' Frieda's eyes were fixed on the view ahead of her, as though she thought she were in fact driving.

'For God's sake, Frieda. You might as well say why does anything matter.'

'But why *this*? Why this particular paper?' She turned to me with an expression that was so unusually solemn it made me worry that I had really upset her. 'Explain it to me.'

'Because it's a historical document! Huysman made, what, twenty designs in his lifetime? This is a unique example of his work. I don't want him to be forgotten. I think he deserves to be remembered. It amazes me, actually, that you don't feel the same.'

'I never said that. As a matter of fact I agree with you. But you're too rash. Play a longer game. Otherwise you alienate people before they've had a chance to think about it.'

'There isn't time for a long game, Frieda.'

'You make the argument too hard and people switch off. I could see her switching off. That glazed look that comes over her. But on and on you went. Digging your own grave.'

'Well, thanks! So how would *you* have gone about it? What would *you* advise, given that they could start ripping this paper down tomorrow?'

'They won't do that. We've got a week or two in hand. There's time to get another professional opinion. In the meantime you can go and find out more about Huysman. What sort of man was he? How did he know the Marchants? These people operate in a commercial world, Ros. They're used to thinking in terms of what they want to buy. We need to sell this to them.'

That was how I came to be relieved of my papermaking duties for a day and dispatched to an archive in the City to find out more about Huysman. Frankly, I was more than happy to get away from Turney House for a day or two; from the studio too, for that matter.

The archive looked severe from outside, but there was an atmosphere of quiet ebullience in the reading room. Predominant among the readers were retired and elderly people who might once have been content to occupy their dotage in crosswords and quizzes but were nowadays impelled by television programmes about genealogy to look into their ancestry. At a long desk under a sign that said 'Welcome', four librarians channelled that enthusiasm into different catalogues and search engines. The newness of the surroundings – there was a plush blue carpet in the reading room, modern computer terminals and downstairs a cafe offering wholesome, cheap food with low-cholesterol options – made researching the ancestors an attractive day out.

'So it's the same name, but spelled *differently*,' cried a woman in her sixties, with short hair that sprang from her head in surprised tufts. 'And look: here he is popping up in France five years later!' The man sitting next to her might have been a husband but was more likely, I reckoned, to be a brother or cousin. A fascination with family roots rarely crossed the marital bond.

Knowing they were never far from a reasonably priced lentil soup or a sticky bun, these modern-day hunters stalked their prey in a comfortable atmosphere of enquiry and discovery – and their enthusiasm was infectious, because the process was so simple. We were fishing in an overstocked pond, pointing, clicking and pulling up information like so much glistening perch. I hooked my own man pretty quickly. Gabriel Huysman was listed in the trade register as a printer and paper stainer in the 1780s and 90s. In the first decade of the nineteenth century he appeared again, as a litigant in a case about the non-payment of debts. I trailed him through several other court cases, finding him variously indicted for drunkenness, public indecency and trying to steal a pig. In less than an hour I had run him to ground in the Clerkenwell House of Correction where he was mentioned in 1806 as one of a dozen poor convicts 'in need of shoes and stockings'. His wife, named as Anna Clancy in one court case, may have been a defendant of the same name in Stepney, 1809, who, 'charged with keeping a disorderly house, petitions for her fine to be cancelled because she is too poor to pay it and her child is ill'. It was sad to think of a skilled craftsman ending this way, his child sick, his wife running prostitutes. Then again, the passing years mould sad events into pieces of heritage to the point where it seems fraudulent to shed tears over the death of a child centuries ago in the way you might grieve a child's death today, even when the historical child was equally unknown, the circumstances equally tragic. Time passes and takes the sharpness out of things. And, although it was a cold calculation to make, I knew that this colourful account of Huysman's descent into penury could only strengthen our case. I hadn't managed to tie him directly to the Marchants through the archives but the date of his death suggested that the Turney papers were the last Huysman ever made. That had to give them some kind of cachet. I took the documents I had found to be copied in a corner of the library 'reserved for quiet study' where three men sat in obedient silence at a line of microfilm readers. Students at a table nearby were poring over papers relating to the Windrush for a university project. They were a mixed group of black and white, male and female, glamorous in this context simply because they were young. Beyond them another librarian was posted away from the fray, at a desk above which a sign encouraged enquiries that were of a 'personal or sensitive nature'. The librarian looked kind. Her nose pointed politely at a mouth that was set in a natural smile and the thick lenses in her glasses blurred the contours of her eyes, giving her a fragile appearance.

Back at my desk I gathered up my papers and pens, and with my eyes still on the terminal, let my fingers do the work of fastening my coat, blindly uniting buttons and holes. The screen was beaming at me with the results of my investigation, the search box still winking at the top of the page. For a few seconds I resisted deleting all this pleasing work before bending over the keyboard to slide the cursor up to 'home'. Then instead, for no reason that I could afterwards bring to mind, I slid it back to the search box and typed in my father's name. I pressed 'return', and straightened up, feeling my nerves singed with an adrenalin burn. Even as I was fastening the last button on my coat, the system returned a file and there was my father's name in bold Helvetica. My heart, reacting more quickly than my brain, took a heavy swing at the ribs. Then the brain got into gear: I'd never seen my father's name on a computer screen before, and it was unfathomably weird to think that modern technology knew about him and had his dates and details. He was pre-digital, I had thought, not seeing that computerisation wasn't confined to the present – it had been reaching backwards too. Vast data servers were churning away day and night, eating up past events and spitting them out as bits and bytes. The file to which my father's name was attached was marked from the collection of South West Thames Regional Authority. 'Scope and Content: Clinical Psychology Primary Care. Access: Not Available for General Access.' The dates covered by the file – 1982–1984 – were the two years before he died.

I sat down to shield the screen from my neighbours while I tried to work out what this material signified and whether it related to my father or somebody else with the same name. It didn't seem likely, given that the dates were right, as well as the name. But – a psychologist? Were these my father's *medical* records? I had a sense of straying into dangerous territory and glanced around to check that nobody was watching. The short-haired woman was still absorbed in researching her family tree, while her companion, eyes moist with yawning, was zipping up his jacket and preparing for lunch. Someone I took to be a member of staff strode past, smiling vaguely in my direction, and my instinct was to look away. I kept expecting someone to tell me that this kind of search was illicit, but how could it be, if the information had come up on my screen? For the first time it crossed my mind that in this archive, in this building, there might be other documents and papers about my father's life. His death certificate could be here and his marriage certificate. And perhaps the holdings weren't restricted to licences and records.

After all, there was a psychologist's report – I looked again at the reference number before me on the screen and the words 'Not Available for General Access'. If there was any doubt about the meaning of that, a line underneath put the same thing differently: 'It is not possible to request this item.' I was being baldly shut out of a document that contained words and opinions someone had voiced about my father – maybe his own opinions and words too. I had his sketchbook, his watch and wallet, and now I so wanted to hear him speak. But through a psychologist? Why a *psychologist*? What had he been going through? The comfort of the deep pile carpet, the areas set aside for quiet study or personal enquiries, made a greater sense to me now and I saw that the archive was a more dangerous place than I had realised.

The distance between my workstation and the desk assigned to personal enquiries now symbolised an entirely different investigation to the one I had expected to pursue today. A new world was opening up. I couldn't get at this file, but perhaps others were accessible. How much should I try to find out, though? Not all discoveries are for the better; what if one of the files contained some upsetting revelation? Once I had seen it, I couldn't un-know it again.

I had overheard a librarian saying that the results of inquests and coroners' reports were kept here. Perhaps they had one about my father's death. Was it acceptable to ask, though? I could take my cue from the sign and own up straight away to a 'personal and sensitive enquiry', appealing to an unknown bureaucrat's compassion. I could take the line of professional research, as with Huysman just now, not acknowledging any connection between myself and this subject of research. I could go home. That was perhaps the most sensible option and it was the one I thought I was going to take until, a few minutes later, I found myself standing in front of the woman's desk.

'I'm trying to track down the results of an inquest,' I said, smiling to disable any professional hauteur. That was unnecessary because, as I had hoped, the librarian was all considerate understanding. Of course, she said, and asked me for the name of the deceased. I spelled out my father's name as coolly as I could because my blood was burning in my veins and I felt like a child who has done something forbidden, who is going to be found out and punished.

'Terence Finlayson Donaghue.' I gripped my hands in my lap to stop my fingers trembling.

'An unusual name,' said the librarian pleasantly.

'You mean it's a mouthful,' I said with a nervous laugh. 'I hope that doesn't make things awkward. Finlayson was his mother's maiden name, I believe.' *I believe* – stuck on to give myself a bit of distance, a little protection.

'No, an unusual name should make life easier for us.' Thin lips pushed a smile into her cheeks. For about a minute, a longer span of time than seemed decent in the digital world, she studied the information on her monitor, scanning lines of text that were reflected as hieroglyphs in her glasses. Unattended, the smile dissolved back into her face and was replaced with an air of puzzlement.

'And it was definitely an accidental death? Because there wouldn't have been an inquest into a death by natural causes.'

'No, it was definitely an accident. A road accident.'

'Do you know where the death took place?

I shook my head. 'I don't know exactly. Is that something I need to –? I only know it was in west London.'

'No, that's fine. London will be enough.' The librarian turned back to the computer, the screen looming up refracted in her glasses, and she made a busy tutting noise with her tongue against her palate. 'Hmm. Those records should be here.' Her fingers on the mouse as it slid along the desk were slender and tipped with unfash-ionably long nails, unpainted. They looked as if they took a lot of buffing and filing. Perhaps that was some-thing she did behind the door marked 'Private' that I could see beyond her desk, when it wasn't her turn to sit out here and help the public solve intimate mysteries. But if you were going to the trouble of a manicure, why not put on varnish? She was in need of colour, I decided. If not on the nails, then on the lips or eyelids. There should be some colour somewhere, otherwise you were too much of a blank, waiting to absorb other people's colours, to be filled up by their personal and sensitive information.

'And it isn't possible that the place of death was different?' A furrowing of the brow endorsed her concern about my mystery and her application to solving it. 'You see, inquests for a death in Surrey, for example, would be held with the county records.'

She could have been throwing me Surrey as a lifeline, I suppose, and I was tempted to take it, because it made no sense that the information wasn't there. I didn't understand why it wasn't there, what this absence signified, or what anything signified. I couldn't place Surrey even on a mental map.

'I've just always assumed that it was in London. That he was going home to Earls Court, from work in Holborn. On his bike. I think that's what they told me.'

'Yes.' The librarian smiled a little, acknowledging that this was a sad way to die, and I realised that with 'what they told me' I had given away more information than I meant to.

A web of consternation encompassed us both now and we moved inside it with cramped motions of pen and mouse. 'You see –' she turned the monitor towards me, buttressing her argument – 'there isn't any file held here under that name.'

'No.' I looked at the screen without seeing anything. 'What if I went through all the files for that year?'

'We can't do that, I'm afraid. They're confidential.'

'Is there anywhere else I could try? Another archive?'

'I'd like to say there is, but if there was a coroner's report it should really be here. Why don't you write down the name of the deceased for me and the year and location of his death, so that I know I have everything right? Then I'll see if I can find anything.' She pushed a pen and a pad towards me. 'Where are you sitting?'

I pointed to the less quiet side of the room, to the genealogists, a merry group of relative-finders from whose success I felt excluded now. They had made it look too easy. Back at my desk I sent some texts and checked my email. About twenty minutes later I looked up to see the librarian plodding over the carpet towards me in an action that was led by her feet and hips, her upper body hanging back. She was smiling sadly.

'I'm afraid to say that we haven't found an inquest for Mr Donaghue. I have also found no death certificate for him. I'm sorry to be so unhelpful.'

'No, it's not your –'

'There is one thing worth bearing in mind, though.' She bent over me and I caught the tight smell of fragrance-free soap on her neck. 'People very often use a different name in their everyday life to the one that appears on certificates. You'd be surprised, the number of people who don't go by the names they were registered under as babies.'

'Ah,' I said, 'Yes, it could be that. I may have got something wrong with the name. I'll go home and check with one of my uncles.' Hoping to distance myself from this troublesome Donaghue, I placed him on a branch of extended family, among a troop of invented uncles. I felt ashamed, of wasting this kind woman's time, of inventing multiple uncles, and of not fitting into groups.

'Yes,' said the librarian, 'and then please do come back and we'll run another search.'

That feeling of being on the edge of life, existing in the margins, was a bit of a knee-jerk thing, a self-indulgence maybe, because it's often easier to stand on the sidelines than to take part. I know there have been times in my life when I could have let myself be incorporated into groups that weren't as hostile as it suited me to believe. For a long time it was easier to scoff at the girls who tried hard at school than to be one of them. As far as the others went, I was never sure which faction I belonged in, the arty ones, the ones who smoked or the ones who didn't care about anything. Cultivating an adolescent disdain for teachers – even the ones who wanted to help me – may have felt like independence but really it was just another form of separation. Like so much else, that marginalisation began in childhood, when I was often aware of imposing on a threesome and not quite fitting in. It wasn't John and Mariel's fault that I felt that way, they were unstintingly kind, and as for Natalie, I loved her like a sister – better than a sister. We may have been on different tracks at school, but I never resented her academic success: she worked hard and deserved her rewards. She knew how to be popular with teachers as well as girls. Then and now, Natalie thrived in organisations, both as a participator and as a leader. I'm sure that an ambition to succeed propelled her from an early age because there are photographs of my cousin looking stout and resolute at the age of three, and she has hardly changed, in either respect. In the last two years of an unblemished school career she was made first a prefect and then head girl. The whole school watched the headmistress pinning the badge to Nat's bust (which was already enormous, a source of wonder to others and alarm to herself) and listened to Natalie's acceptance speech in which she exhorted us schoolgirls to do our best and to do the right thing.

My aunt and uncle were burstingly proud of her that day and Granny Pea went out to buy Italian ice cream and organised a celebratory meal which I remember as being an awkward occasion. Natalie was bad-tempered, perhaps because she felt uncomfortable being such a focus of spoiling admiration, or maybe she just had too much homework or other things on her mind. She'd been sent off to take part in national debates recently and often won – even against the girls from private schools – and that had got her into the habit of declaiming at home too, on politics or justice, subjects on which her audience were almost always in agreement anyway, though it didn't stop her dripping scorn on us.

On the evening of the celebratory meal at Alma Street I'd been drawing in my room and by the time I came downstairs the others were already at the table. I rounded the bottom of the staircase and saw them, from the darkened hall, sitting in a circle of light: Natalie, still in her uniform with her head girl badge, tie tugged to one side, and across the table her father, whose back was to me as I approached the door. I was curious to see her glaring at him but not surprised – she often glared at us in those days.

'No, Natalie, I have to disagree,' I heard my uncle say. 'Being eighteen does not automatically entitle a person to know *everything*. Some things are complicated and there is a time and a place for finding them out. Not necessarily at the age of majority.'

As I came through the door, Mariel had murmured, 'Don't spoil things, darling,' at which Natalie seemed to stiffen into a block of indignation and continued in this attitude, huffy and obtuse throughout the meal, not even pretending to enjoy the toad-in-the-hole, which had once been her favourite meal and was now rejected as too fattening (not that anyone had thought to let my grandmother know).

Afterwards, when we were tidying up and my cousin and I coincided in the dining room, I had whispered conspiratorially: 'What was your dad saying you're too young to know?' Natalie blushed and made a tetchy remark about it not being important, and I had guessed that it was something to do with sex, though it was hard to believe that there was anything left for Natalie to find out, given the thriving exchange of such information in the toilets at school, or that she would ask her parents about this anyway.

And it was only now, sitting on the bus back from the archive and idling with some of these memories, that I saw the scene differently, and I wondered if the eighteen-year-old John had warned shouldn't be told something wasn't in fact Natalie at all – but me.

EIGHT

The man's expression behind the visor was hard to interpret. His eyes were narrowed in a squint that almost completely closed them and he seemed to be partly relying on the evidence of his neoprene-gloved hands. He was half feeling, half seeing, and whatever it was he was straining to discern seemed to cause him a kind of pain, either physical or existential, that sent lines radiating from his eyes and across his forehead. The lower part of his face was covered by breathing apparatus from which rubber tubing curled round to the oxygen canister on his back. He had on a lurid orange zip-up outfit – a colour universally understood to advertise the proximity of hazardous material. The source of that hazard, reflected on the man's visor as he scraped microscopic particles of green pigment into a dish, was Gabriel Huysman's 1795 patterned wallpaper. Beside him, a colleague, dressed in the same orange chemical protective suit, was guiding a spectrometer in his gloved hand over another section of the paper as information was fed back to a laptop computer where it appeared as long strings of data, recording the presence of chromium, mercury, lead and arsenic.

'Those two aren't going to get lost in the park,' said

Roger with a smirk, tipping his shoulder against mine. We had been instructed to stand by open windows at the far end of the room while the heritage inspectors did their work. One of them had pointed with his booted toe at a mark on the floor and warned us not to advance beyond it.

'It's totally excessive,' I murmured, turning away from the men so that they wouldn't hear me. 'They really don't need so much gear.'

'Oh, I don't know,' said Roger. 'Arsine gas can be pretty nasty. Blood vessels rupturing, kidneys failing, encephalitis . . .'

'I know, I know,' I conceded. 'Lots of horrible things can happen. And we also don't know how the chemicals in the paper will have reacted with the fungal material over time. Even so, I think a normal mask and disposable gloves would be enough.'

'There was that girl, wasn't there, who breathed in spores and her lungs collapsed.' Alexandra Marchant was leaning against the windowsill, looking wonderingly at one hand which she held up in front of her, waggling the plum-tipped fingers. 'Shellac's bloody amazing stuff, isn't it? Lasts forever.'

'I don't know if it was both lungs,' said Roger. He didn't look back at Alexandra but pressed his lower lip upwards so that his chin crumpled into divots like a peach stone.

The first inspector had stepped away from the wall and signalled with a hand gesture to his colleague that he had seen enough. Looking towards us he waved the same gloved hand in the direction of the library and we obeyed his instruction, filing out of the room while the men took off their suits and placed them in a plastic bin for decontamination. While one of the men took charge of the packing up, the other came into the library to deliver their verdict. I had met him before; he was an inspector known in conservation circles as much for his work as for the similarity of his name to a famous actor's.

'Ros, do you know Nigel Mavers?' Alexandra said.

'We've met,' said the inspector, nodding at me. 'Couple of years back?'

'That's right,' I said. 'The house in Norfolk.'

'With the terrifying owner. She bred Rhodesian ridgebacks,' Nigel explained, rubbing the back of his head and looking around at the others with a sheepish smile. The removal of his helmet had left his black-and-grey hair in static clumps and he had small, juicy lips that, when he wasn't speaking, were shaped in a kind of 'o'.

'Well,' he said, 'what do you want first – the good news or the bad?'

Alexandra laughed. 'Believe me, Nigel, when it comes to bad news nothing shocks us. You can shoot from the hip.'

'Right.' He nodded and planted his feet wider, swaying into the stance as though the allusion to weaponry had reminded him to be manly. 'I'm sure you know that any time you disturb a very old piece like this, there's a potential to stir up problems. These pieces don't like to be moved. If they're put on hessian that makes life easier, but this was pasted onto the wall. That means the paper is very fragile, and the chemicals are unstable. We don't know what's going on under it, either. That's a whole other story.'

'So really it should be left where it is?' I asked.

Nigel smiled. 'We would always rather that a paper remain in situ. Our motto is, "If it can be left, leave it." Otherwise the historical integrity is bound to be compromised. Let's imagine that the eighteenth-century hanger accidentally put in wrinkles which then get smoothed out in the conservation process. It means that we end up rewriting history, albeit with the best intentions. Plus, as soon as you take something off the wall it becomes a much more expensive job.'

'What if it can't be left?' said Alexandra, adding firmly, 'Which, in this case, it definitely can't.'

Nigel breathed a gentle whistle through the little 'o' of his mouth. 'Well, then we have to proceed very carefully.'

'But moving it could be disastrous, couldn't it?' I asked.

'Look, we still live in a democracy. There's no authority that can compel someone to keep a piece of wallpaper they don't want. And if it can't stay where it is we would obviously rather see it removed than destroyed. But the logistics of dealing with such a fragile paper are complicated. This paper has just been exposed after more than 150 years under wraps. It's been subjected to extreme heat, water, chemical and bacterial change. To be honest, it should now be left undisturbed for a year, so that we can monitor the effect of a full range of seasonal change before we do anything else.'

'A year?!' shouted Alexandra. 'Sorry, but that's actually not going to happen.'

'Even then,' said Nigel, 'we would to need to take advice from a medical toxicologist before doing any work on it.'

'A toxicologist?!' It was my turn to shout. At least Alexandra and I were united in outrage, if in nothing else.

'This is where somebody says it's health and safety gone mad,' said Roger wolfishly, and Nigel marked the observation with the resigned smile of someone who often encounters a lack of understanding in the course of his work.

'You just don't take risks with this kind of stuff,' he said, shaking his head. 'Anybody working in the Rose Room is going to need the place fully ventilated – you'd need an elephant trunk for starters.'

'Elephant trunk?' said Roger.

'It's a fume extractor,' I said. 'But the room's got five massive windows, Nigel – we couldn't just open them?'

'Ros, we're talking about spores that have been lying dormant for centuries. Exposure to air and water activates them. I'm sure you don't need a chemistry lesson from me.'

'We could be bringing back to life some deadly eighteenth-century disease,' said Alexandra brightly. 'I can already see the headlines: "Lord and Lady Marchant cause outbreak of bubonic plague".'

From the garden came the sad call of a wood pigeon.

'I really don't think so,' I said. 'I mean –'

'Who would pay for all of this, anyway?' Alexandra said.

'Well, that at least is fairly straightforward,' said Nigel. 'It's whoever wants to keep the paper.'

'No grants?'

'No grants.'

'Looks like the Huysman paper's yours then, Ros,' Alexandra said, looking at me with a stiff smile. 'If you think you can afford it.'

At the entrance to the Ravenslea Care Home, I hesitated and almost turned away. It was the last in a series of hesitations that had detained me first on my own front doorstep then at several points in the tangle of streets between Battersea and Balham as I made my way in a dithering zigzag to Granny Pea. This time, before I could change my mind again, the receptionist saw me and the polished wooden doors swung open, sweeping me inside. The reception area was like a cautious hotel lobby, with no marble, rugs or anything slippery, but a fitted, tufted carpet and a linoleum pathway for wheelchairs. A display of calla lilies seemed designed to cover all emotional states. I signed into the visitors' book and walked on to the lounge, where the morning 'Reminiscence' session was drawing to a close. My grandmother was among a group of old people making collages at a long table on one side of the room. A bright woman in her thirties was guiding the group through the creative interpretation of a particular memory. She was the Outreach worker, reaching out from the certainty of her canary-yellow dress and peroxide hair to whatever crystalline memories she could find buried in the recesses of her students' foggy minds. Memories were the currency at Ravenslea. Nobody ever talked about the economy or the coalition government, but about what they remembered, and what they remembered was getting progressively further back in time. You could have an enlightening conversation so long as you backdated it thirty years. Vietnamese boat people or the Winter of Discontent were safe territory.

I approached cautiously, not wanting to disturb the group, but Jackie, the deputy care manager, had no such scruples. 'Somebody here to see you,' she shouted over Granny Pea's shoulder as my grandmother bent to her task.

Granny Pea turned jerkily from the table, her hand fluttering onto my wrist, which she then gripped very hard.

'Oh, hello, Natalie darling.'

'It's Ros, Granny.' I planted a kiss on my grandmother's forehead.

'Of course it is. You look different, though. Have you put on weight? Or lost it? I can't tell.'

Others at the table examined me critically, old age exempting them from a requirement to be polite or circumspect.

'I don't know really. I'm a bit stiff,' I offered. My back and arms were still complaining from that twelve-hour shift at Turney.

'Perhaps that's it. Well, you'd better rest, love. Let's go and have a sit together.' I helped my grandmother get up from the table and fetched her stick, then followed her towards her accustomed chair, where Granny Pea hovered, lowering herself by increments, and finally falling backwards with the faith and flair of a daredevil.

'Where are the others?'

'It's just me today. Since I couldn't come on Sunday I thought I'd make up for it. I had spare time.'

'Well, let's hear all about it. What have you been up to?'

'Working, mainly.'

'What kind of work is it you do, love?' It was clear from her attentive expression that this was a genuine enquiry.

'You know what I do, Granny! I work in old houses, mending things that are broken.'

'Oh, I see. That sounds very useful. I used to work in houses, too.'

'Yes, I remember that. You worked for Mrs Saunders. Sometimes she sent you home with sweets for us.'

'Mrs?'

'Saunders.'

'Flanders?'

'No: Saunders. Look, Granny, I hope you don't mind but I wanted to ask you a few questions about Dad.'

'My dad, darling?'

'No, I mean Terence – you know, Mum's husband.'

'Oh, Terence. I'm with you now. What would you like to know?'

'What do you remember about him? What was he like?'

'What would I say about Terence?' Granny Pea made a great effort of concentration that the softening effect of senescence reduced to mere crumpling. 'Was he the chap who –' One arthritic hand flew up, snatching at a memory and just missing it. 'Remind me, darling.'

'My mother's husband, Granny. Your son-in-law,' I said, and added, rather priggishly, 'He was my father.'

'Oh,' said my grandmother, shifting in her chair and giving a little sniff of surprise. 'Well, I'm not sure what to say about him. He's a peculiar chap.'

'Why do you say that?' 'Peculiar' was not a word that

fitted with the mental image I had of my father. 'Peculiar' didn't go with the salty smile and the sea.

'It's just hard to know what's in his mind, love.'

'You found him hard to understand?'

'Underhand? Maybe. Yes, I think you're onto something there.'

'No, I said –'

'I liked him, mind, but your mum and he didn't always see eye to eye.'

'You mean they argued?'

'Did they argue, love?'

'I was wondering – asking you really – if they used to have arguments.'

She stared at me, the pale eyes fixed on some point just above my eyebrows. The thirty-second lag that preceded all my grandmother's responses felt uncomfortable; in our chat-based culture that counts as quite a delay. But if the conversation seemed stilted to me, Granny Pea showed no sign of awkwardness. After giving my question a minute's thought she wrapped one hand around the other in her lap, as though arriving at the end of some process, packing her conclusion up as neatly as she had once packed away the baby clothes we'd found in the loft.

'Well, there was a terrible row, the day before he left.'

'The day before he died?'

'Yes, before he went off.'

'Went off on his bike?' Out of the corner of my eye I caught sight of Godfrey looking goofishly in our direction and remembered the elderly resident's ambition to be scattered over London after his death. 'Went off like a rocket?'

Granny Pea cast me a withering look. 'Like a rocket?

You could put it like that, I suppose. It was sudden, the way he went away. You know, from one day to the next.'

'Very sudden,' I agreed, hoping to level with my grandmother without abusing the difference in power so starkly illustrated by the doily halo on which Granny Pea's head rested. Our exchange had locked into a repeating pattern of euphemisms and it was hard to tell who was humouring whom.

'Very sudden,' murmured Granny Pea again and looked exhausted. Her attention drifted and her head went doddering around the assembled residents, some of whom were looking in our direction, following the progress of this halting exchange with the uninhibited curiosity of small children. Granny Pea's eyes closed, she heaved one of her classic sighs and seemed about to fall asleep. I sat back in my chair feeling annoyed about the collage session; that Outreach woman, with her bright clothes and silly chirpy banter, had robbed my grandmother of the energy required for this conversation. Outside heavy clouds were pressing into the sky and the shifting balance of light pieced patches of reflection into the view through the long windows. Old, frilly heads popped up among the flowers in the herbaceous border. Two children were wandering in the garden with their mother who must have brought them to visit a relative. The younger strained against his tether, falling every so often, with a soft wallop that prompted a wave of chuckles through the room. His mother looked towards her audience inside with a tentative pride, trying to pick out through the reflecting window which old lady was hers.

'I hope it won't rain on those kids,' said Granny Pea, who wasn't sleeping after all.

'Yes,' I said. 'Well, they can always come inside.' I wanted to press on with my questions, but knew that there was a fine line between pressing and pushing. I might not have my grandmother's attention for long and Jackie was watching us as she wove among the chairs.

'Who is the fellow in the cape?' asked my grandmother, knitting together sparse eyebrows. 'Is it the Pope?'

'Where are you looking, Granny? Oh, I see. No, that isn't a person, it's a closed sunshade. On a garden table. It does look a bit like the Pope though, the way the material is draped and the colour.'

'Oh.' My grandmother took this information at face value, neither laughing at her mistake nor expressing wonder at the visual illusion. She was like a person discovering the world for the first time, for whom every kind of explanation was possible. I thought, with a pang, how easy it would be to take advantage of that innocence. *Yes, Granny, it's the Pope. He's holding Mass in the garden and then coming in for cakes and a sing-song.* To hold any sort of straightforward conversation with her might count as abuse, because straightforward was a line my grandmother couldn't count on following any more.

'Granny?'

'Hmm?'

'You said Dad went away. You mean, like "passed away", right?

'Passed away?'

'Passed away. You know – passed on, passed over.'

'Passover. Is that the same thing?' asked Granny Pea,

looking suddenly intellectual. 'I've heard people in here talk about Passover. Mrs Henry could talk to people who passed over.'

'That's right, I remember Mrs Henry.' She was a neighbour, a West Indian who had lived opposite the house in Alma Street and used to stand at her kitchen window watching Natalie and me with disapproval as we clattered past on roller skates. Mrs Henry claimed to be able to connect people to their relatives in 'the other world' and Granny Pea visited her several times, as I remember it, in hopes of reaching her husband. Mrs Henry's own husband, whose name – Prince Henry – caused Natalie and me great merriment, was as thin as his wife was fat and as given to the outdoors as she was to her kitchen. Most days we saw him in the street, waxing and polishing the bodywork of his mustard-coloured Ford or sometimes just leaning on it with a look of quiet pride. Only on Sunday mornings did Mrs Henry sail forth from the house, like a member of the royal family, in a brown coat and matching hat, a shiny plasticated handbag looped over one arm. Then Prince would open the door of the Ford for her and bear her away to the spiritualist church. I hadn't thought of them for years though once they were a significant, unquestioned presence in my life. The past, jewelled with bright memories like these, was also full of snares. I had a sensation of pulling bright knotted handkerchiefs from a magician's pocket. At the end of the string might be the silken memory I needed, but there was no guarantee of that.

'Coming back to Dad, Granny. Do you remember the day he passed away – or passed on or passed over?'

'Or passed out!' cried Granny Pea.

'Over and out!' called Godfrey with a salute.

'Out and about!' Granny Pea's bandaged feet scooted off the ground in a display of girlish frippery.

'Shake it all about!' shouted Godfrey, and a woman sitting nearby chimed in: 'That's what it's all about!'

Jackie, standing close to Godfrey's chair, wiggled herself gustily.

'Are you joining us for tea, my love?' she shouted across to me. Jackie was a stranger to modulation, using the same pitch and volume for everyone. 'Well, I must say, we've got a right old party going on over here now. We should have you in more often, my love. You're the life and soul!' Everyone was 'my love' to her. I smiled, but smiling upset the mask I had been relying on and I felt my eyes pricking.

I moved my hand over my face, plucking away tears with my thumb and forefinger, as though a tear were something you could pick up and put down somewhere without attracting attention. It saddened me the way the old people here all behaved in such a similar way, as though time had stripped them of difference as well as youth. Ravenslea's residents might as well have adopted a universal code of conduct: only to make elusive, bird-like movements of the head, to love a dirty joke and a sing-song, to make eager faces at the tea trolley. I didn't remember my grandmother ever singing aloud when she lived at Alma Street, though she may sometimes have accompanied *Songs of Praise* with a tuneless hum. Now she was quite happy to join in a chorus of 'Knees Up Mother Brown'. She wasn't the person she used to be and for that reason I decided it was pointless, and probably unkind, to try to make her remember her earlier incarnation. Reaching around to pull the jacket off the back of my chair, I prepared to leave, but either the exchange with Godfrey or the promise of a cup of tea had invigorated Granny Pea, who caught my wrist in another painful grip.

'Don't go, doll. It was a bit boring when you first came, but we've started having fun now. Why did you come, by the way?'

'I wanted to ask you about my dad, Terence. I wanted to ask you about the day he died.'

Granny Pea tightened the grip, her eyes widening in alarm. 'He's died! When?'

My poor, senile grandmother. I held her hand against my cheek, shielding my eyes from the attention of the other residents.

'I miss you, GP.'

'I miss you too, darling. But I don't think you'd want to come and live here with us lot. Not much laughs around here, are there?' She said this to Godfrey and some of the others who were sitting nearby and they agreed, but with a gusto and laughter that refuted her observation. Plainly there were laughs at Ravenslea. They did seem to be happy, so perhaps I should stop feeling that my grandmother's confinement was tragic. She hadn't said anything about coming back to Alma Street. It could be that she was resigned, then, to staying here.

'You know that we've been talking about my dad, about Terry?'

'Yes, love.' Granny Pea met my eye again with new determination to concentrate. 'Terence, yes, a handsome man. I never call him Terry. Do you call him that?'

'I was little. I suppose I just called him Daddy.'

'Yes, most likely.'

'You said he died that day after the row you heard. He had an accident and died.' I had put the euphemisms behind me now, dispensed with passing on and passing away, and although it was brutal to keep repeating 'dead' and 'died', it was a relief too, after thirty years of silence on the subject.

'Dad died. I went swimming with the Coopers. Mrs Cooper came to pick me up. Remember?' I saw the scene myself now, in vivid artificial 3D, like something a child might watch through a viewfinder: Mrs Cooper, broad-hipped and smiling on the doorstep and the car behind her on a distinct plane, the three children scrambling in the back to get a view of my fresh bereavement. It was obvious that they had been warned not to mention my father's death. I remembered their recoiling limbs in the back seat, warm and sticky from eating ice lollies, the wrappers discarded on the floor and the seat. They had thought I was too delicate to touch, or perhaps they wanted to avoid my cool contagion of death. At the swimming pool I had waited for ages, dripping in my cubicle, for Mrs Cooper to bring my clothes from the locker, convinced that they had forgotten I was there and wondering if I would have to walk home in my wet swimsuit. Looking back, I felt a scouring sorrow for myself on that day, for that child whose world had been turned upside down but who still had to be polite and pretend that everything was fine. At the very least they should have given me a lolly.

Granny Pea looked hard at me for a moment, then

blinked and looked away, out of the window at the herbaceous border. 'Mrs Cooper always was a nosy old bag. You liked going to their house because she let you have sweets before tea. The children ran wild. Not a hairbrush between them.'

I smiled, taking heart; it was a long time since I had heard my grandmother rant about hairbrushes. I wished we could spend some time resurrecting these ghosts of childhood, the Coopers and the Henrys, the girls from school, but I felt that Granny Pea's attention might not be with me much longer: 'I went with Mrs Cooper, because you needed me out of the house, there were arrangements to make. Dad had died and Mum was going to his funeral in Ireland and –'

'Well, that's just it, love,' said Granny Pea, interrupting with a frown. 'You keep saying that but I don't think he could have died then, because he wrote to me afterwards, saying he was sorry about everything.'

'He was sorry? What about? When did he write?'

'I can't remember exactly when. He was sorry about the trouble he'd caused us, I suppose.'

'Perhaps you dreamt that, Granny. When someone dies people often do dream about them.'

'Yes,' she agreed. 'Dreams and life are hard to separate sometimes. Last night I dreamt I was with Ray. We went down to Brighton, sat on the front and ate winkles and that. He rolled up his trousers and started walking into the sea. It was funny. He kept turning round and smiling and waving. I was waiting for him to come back, but he never did. Just kept walking into the water.'

I leaned back in my chair again, defeated. It was painful

witnessing my grandmother's retreat into this felted world where there were no certainties or absolutes, no hard edges. Jackie, with the tea trolley, had reached the far side of the room where two visitors were sitting with one of Ravenslea's most decrepit residents, a woman in her nineties whose mouth hung open in a lopsided grin. Awful to be among invalids and to know that there was no chance of them getting better, only of getting worse.

'It's coming back to me now,' said my grandmother, delicately fingering the edge of her cardigan. 'I do remember something he wrote in the letter. He said that he loved you and we must always take care of you. And we have done, chick, haven't we? But I don't really know if I was supposed to tell you that.' Her fingers moved to the blanket over her knees and a grimace changed the topography of her face, gathering lines to her eyes and around her mouth. 'I hope I haven't got it wrong. She did say there were things I shouldn't tell you.'

'"She"?'

'Iris. There were things she didn't want said and I can't remember exactly – Oh dear, I hope I haven't done the wrong thing. I do get muddled up.' Her mouth seemed mismatched to the words coming out of it, her lower lip hanging away from the bottom teeth so that I could see the tender, glistening inside of it.

'It's fine, Granny. Don't worry. Look, Jackie's coming with the trolley now, let's have a cup of tea,' I said but I had to brace myself against the back of the chair because for a moment it felt as if everything around me was rising up in a fluttering, scraping and flapping and the room itself was filling up with birds. My throat felt full of something light and choking, like feathers, and I was struggling to breathe.

There were birds in Kensington Gardens too, among them green parakeets that looked outlandish in the chestnut trees and even sounded foreign, shrieking when round here tweeting was the general rule. I had seen flocks of parakeets on Clapham Common before. Uncle John said that they were descended from a pair released by Jimi Hendrix in Carnaby Street. Either that or they had escaped from Shepperton Studios in the 1950s during the filming of *The African Queen*. You could pick your myth, I thought, as I walked through the park down an avenue of London plane trees. Their leaves, curling as they caught the light, filled the eye with prismatic greens. Not even the golden statue at the avenue's end could compete with such a sumptuous effect. It was the first hot day of the year and Londoners were overreacting in large numbers, chasing the sun with picnics and bottles of wine or lying splayed in their underwear in the long grass. A group of paunchy pensioners stood smiling around the boating pond, sending their model yachts and clippers on very short adventures. At the park's edge, I stopped to watch a family group pose for photographs after a baptism at the nearby Catholic church. The presence of an official photographer had drawn a small crowd anxious not to miss any moment of record. Then some Japanese tourists, seeing the crowd, started rummaging in their bags for cameras without even knowing what sort of photo opportunity awaited them. The members of the christening group looked smart in an unspecified European style, elegant enough to be French although their frank joy in the child suggested Italian blood. In between shots each of them held the baby in turn, inspecting it with bewildered smiles, as if they had never before seen humankind represented in miniature form and found it a wonderful novelty. Their delight delighted the baby, who bit her fist, laughing as she swooped through the air to the next pair of arms. Finally, at the command of the photographer, the baby was settled in her father's arms and the mother joined them. The father looked down at his baby with a fearful joy I could scarcely bear to witness. I checked my watch or, rather, my father's watch – it was 12.45 p.m. – and set off down Exhibition Road.

My mother worked at the college here, a glass-fronted monolith that was one of the world's foremost scientific institutes. On a more modest level, it was also a family base for us because my Uncle John was a professor of particle physics in the department where my aunt was also a secretary. Mariel had applied for the job when Natalie started secondary school. Soon after she helped my mother, who was also a trained secretary, to get work in another department at the same university. For nearly thirty years Mariel and John had been helping my mother and bailing her out. Most of what she had she owed to them: her job, the care of her child, occasional loans. Once, in flight from an abusive relationship, she had even sent my uncle to rescue her belongings from the boyfriend's flat. These were the debts I knew about but maybe she owed them something greater – some collusion or deception that had bound them for thirty years.

I reached the university and waited inside while a receptionist telephoned my uncle's office. The lobby was two storeys high and dominated by a giant abstract work which insiders knew to be a coloured CT scan of the rector's brain. It was brave of him to put his brain on display, John sometimes said, considering the number of Nobel laureates on campus, 'because his is by no means the most evolved cerebrum'. I wondered how long it would be before people could see illustrations not only of the brain's tissue but of the thoughts flashing in electrical bursts through it: the rector's appetites and secrets laid bare. After a few minutes my uncle appeared, taking the stairs at a youthful trot.

'I'm sorry this is such short notice,' I said as he walked towards me.

John gave me a bristly, avuncular kiss, banging my nose with his glasses. 'Not at all. I'm delighted to see you any time, Ros, you know that. And you haven't been here for a while. When was the last time?'

'I think when you got the endowed chair.'

'A long time ago.' He folded his arms across his middle, each hand investigating the peculiarities of the bony elbow in its grasp. 'That was a good party.'

'Mariel got rather giggly, I seem to remember.'

'Yes, indeed.' He frowned at a patch of the concrete floor between us. 'Well, a lot has happened since then. Can you come upstairs for a moment before we go for lunch?'

'I'd love to.'

In the physics lab banks of computers spilled wires across every surface and tangled cables on the floor constituted a tripping hazard that would never have been permitted in my line of work. There were a few postgrad students present, lolling in chairs, inert and unwashed, blinking at the multiple monitors. Food packages and empty coffee cups were strewn about the desktops, and in one area chairs and beanbags were grouped around a whiteboard covered in equations. Beside it a trolley sagged under the weight of stacked cups, a coffee percolator and a kettle. A mushy pyramid of used tea bags was two or three brews away from collapse.

'Come,' said my uncle, striding ahead. 'Come and see this.' In a workshop adjoining the lab he stopped and pointed proudly at something that looked like a deconstructed washing machine on legs attached to a catering urn.

'This is our new baby, funded by the European Union,' John said fondly.

'I hope you're not going to ask me to guess what it is.'

'What do you think it might be?'

'I don't know!' I laughed helplessly. Uncle John made me feel eternally fourteen. 'Is it a particle accelerator?'

'Good guess! It's part of a dark-matter detector. We're building it here and it'll be used in an underground laboratory in experiments to detect the heat produced when a particle hits an atom.'

'There's an underground lab here?'

'No! Not in London. They have to be as far as possible from light contamination. There's one in Yorkshire, half a mile underground, but this one's going to be used in Canada.'

'So you're finally going to solve the meaning of the universe, Uncle John. I always knew you would.'

He laughed. 'Not in my lifetime, Ros. Perhaps in Sadie's.'

'I don't know,' I said, as we walked back through the main lab. 'People say I spend all day looking into the past. It's nothing compared to your work. You're looking right back to the beginning of time.'

'A traditional concept of time doesn't really apply at this level. It's time to eat, though, I do know that. Let me treat you to lunch in our incomparable canteen.'

Along the corridors, doors were opening in anticipation of food. Behind them were small offices in which staff and students could be seen grouped together behind desks or perched on them, bent over computers in attitudes of rapt attention. They clearly directed all their enthusiasm into their research, because the walls of the corridor were bare of any creative overflow; no posters advertising parties or performances, no invitations to sign a petition or join a demo. We passed through two sets of doors, opened by John with a flourish of his security pass, and emerged onto a concrete concourse, where we were swept into a gathering swarm of people urged by hunger towards the two canteens and a number of concessions selling crisps, chocolate and other student fodder.

In the canteen John led me on a circuit of the carousels offering hot and cold meals, salads and desserts. All of it looked revolting to me.

'Choose anything you like,' my uncle kept saying, 'anything you like,' but at the same time he was making the choices for me, piling my plate high. At the till, chiding me for not taking a dessert, he tossed a chocolate brownie onto my tray.

'Let's go over there.'

We took seats beside a window overlooking a rectangle of grass on which about a hundred Muslim students were standing together, their heads bowed in prayer, a statue of the university's founder, a glum Victorian, rising incongruously in their midst. The men were ranged in rows at the front of the rectangle, the women behind them. As I watched, all of them bowed and kneeled, touching their heads to the ground in unison.

'Wow. That's quite – unexpected.'

John glanced out of the window. 'It's a move by the Islamic Society to hold Friday prayers outside. A gesture of openness. There have been some tensions on campus recently.' He dismissed my raised eyebrow with an impatient shrug. 'There always are, in any university worth its salt. You've got all these competing ideas and energies – which is a good thing – but when they collide it can be an explosive place, much like the universe itself. So people find ways to defuse the tensions.'

'That looks more like a statement than a gesture.'

John shrugged and waved his fork at my plate. 'Eat something.'

'I will – but I'm not that hungry. You've given me loads.'

That food was merely fuel to my uncle was obvious from the peculiar melange of flavours and textures with which he had filled both our plates. Chicken curry sat alongside tuna mayonnaise, beef and gravy with potato salad. Cheerfully he shovelled in these elements together, using one elbow on the table as a lever for the fork that went up and down between plate and mouth. I could imagine the sad remonstrations my aunt might have been moved to make had she been sitting at the table with us.

'Is today Mariel's day off?'

'Yes, she only works three days a week now. This afternoon she'll be heading out to her "knit and natter" group, God help us.'

'I don't know – it sounds like fun.'

'Do you think so?' He looked up at me, deliberately aghast – 'I can't think of anything worse' – then jabbed his fork at me again. 'You realise that *I* am the one she's knitting for?'

'Of course. I expect she's nattering about you, too.'

Laughter sent him not one way or the other but straight up in his chair, like a popping cork.

'Yes, yes. And none of it good, I fear,' he said, but then he sighed in a way that suggested he didn't really care what Mariel might be saying about him. He was much more interested in the deconstructed washing machine waiting up in the lab. I watched his fork circle above his plate like a grab claw in an amusement arcade, before descending onto a piece of curried chicken. 'So, Ros, what's new? What brings you here? How are things with you and Chris?'

'They're not too bad. We're in contact. We've seen each other a few times,' I said. The night I wrote that I missed him, Chris had texted back saying he missed me too and we had agreed to go down to the coast together on the next day both of us were free. I didn't mention that to John. It amused me to think of him finding the patience to listen to my marital problems. He hated any talk of emotions – though, as the only man in our extended family, he often had to hear it.

'I haven't come because of that. I'm here partly because – I don't know – I wanted to thank you for everything you've done for me over the years.'

John's head shot back in alarm. 'What's this? Are you going away somewhere?'

'No! I just wanted you to know that I don't take it for granted, the way you stepped in and did so much for me when Dad died. It can't have been easy. I don't think we've ever spoken about it.'

My uncle seemed absorbed by the contents of his plate, especially a thick slice of meat that he had tried to sever with the edge of his fork, before accepting that the job demanded a knife. When he looked up he glanced out of the window first, taking his bearings it seemed, before meeting my eye.

'It wasn't a chore. You and Natalie are the same age. You got on and you were good company for each other. That made things easier. It was the obvious thing to do.'

'It meant that you had to be a father figure in a sense.'

'Not really, Ros. No, I think this idea that everyone needs a role model is overdone. People get on with life, don't they, whatever hand they've been dealt? I can't take any credit for bringing you up. You had determination and a strong character and I'm sure you would have turned out wonderfully, no matter who was looking after you.'

'Even if it had been left to Mum?'

Mention of my mother seemed to make his wrist go limp; the fork dangled in his hand. 'Your mother wasn't best placed to look after you at that time, it's true. She was struggling. She found it hard to come to terms with . . .'

'Losing Dad?'

'Yes.'

'Losing him, or being left by him?'

I heard my heart beat one, two, three times. My uncle looked hard at me, as if he had not properly seen me before, and at the centre of his lenses, his pupils contracted into sharp black points. A miniature version of the college's Victorian clock tower was reflected in each lens. At that moment, I felt sorry for him and for myself a kind of disdain for stirring up trouble, when it would be easy to let things lie.

'I don't believe my father is dead, John. There's no record of an inquest in the London archives. And Granny says she had a letter from him after he left, saying that he was sorry for the trouble he'd caused. I know she gets confused, but . . . please tell me, if I'm wrong. I trust you to tell me the truth.'

John laid down his fork and pushed his plate away. 'I suppose I knew this day would come.'

'Oh God.'

'Are you all right? You've gone very pale.'

I laughed because – what else could I do? Awkward, apologetic and frightened all at once: there's no recognised gesture for that combination of feelings. 'I thought you were going to tell me I was wrong. I think I wanted you to.'

He glanced around him. 'This isn't the right place. Let's go somewhere quieter. We can go back to my office.'

'I don't think I can. I'll be sick if I move. It's fine here.'

The crowds of people pushing past the end of our table with their trays looking for places to sit were a line that looked too daunting to break through, but at the same time they provided a kind of human insulation. The chatter and hubbub gave us privacy.

John bent over the table, head bowed. 'Good God, Ros, I'm so sorry. Iris should have told you long before it came to this. I pressed her to tell you, I always have done. In retrospect we should have taken matters out of her hands. I just – I felt that it was incumbent on her, as a parent –'

'Oh my God.'

'Here, have some water.'

'OK.' My hand shook as I drank. While we had been invoking our notional God the Muslim students outside were coming to the end of their more considered ritual. I watched as they got to their feet, slipping off their piety as they slipped back into their shoes and trainers. Some spotted friends and walked towards them with the lolloping gait of self-conscious youth. The water made me feel a bit better.

'Is he alive, then?' I said. 'My father?'

John shook his head quickly. His leg, jigging up and down under the table, was making our plates rattle together and I moved them apart. Of the two of us, I seemed to be the calmer. 'I can't tell you that, because I don't know,' John said. 'All I can tell you is that he didn't die then. There was no accident. That didn't happen.'

'So what did happen?'

My uncle took a deep breath that filled out the front of his fraying checked shirt. 'In a way it's very simple: they decided to split up and Terry went back to live in Dublin. Iris came up with her story and we all agreed to back it, I don't know why –'

'Well, why did you?' I said quietly, but I could hear my

voice begin to shake with anger. 'How could you? You kept this from me, all of you, and I was a *child*. And then afterwards letting me be the only one, for years and years, for nearly thirty years, who didn't know? It's cruel. When I think of all the times we sat together at that table, and everybody knew apart from me. And there was never any intention to tell me –'

He shook his head sadly. 'There is no defence.'

'You could at least try to defend it!'

'Well.' John brought his fingers together in the shape of a diamond on the table, leaning over it. 'I suppose I would say that your mother was unstable. She told us, announced to us really, that she had decided to take this line and that Terry had agreed to it. You see, Ros, by that stage he had already gone –' He glanced up at me and the little clock towers swung back onto his lenses. 'Let me go back a bit. The night before there had been a supper at Alma Street where the atmosphere was very tense. I think your mother had discovered something.' He frowned and blinked quickly several times. 'She'd found a letter, or a diary or something. I don't know what exactly, but she suspected an affair. The atmosphere that evening was terrible. They could barely bring themselves to speak to each other and it was very uncomfortable for everyone. Once you and Natalie had gone to bed, it all started coming out.'

'What were they saying?'

He looked anxiously at some students filing past our table and I followed his gaze, but the expressions they returned were blank and uninterested. 'Oh, I don't know, your mother was saying that Terry was a liar, that he disgusted her, she hated him. It was a rambling diatribe. She – your mother – had been drinking and she was incoherent. Granny was very upset. We wanted to protect her, and you, of course. But nobody really understood what was going on.'

'And my father?'

John opened his hands from the diamond shape, palms up on the table. 'He didn't defend himself or disagree. He kept saying that they should go back to their flat and sort things out there, on their own. He said that she should keep her voice down, he didn't want you to hear her and be upset. But Iris was hysterical. She said she couldn't stand to be alone with him. I wondered if –' Then he stopped talking, so absorbed in the mental re-enactment that he forgot to follow it aloud.

'If what?' I prompted.

'Well, if he had been violent to her. But it didn't *feel* like that kind of situation. If anyone seemed likely to be violent, it was her.' John looked up at me with an apologetic little laugh. 'Terry was actually the one I was afraid for.'

He leaned back in his chair, frowning at his hands.

'So? What happened then?'

'I said that I would take them home, that I would stay there with them while they talked things over, although quite what I would have been able to do . . . Anyway, Mariel and Granny were going to look after you and Natalie at Alma Street. To start with your mother refused to be in the flat with him so Terry said, "It's all right, I'll find somewhere else to go."'

These salvaged, possibly misremembered, words of my

father gave me a jolt. For an instant I saw him clearly, with his salty hair blowing across his face, standing in my grandmother's front room, his hand on the door handle. 'I'll find somewhere else to go.' He was alive in my imagination and the illusion reminded me that he could be alive outside it too, an idea so overpowering that I was moved to hide my face in my hands.

'Are you all right?'

'Yes, just taking it all in. Keep going. What happened next?'

'Then –' My uncle sighed again, sending out a stream of breath that lifted the corner of a napkin on the table. 'It's hard piecing it all together so long after the event. I think what happened was – yes, they agreed that I would take them home and by the time we got to Earls Court your mother had calmed down – perhaps because of the drive, during which things had been mercifully quiet. Anyway, she decided they didn't need me to stay. They could sort things out between them.'

'And he agreed?'

'Yes, as I said before, he didn't stand up for himself in any way. He seemed defeated, somehow, prepared to go along with anything. The next morning your mother told us that it was over; they had decided that she would divorce him and he wouldn't contest the divorce. She told us he had already gone, that he didn't want to say goodbye – that this was all decided on, he had agreed to it. That was very hard because we were fond of him, but I just assumed that –' he made a guttural noise that could have been the beginning of a laugh or a sob – 'that we would see him again. I thought this rift was temporary, that things would settle down in some form or other. And in the meantime we let ourselves believe that we were doing the best thing – for you and her. When with hindsight –'

'Did Natalie know?' I asked impatiently. There was a discrepancy between the amount of information I wanted to know and the time I could bear to spend hearing it. It was taking all my energy just to sit still.

John nodded silently. 'Yes. She found out a few years later. I'm afraid she overheard a conversation between Mariel and me.'

'Jesus. Even Natalie.' My arms were pressed together on the tabletop, my hands in fists under my chin but when Uncle John reached across the table, I drew them away, sitting back in my seat with my hands in my lap. I didn't want him to touch me, or to be touched by anyone. This betrayal shouldn't be so easily salved – but there was more to it than that: I felt like a pariah, rejected by my parents, deceived by my family, distant from every sort of love.

'I'm sorry,' John said.

I nodded. I was hardly going to say 'It's fine'.

'Why would anyone keep a secret for so long?' I said finally. 'People fall out of love or leave each other *all the time*. It doesn't mean you write them out of history. Only an idiot would do that, or someone trying to get revenge. To declare somebody dead? It's so extreme, so pathetic and vindictive. And why would he let that happen? Unless – maybe it was what *he* wanted? Perhaps my father didn't want to be a part of my life and this was the easiest way to opt out. That makes a kind of sense.'

'No, Ros, I can't believe that's true. He loved you very

much.' John's eyes shone with tears. 'He was immensely proud of you. I can't believe he went along with this willingly. He must have felt that he had no choice.'

'You mean he felt dead. So he didn't care if she made out that he was.'

He shook his head then shrugged and slumped back in his chair. 'I don't know if that's what he felt. Only one person knows the truth and she's here, just two floors above us. Shouldn't we go and talk to your mother?'

NINE

The inability to love a parent is a peculiar kind of failure. Antagonism isn't rare in families, of course, but it ought to be a developmental stage you grow into and out of on the way to reaching a stage of mutual respect and affection. We never reached that stage, my mother and I, but were indefinitely detained in the adolescent phase. Almost everything she said raised my hackles, and I couldn't seem to please her either. In fact I don't remember ever feeling comfortable with Iris, as a child or as an adult. Simple expeditions that were so enjoyable with Mariel and Natalie, Saturday afternoons in the 'pedestrian precinct' (as a child I didn't know what the words meant, only that they made me happy) were miserable and complicated when I tried to replicate them with my mother. Whether struggling to find school shoes we both liked or vainly making the case for pick 'n' mix, I seemed always to exasperate her. Things were easier once I was eighteen and there was no longer an implied duty of care, at least not on her part. We loosened the ties with relief on both sides and for a few years saw each other rarely. It used to bother me, though, that we weren't closer. Those early years together had been so hard, so bleak, they should have made a bedrock for us.

Now it all made sense: we weren't close because our

relationship was built on a lie. Since I had no way of knowing that, as a young woman I used to wonder if we just associated each other too much with bad times, with failure and desperation, and were better off apart. I think my mother met Chris only two or three times before we got married. I didn't involve her in planning the wedding though she was invited, and came, on the same footing as the other relations. I remember how, at the registry office, she seemed awkwardly deprived of her role as mother of the bride and that I didn't feel sorry for her; she hadn't earned it, as far as I was concerned. As time went on, though, I began to feel that, even if she had failed in her duty to me, I still had one to her. She was my only parent and I was her only child; we ought to make something of that singularity. And I did try: I made an effort to see her regularly and we pieced together a relationship, around family occasions and phone calls.

Every couple of months I came to visit her here at the university. My mother, a student accommodation officer, worked in an open-plan office at the top of the administration block, a glossy, impersonal area on which the occupants strove to leave marks of identity through screensavers, photographs and knick-knacks. Each workspace was backed with a felt-covered board on which people could pin papers and photographs. Over the years that I had been coming here I had got to know my mother's colleagues through the evidence presented on their desks. There was Rory, a fruitarian and yoga enthusiast, Susie, a FarmVille addict, and Sandra, who had a collie and a timeshare in Mallorca. Further down the same arm as my mother sat Hen, short for Henrietta, I suppose, though 'Hen' suited her perfectly: she often seemed flustered and afraid. Hen's screensaver was 'God is Love'. Every few seconds these words appeared at the bottom left-hand corner of the screen and wafted up to the top right-hand corner, evanescing only to resurrect themselves at the bottom left-hand corner. My instinct, when I first met Hen, had been to avert my eyes from the screen. It surprised me that someone would make such a public statement about something so personal – it would be like Rory having the words 'Out and proud' dancing on his screen, rather than allowing that information to be expressed subliminally through his fruitarianism. But in a way my mother's booth was the strangest of all: pinned onto her board were seven or eight photographs of Marlon Brando, sitting astride his motorcycle, looking moodily into the camera lens as he stroked the bruised bump of his lip or strained against a vest. This wasn't a fixation my mother had ever mentioned to me and it was symbolic of how little we knew one another. Actually it embarrassed me, though I told myself that she had probably supplied only two or three of the photographs herself; colleagues and grateful students must have given her the rest. In fact one had some words scribbled on it: *Thanx Iris! Loadsa luv xxxx*. Among all the pictures of Brando, there wasn't a single photograph of my father. I'm not sure that my mother's colleagues even knew she had ever been married.

My heart felt bulky in my chest as John and I came out of the lift and walked into the Admissions office. It was the end of the lunch hour and the air was heavy with resignation and a smell of spoiling soup. Scanning the room for my mother, I spotted her close to the wall, wiping her hands then tossing a napkin into a flip bin with dispatch. Turning to walk back to her desk, she smoothed down her skirt and dabbed at the corners of the mouth and had almost reached her chair when she saw us coming towards her.

'Ros,' she said, and then, 'John?' and immediately drawing the wrong conclusion she raised her hand to her throat and said, 'Is it Mum?'

'No, no,' said John quickly, patting the air in front of him. 'It's nothing to do with your mother; she's fine. This is to do with Ros.'

My mother looked critically at me. 'What's happened, Ros? Is there a problem with the house? The boiler?'

The way she was wringing her hands looked like a signal for me to be quick, which only made my thoughts clumsier and harder to express.

'No – everything at the house is fine,' I said. 'It's something else. It's us – you and me – we need to talk about something.'

'Privately,' John added. 'Perhaps you could use the conference room.'

Standing behind her chair, Iris struck a defiant pose. 'Well, not right now, John, I can't, no. I've got a pile of application forms to get through this afternoon. Today's the last day for getting them in. And anyway, there's a booking system for that room. I don't think we can just waltz in –'

'It seems to be free at the moment,' John said, 'and this needn't take long.'

She gestured at her desk. 'I've got so much on. And I'm expecting calls.'

'You go on!' said Sandra, cheerfully taking Iris's excuses at face value. 'I'll watch your phone for you.'

My mother turned to look at Sandra and her other colleagues either for guidance or to buy herself time. As she turned back she caught John motioning to me that he might leave and me urgently motioning back that he should stay. Her eyes narrowed under the shimmering grey lids.

'I don't know what this is all about, but whatever it is, it will have to be double-quick,' she said.

The conference room was glass-fronted and sound-proofed, allowing people inside it to observe the office life continuing outside as though it were a television drama switched to mute. The oblong-shaped walnut table could accommodate twenty and on a sideboard at one end of the room were a hot-water urn and trays bearing meticu-lous presentations. Jammy dodgers, custard creams and bourbons were lined up on one. On the other were tea bags, colour-coded for flavour. Somebody had taken care to make the arrangement perfect.

My mother had followed me into the room – my uncle coming after her – but advanced only as far as the head of the table, where she took a commanding position, the fingertips of one hand splayed on the surface in front of her in the pinch grip of a basketball player. 'Now, Ros, what's this all about?' she said. I recognised the hectored, parental tone that had undermined me so often in the past and was interested to find that today it didn't reach me. It sounded hollow, as though she were appealing to some long-exhausted authority.

'Can we at least sit down?' I said.

'I'm afraid there isn't time for that.'

'Come on, Iris,' said John sharply, and my mother turned instantly towards him with such a fearful expression that I felt sorry for her.

'It's just that if you don't sit down I'll have to stand up again,' I explained, 'and that's going to look silly.'

With a glance over her shoulder at her fellow office workers beyond the glass, my mother pulled out a chair and sat down. John, who was leaning against the sideboard, picked up a custard cream and absently crunched off half of it. Since visiting Granny Pea I had been wondering obsessively about how I was going to tackle my mother on the subject of my father's disappearance, a prospect that had finally seemed so difficult I made the decision to talk to John instead. Now it was here, though, that moment of confrontation I had hoped to avoid, and I felt sick with apprehension. The complacency of my mother's trim figure in her close-fitting clothes, the hair that was coloured and teased and sprayed into shape – I hated to think I may be about to send a wrecking ball through such a careful construct.

'Let's get this over with. I haven't got long, Ros.' She looked pale; she must have an inkling, I thought, of why I was here.

I began falteringly: 'It's about Dad.' There was a knot at the base of my throat and rising from it an ache provoked by saying this word that was taboo between us.

Iris looked steadily at me for a few seconds, then said: 'Well, what about him? What is there to say?'

'There's everything to say,' I began, a sudden grief loosening my eyes. 'You've never said a single thing. You've never told me what books he read, what music he liked, where he liked to go.'

'So you've interrupted me at work to ask –'

'Listen to her,' John said. 'Hear what she has to say.'

'You've never even said that he loved me.'

'Obviously he would love you!' my mother snapped, but just saying the word 'love' had the effect of defusing her anger. 'You were a lovely little girl. He adored you.' Instead of projecting words, she seemed to be trapping them in the air and swallowing them.

Hearing how much it cost her to say even this, I sniffed and smiled. 'Thank you. I needed to know that.'

'So is that all?'

I was tempted to say that it was, since every transaction felt so difficult. Who knew that it could take so much energy just to speak?

'Iris,' said John, taking matters out of my hands, 'Ros knows about Terry. She knows the truth.'

My mother turned to look at John again and for a few seconds stared at him, uncomprehending. He held her gaze, still leaning against the sideboard, arms resolutely folded.

'She asked me to tell her the truth,' he said, 'and I did. Somebody had to.'

My mother looked away and seemed to shrink bodily, as though crumbling inwards.

'Why did you tell me he'd had an accident, Mum?' I said. 'Why have you let me believe that all these years?'

She turned to look me with no hint of an apology. 'It was for the best, Ros. We needed a clean break.'

Behind my mother, I could see people moving smoothly

between workstations, carrying piles of paper and styro-foam mugs of coffee. Three women standing together were sharing some amusing episode, bending their heads in classical poses. They made office work look easy and mechanical. No fear of getting spiders in your hair or arsenic under your fingernails.

'But does that justify telling a gigantic lie?'

I didn't mean to sound confrontational – at that moment I didn't feel angry, exactly – but the word 'lie' woke her up and she hissed across the table: 'It wasn't a lie. Why should it be anything to do with you, what happened in the past, between your father and me?'

'It concerned me too! People need to know who their parents are. I'm pretty sure it's in the Declaration of Human Rights.'

'Oh, for goodness' sake, Ros,' said my mother, trying out her parental tone again. 'Now you're being silly. You do know who your father is. I've never hidden that from you.'

'But *why* he disappeared . . .'

'You've always been very demanding, Ros, right from being a little girl. Very challenging. It wasn't just me that thought so . . . I had a lot of trouble with you.' She smoothed down the material of her skirt, brushing away imaginary specks from its glib pattern of coffee pots and cups. I pressed the heels of my hands into my eyes, damp-ening my wrists.

'That's not fair or true, Iris,' John said sternly. 'You're evading the question. Ros needs to know why you fabri-cated this lie and I would also like to know.'

'But why now?' she said. 'Just tell me that. Why are we here, talking about this today?'

'It was something Granny said. She said that Dad had gone away, that there had been a row the night before and that he left.'

'You shouldn't have gone to speak to her!' my mother said sharply. 'Granny doesn't know what happened yesterday, let alone thirty years ago. You know she mustn't be upset.'

'I didn't upset her,' I said, awfully aware that I had in fact upset her. The thought brought tears to my eyes. But I knew I was getting closer to the truth, I could feel the contours of it, how it changed the shape of the air between us.

'Iris,' said John softly, 'it's been a long time now. You need to let this go. Why did you say that Terry had died?'

'Because,' and she teetered, her tongue pressed against her teeth.

She looked down at her lap and seemed ready to break down. Instead she looked calmly up at John again and I saw what it meant to them, their thirty-year collusion, how heavy and uncomfortable it must be but also how familiar, how difficult to break.

Quietly she said: 'He didn't love me. He was gay.'

For a moment nobody spoke, and the moment felt so prolonged that there was time to notice such details as the windscreen-wiper motion a cleaner had used to polish the table; the few grains of sugar that had escaped her cloth; the low hum of an air-conditioning unit, which made the corner of my uncle's eye twitch with irritation. The only movement was contained within the frame of the window, which showed people going back and forth as if nothing momentous had happened. Then John edged forward from the sideboard, gripping the tabletop.

'Only that?'

My mother nodded slowly. 'But you don't know what it's like to love somebody and not be loved back. He did try. He tried – and he couldn't. That's all.'

And then she turned to me. 'It wasn't all my selfishness, Ros. He didn't want to be in our lives. I let him go.'

I think I must have stared at her for a few seconds without saying anything. I didn't recognise her: all the elements of her face looked strange to me. Then I said, 'He wanted you to let me think he was dead?'

My mother looked down at her skirt again. The angle made moisture rush to the edges of her nostrils and she wiped her nose with the heel of her hand. 'No. He didn't know about that. His plan was to get in touch with you once he'd found a job and somewhere to live. But then when he did write, I told him that you thought he was dead, that you had settled down and it would upset you very much if he tried to come back into your life. So he agreed to stay away.'

'Upset me? I would have loved him in my life! I wouldn't have cared – I would have understood!'

My mother nodded without expression, as though she were listening to the findings of a company report, then began to reach across the table – I think she was going to take my hand – before something made her flinch away.

'You're wearing his watch,' she said, and as she looked back down at her lap, her face contorted with grief. A black tear slid over her cheek and when she spoke again the quality of her voice was quite different, pain pushing through the cracks in her composure.

'I was so angry, and it seemed a simple thing to do, and

then time went on and I didn't know how to –' she touched the side of her eye, she had felt that the make-up was running – 'I didn't know how to go back. It was too late.'

'But it doesn't make sense,' I said. 'I mean, you went away. You went to Ireland, for the funeral . . .'

From the cuff of her dress my mother pulled out a crumpled handkerchief and dabbed at her eyes. 'Not Ireland. I went to Bournemouth. I stayed in a bed and breakfast, to make it look like – well, you know. I had to go somewhere.' She looked up at me, blinking hopefully. 'Can you understand, Ros?'

'No. How could I possibly?'

My mother shrugged, her mouth an ugly, upended smile. 'He never forgot you. He wrote you letters. I've kept them and I'll give them to you. They have his address on the back.'

Behind the room's silence a turbulence was gathering. We were braced for it, holding on to the furniture. A cyclone was going to rip through this space, tearing up the fittings, whipping the biscuits and tea bags into a vortex. John was already leaning forward, a captain at the helm with his face screwed up, ready to sail into the storm.

My mother felt the building pressure and identified this as a good moment to leave. 'I'll give you his letters,' she said again, as she backed away towards the door, 'so that you can get in touch. I need to go now. I need to –'

But she left the room before she had finished saying what it was she needed to do.

My phone rang and somehow that small event caused me to drop my bag, which was unzipped and spilled onto the gangway an assortment that included make-up boxes, an open bag of sweets, a novel, tissues, lip balm, the broken handle of an old palette knife, tampons, tickets and my purse which – because it wasn't properly done up either – unloosed coins that rolled away among the feet of people sitting across the gangway who moved their feet, in stolid leather shoes or boots or trainers, inches to the left or right in a blind effort to be helpful. As we scrambled together to retrieve my things, it felt as though everyone in this section of the waiting area was invested in the success of my phone call. And when I took up my mobile in trembling hands they had a right to feel that this farcical scene was due some kind of romantic pay-off. Frankly, I was hoping the same thing; I had been waiting two days to hear from Chris, after leaving him a voicemail and getting nothing back, and then been so scared of missing his call I'd slept with the phone beside my pillow two nights running. He wasn't the one calling, though.

'Hi, Frieda. Can you hang on a sec?'

I collected back the last of my belongings with thanks and apologies then said into the phone, 'Sorry about that. What's up?'

'Good news!'

'Oh?'

'I've found a home for Gabriel Huysman.'

'Seriously? That's fantastic!' My new friends in the waiting area lifted faces of furtive curiosity. A woman smiled. When something's 'fantastic', everybody wants to know more; it's the best hook after 'terrible', which is still the quickest way to silence a bus.

'Where?'

'I think you'll approve. It's a first-rate collection with some nice papers from the same period. They've got a James Wheeley and some wonderful pieces from Spitalfields.'

'So will they come and take it down?'

'No, they need someone local to do that. They'll pay you to do it if you like – and they'll fund the benchwork and the transport. I've just got off the phone with them. It's worked out really well.'

'I could deliver it myself probably.'

'I don't think so, Ros, not to America. It's going to the Museum of Philadelphia.'

'To America?' Consternation loomed on the faces opposite.

'It's the perfect home. They're expanding their collection of eighteenth-century papers and they've got wonderful facilities. A conservation lab to die for, about ten times the size of ours. Sebastian was very helpful, I must say. He arranged a donation from the American Friends of Turney that made the project much more attractive to the curator in Philadelphia. I take back those mean things I said about him.'

'That's all great but . . .'

'But?'

'There wasn't a way to keep it here?'

'Nobody here wants it!' Frieda cried with an easy laugh and, not for the first time, I envied that lack of sentiment. For Frieda there is nothing emotionally complicated about an object. Things are things and don't alter through their connection to people. 'If this had been another year it would most likely have been a different story, but you know how it is – everyone's budgets have been cut.'

'It's a shame we couldn't have waited until someone had enough money to buy it and keep it here.'

'Come on, Ros, I thought you'd be pleased. What counts is that it's going to a good home. The world's a small place. This is a happy ending.'

'Is it? I suppose so. It's sad too, though. It's another loss.'

'In that case we'd better get used to losing things. A lot of the best work is being done in America now. The reproduction papers for Ostley Hall are all going to be made there.'

'I know. We'll have to watch our backs.'

'Yes, I think we will. What on earth is that noise?'

A low horn resounded through the waiting area, rippling the coffee in my takeaway cup.

'I think that might be my ship coming in. Literally.' The line went blank with mystification. 'I'm at the port. Remember?'

'Of course! Your weekend away. I forgot, in all the excitement.'

'A long weekend. Three nights. I'll be back in the studio on Tuesday. I'm sorry I haven't been there the last few days.'

'You haven't been well, darling. And anyway, there isn't much happening at the moment, so it's a good time to be away. Have you been to Dublin before?'

'No. It's a first.'

'You'll love it. Well, I'd better let you go. You can tell me all about it when you get back.'

I hadn't told Frieda anything, yet, about my father. The information I had about him didn't feel solid enough to be committed to a conversation with anyone outside the family. Even then, I had waited four days before talking to Natalie about it, or trying to reach Chris. I'd spent those days at home, reading the letters my mother brought over, letters that revealed my father to be a man of kindness, curiosity and undiminished sorrow. They had moved me in an abstract way because I still could scarcely believe in a person who was supposed to have been dead for so long. I hadn't seen him for thirty years. I had heard him though. In the evenings, after closing time, I telephoned the bookshop and listened to the voice on the other end listing the hours of business with an equanimity into which I read a hundred different virtues. Then I tried listening to this message the other way, testing it for signs of cowardice and treachery, and in fact they could have been there too. You can read almost any attribute into the way somebody says 'Monday to Saturday, ten until six': it's infinitely open to interpretation. I had to believe that my father was a good man, though, otherwise there was no reason, no rhythm to anything.

Remembering a person who has been dead for a long time requires an effort of concentration because imagination keeps taking over where the evidence ends. You try to conjure, from some fragile recollection of the smell and texture of a jacket, the memory of worn clothes and of the body, warm and lively inside them. You try to hear that person's heart, his voice resonate within his chest, the way you heard them as a child sitting on his knee. The voice is elusive – after smell, it's the first thing to go. You try to see the hands that used to do up your shoelaces – you should be able to see them, you looked down on them every day as you sat on the kitchen chair, legs swinging. Even more so the face that was often held beside your cheek, that smiled on you at the beginning and end of every day. Whatever fragments you can find are quick-silver because the harder you work on your reconstruction, the more fragile it becomes. Pieces of memory fall away until, everywhere you look, there is nothing. How strange it was, then, to reverse the process, to bring the ghost out of the shadows and put flesh on the bones, reclothe him and make him real and breathing. Discovering that my father was alive was like an amazing feat of time reversal: the world had stopped on its axis and spun the other way. I felt that I was living at something better than the human level, in the company of sorcerers and alchemists. Flying, not falling. To find out now that my father was callous or even indifferent would bring me crashing back down to earth.

'Tell me that I'm mad to go, that I should stay at home,' I had said to Natalie, as she drove me to the port.

'No, I think you should, no, no, I think you, I think if you –' She'd been like this, babbling and gasping, streaming tears, ever since arriving to pick me up from home that morning. However much I said that I understood why she hadn't told me what she knew about my father, that I forgave her, that in any case there was nothing to forgive, Natalie was set on a course of self-punishment that didn't go well with driving. Not to talk at all would have been safer, but she seemed determined to unburden herself.

At the service station where we stopped to eat something and feed Sadie she fell back into a red bucket chair, bruised around both eyes, finally silent. We focused our attention on the baby, who had recently acquired a set of ringlets that framed her face like a Regency heroine's. She looked adorable bending over the table, her golden curls catching the light as she used her top-scoring pincer movement to retrieve crumbs of batter from her lunch box. It was enough, for a while, to fill the eye with her.

'Her first ever chicken nugget,' Natalie said finally.

'Ah – something you'll always remember, like her first step and her first word.'

My cousin didn't look amused. Perhaps this was one milestone that wasn't going to be cast in silver and turned into a piece of jewellery. It would look nice though, a little silver nugget on a chain or a charm bracelet. Better than a fingerprint, I thought.

'Hate to say it, but I've never seen anyone enjoy a box of chicken nuggets more,' I said.

'More! More!' agreed Sadie.

'Well,' Natalie shrugged. 'I don't know. I suppose it's not that big a deal.'

'All parents abandon their principles sooner or later, so I've heard.'

'I'm not sure I was ever very good at principles, anyway,' she said, and I was dispirited to see that she was going to cry again. 'If I had known your mother's reasons for lying about your dad I would never, ever have kept quiet. I would have told you, or made them tell you. I sort of stumbled into this massive secret and –'

'I know, I know.'

'I was in the dark almost as much as you. They told me some things, yes, but I didn't fully understand, and actually I did try to get them to –'

'I know. I get that. I remember you trying. Don't beat yourself up about it.'

'I mean, your *mum* . . .'

'Yeah, right.'

'I should have asked questions. I've always thought of you as my sister, but I haven't behaved like a sister should.' The last words came interspersed with rasping sobs. Sadie, who seconds ago had been smiling and laughing, turned red and set up a piercing wail.

'I don't want a sister,' I said over the clamour. 'I'm happy with you the way you are.' I pushed my chair away from the table and stood up, collecting up our rubbish ready for the bin. 'I know you couldn't have done things differently. I totally understand that. Please don't use this as a reason to fall apart, Nat. It's my drama, not yours. If anyone's going to have histrionics it should be me. Look, I'll drive the next bit and you can sit in the back with Sadie.'

The sky overhead was packed with grey clouds, one streak of sheer blue showing to the west. The certainty that behind this mottled outlook lay an expanse of vivid blue united those waiting on the upper deck in a gentle frustration. Some passengers looked upwards, with practised British optimism, and murmured to one another that the blue was 'trying to break through'. Others looked at the view without interest, or down at their hands or at nothing much; they were waiting for the bar and the duty-free shops to open and as the ferry clanked and moved away from the dock they headed for the stairways. The deck shone in the metal-coloured light and turned people walking across it into dark figures who moved uncertainly on legs that were twice as long and dissolved into reflective shimmers. I had thought there weren't that many of us boarding this night-time ferry, but now dozens more were arriving on deck, coming up from the lower levels where they had left their cars. Some looked like regular travellers, already weighing up the relative merits of an à la carte dinner and the all-you-can-eat buffet. They may have had cabins booked. They were going to sleep all the way across the sea and wake up in another country. I let my eyes drift in this amorphous crowd, figures gliding in and out of groups. Then the phone buzzed in my hand and there was Chris, smiling in Prague.

'Hi,' I said, pressing the phone to my ear against the wind. 'Can you hear me? I've been trying to reach you.'

There was a mumble on the line, some low music that sounded like contrition or discouragement. A tone of defeat.

'I can't really hear you. Hang on a sec.' Running now for the stairway, ignoring a sign that said not to run, I got on the quieter side of the first door I came to.

'And so that's why I didn't get your message until this morning,' Chris was saying. 'Because I've spent most of the last two days underground and then I accidentally left my phone in the Portakabin so I couldn't check it and just – God, work's been a total nightmare.'

'Why, what happened?'

'I won't bore you with the details. Basically, a problem with one of the tunnelling machines.'

'Elizabeth or Victoria?'

'Actually Mary, the new one. She ground to a halt forty metres under Whitechapel.'

Nerves had made me giddy and I laughed, louder and longer than this image warranted, all the way down the stairs to the door of the James Joyce Bar and Bistro. On the other side of the glass diners were contemplating their plates of fish and chips with expressions of deep contentment.

'Are you OK?' said Chris. 'With everything that's happened in the last few days you must be feeling –'

'Definitely quite weird. It feels like a dream. It's good to hear your voice, though. So you got my message? About my father and Ireland and everything?'

'Yes, I heard it. You think it's for real?'

'I don't know,' I said, and then: 'I'm pretty sure it is.'

'I should have been there to go with you. I've let you down.'

'No, don't say that. If anyone's let us down it's Mary. Anyway, it's better for me to do this alone. Nerve-racking, but better, I think.'

'You'll ring me when you get back?'

'I'll ring you from Dublin. Let you know how things went.'

'I want to see you.'

'I want to see you too.'

Back outside the clouds were clearing, rewarding those who were still on deck with the promise of a periwinkle sunset. We were passing through container land, a landscape of twenty-foot metal boxes guarded by gantry cranes. No knowing what was in all the boxes – Chinese toys or German dishwashers? Gangland murder victims?

We sailed on untroubled, past the last crane, the last landing pier, the last buoy, and on either side the coastline stopped putting up defences and bumbled down to nothing. On we went, past the lighthouse and out to the sea.

There's an urge to breathe deeper when the sea is all around you. It feels like a chance to get more life in, to redouble your efforts, be more and more alive. And there's a sense of vertigo you get setting off from somewhere into the blue. It suited me, being on the edge of things. I think I prefer edges to middles.

I looked back, for a moment, at the dwindling houses on the shore, each one a depository of joy, turmoil and secrets. And when I turned to face forward again the sea, and the world, seemed to be opening up in front of me.

ACKNOWLEDGEMENTS

The inspiration for this novel came from the story of Uppark, a National Trust property in Sussex that was gutted by fire in August 1989, then meticulously restored to its appearance 'the day before the fire'. I was as fascinated by the philosophy behind that idea of a total restoration – resurrecting one moment in time – as I was by the scale of the job, which took six years and a workforce of more than 250. In order to recreate the eighteenth-century interiors, a generation of craftsmen and women had to learn methods that had been forgotten for 150 years. By the time the work was finished, Britain could claim to have the best conservational expertise in the world. I'm grateful to Christopher Rowell for telling me more about Uppark and for the book he wrote with John Martin Robinson, *Uppark Restored*. Two other books – *Restoration: The Rebuilding of Windsor Castle*, by Adam Nicholson, and Michael Fishlock's *The Great Fire at Hampton Court* – were also invaluable.

Andrew Bush, the National Trust's paper conservation advisor, helped me understand the practicalities of working with historic materials and was often available to answer obscure queries about methods and materials. Gill Saunders at the Victoria and Albert Museum was equally generous with her time and expertise. Her book *Wallpaper in Interior Design* is an engaging, and beautiful, survey of the cultural history of wallpaper.

Meeting practicing conservators was the greatest pleasure of this research. Allyson McDermott made me lunch and showed me round her paper conservation studio in the Forest of Dean. Lucia Scalisi was fascinating on the history and uses of pigments. I'm especially indebted to Louise Drover, who tirelessly answered questions about her work – sometimes while in the process of trying to do it – and generously gave me ideas and contacts. Susan Catcher took me behind the scenes at the Victoria and Albert Museum, introducing me to the idea of 'there and not there' restoration. Thanks also to Graeme Storey and to the trustees of Strawberry Hill, once home to Horace Walpole, who let me visit while restoration was in progress.

I had absorbing conversations about pattern with Neisha Crosland, Humphrey Boyle of Zoffany, and Richard Rhys of the experimental design group Pattern Foundry. Carole Milner was eloquent and illuminating on our reasons for loving things simply because they are old.

I was lucky to watch conservators working at Carvers and Gilders, and at Plowden-Smith in London. Andrew Meharg and Treve Rosoman answered searching questions about arsenic. Mr Rosoman's book, *London Wallpapers*, was also very useful.

Frank Cockerill and Philippa Mapes at the Wallpaper History Society have given me some valuable pointers and I'm very grateful to Wendy Andrews, a wallpaper researcher whose enthusiasm for her subject is infectious, and who passed on some useful ideas. Many thanks to my friend

Beatrice Colin, who read an early draft, to my agent Patrick Walsh and to my editor, Becky Hardie, for her patience and her unerring eye. Barbara Bibb, an art restorer and a friend, has been talking to me about the ethics of conservation for years. She taught me how to look at things more closely and sparked the interest that led to this book.